THE
LAST
ONE TO
SEE
HIM

BOOKS BY KATHRYN CROFT

Kathryn Croft

THE LAST ONE TO SEE HIM

bookouture

Published by Bookouture in 2025

An imprint of Storyfire Ltd.
Carmelite House
50 Victoria Embankment
London EC4Y 0DZ

www.bookouture.com

The authorised representative in the EEA is Hachette Ireland
8 Castlecourt Centre
Dublin 15 D15 XTP3
Ireland
(email: info@hbgi.ie)

ISBN: 978-1-83618-338-9
eBook ISBN: 978-1-83618-337-2

For Oliver & Amelie

PROLOGUE

I stare at his lifeless body and watch the pool of blood fanning around his head, soaking into his hair, turning it darker. There's no chance he's alive.

Slowly, I walk over to him and pat down his pockets. There's something in one of them that feels like a wallet, so I pull it out and prise it open. A photo of him and a woman stares back at me – both of them smiling with their arms around each other.

I throw his wallet down and it lands by his body. And then I sink to the ground, my knees scraping on concrete, and scream – a wail I don't recognise as coming from me.

I can't make it stop.

'Kate?'

Rowan's voice forces her back to the present. She's not back in that desolate place, standing over a dead body; she's in her therapist's office, a mews house in Kensington with magnolia walls and teal green cushions. She's safe.

'Are you thinking about him again?'

The stream of winter sunlight flooding through the window

obscures Kate's view of Rowan so that she has to squint. 'No, actually I wasn't. Ellis has finally moved out and we've set things in motion for the divorce – I'm not going to let him get under my skin. We're over. He's Thomas's dad – that's all now.'

Rowan tilts his head and studies her. He won't believe that it's as simple as she's making out.

'I wasn't referring to Ellis,' Rowan says.

'Oh.' Kate knows exactly who he's talking about, and she doesn't want to go there right now. 'Never again will I be a victim.' She searches Rowan's face, wondering what he's reading into her statement. One day she'll tell him how she chose him as her therapist. It was his photo on the clinic website that drew her in – nothing to do with the text underneath it, detailing his long list of credentials. None of that mattered; it was his hazel brown wide-set eyes that grabbed her attention. His reddish hair. The modest smile that told Kate he was someone she could trust. He was the person she needed to talk to.

'I'm glad to hear that, Kate,' Rowan says. 'You're a survivor.' His lips twitch, restraining all the questions he wants to ask but holds back. He knows all about her childhood, the horrific incident that made her the person she is. But how can Kate ever tell him about what happened six days ago? That, for the second time in her life, she's come face to face with a dead body.

'I feel like you want to tell me something,' Rowan says.

Of course he can read her by now; it's been two years since a podcast episode led Kate to seek the therapy she's needed since she was fifteen.

Kate glances at the clock. Ten more minutes to fill and then she can get out of here. 'I need to know that you'll believe me,' she says. Whatever I tell you. That you won't question it, no matter what you think. That's important.'

'Kate, it's not for me to—'

'I need someone to know this, and it has to be someone I can trust.'

Rowan nods. 'That's why you're here. Because you can trust me.'

Kate pauses, selecting her words carefully. 'I think a woman I know wants to kill me.'

ONE

'I can't believe you've persuaded me to come here,' Kate says to Aleena. They're in an Uber heading towards Putney high street, and doubt creeps over her, engulfing her in intense heat. The driver is speeding, tearing around corners so fast, it feels like he'll lose control of the car any second.

'You have to celebrate your freedom,' Aleena says. 'It's important to mark this occasion. Ellis has moved out – it's a new beginning.'

'This isn't really something to celebrate,' Kate protests. Even though she and Ellis have been over for months now, him moving out today has hit her harder than she'd expected, and she's in no mood for drinking, or dancing, or whatever it is Aleena intends for them to do.

'Of course it is,' Aleena says, peering round from the front seat. 'You're finally free. Better it happened now than later.'

Kate rolls her eyes. 'Ellis and I are still friends,' she insists. She's grateful that there's no animosity between them, and that they can co-parent Thomas together amicably. Kate still loves him, that will take time to fade, but she will never let him get close to her again.

'Think I'll just message him,' she tells Aleena. 'Make sure Thomas got to bed okay.' Kate can picture her son now – trying his best to convince Ellis to give him ten more minutes on his iPad.

'Thomas is *fine*,' Aleena says. 'Both our kids are fine. They're ten, not two. Tonight is about *us*. For once. We have to forget we're mums tonight.' She pauses. 'Oh, that sounds heartless. What I mean is, not *forget*, more like just put it to the side for a few hours.' She flicks back her curly black hair and flashes Kate a dark red smile. It's strange seeing Aleena dressed up, out of the joggers and T-shirts she wears for the school run, her hair floating around her shoulders instead of scraped back.

In the mirror, the Uber driver grins.

'I know, you're right,' Kate says. Still, she ignores Aleena's frown and pulls out her phone, quickly sending a message to Ellis.

It's Friday and the bar is busy; it seems like everyone is out in Putney tonight. Kate's never been to Tequila Mockingbird; in these colourfully painted walls is a world she doesn't inhabit, and she feels conspicuous as they walk in. 'Maybe we could go somewhere else,' she suggests, stalling by the door. 'Somewhere quiet? We won't be able to hear each other speak.'

Aleena grabs her arm. 'Nope. Don't even think about it. You're thirty-seven not ninety! We can talk any time. We are *not* doing quiet tonight. This place is great. There's a basement bar downstairs with a dancefloor too.' She points at Kate's patent leather Mary Jane shoes. 'You'll be fine in those block heels.'

'I'm not dancing!'

Aleena chuckles. 'Come on, let's get you something to help loosen you up.'

Surprisingly, Kate feels a lot better with a drink in her hand. She's barely touched alcohol since her separation   a subconscious choice she hadn't been aware she'd made until tonight.

The memories of sitting down with Ellis in the evening and sharing a bottle of wine are too raw.

'Are you really okay about it all?' Aleena asks, once they've found a seat. 'I've known you long enough to sense when you're... blocking things out.'

Kate shakes her head. 'Nope. Not at all.' She takes a swig of her drink, hoping her friend will stop digging.

'I know it must be hard,' Aleena continues. 'My mum's divorce nearly finished her off.'

Kate nods, and takes a huge gulp of her cocktail. 'Affairs destroy people. *Both* people.' Like other things, she hasn't talked about this to Aleena, and her voice sounds like it belongs to a stranger. How can this have happened to her?

'Yeah, I guess. I've never thought of it like that,' Aleena says. 'We always just think of the person who was cheated on being hurt. But I suppose the one who did the cheating loses out too.'

'Let's change the subject,' Kate says. She doesn't want Aleena's pity; she's not going to crumble because her marriage is over. She's got Thomas and that's all she needs in her life. *And to keep the past at bay.* 'Everything's fine.'

'I salute you for being so forgiving,' Aleena says. 'It's a sign of strength.'

'Aleena? I thought that was you!'

Kate and Aleena both look up as a tall, dark-haired woman grabs Aleena and gives her a hug.

Aleena jumps up. 'Oh my god, it's been years!' She turns to Kate. 'This is my old school friend, Heidi.'

'You have to come and join us?' Heidi asks. 'There's a whole group of us – you'll love everyone.'

'Yeah,' Aleena says. 'Maybe we will.'

This is the last thing Kate wants, but she doesn't want to seem antisocial. 'Why don't I get some drinks and I'll meet you down there?'

'Are you sure?' Aleena asks.

'Yep. Go. I'll be right there.'

They disappear downstairs, and Kate makes her way to the bar, unsteady on her legs, as if she's detached from her body. At the bar, she finds herself merging into a huddle of men, their booming voices fighting to compete with the music. They look like they've just come from the office, but their jackets and ties have been removed, along with their inhibitions it seems.

'Hey, make room,' one of the men says, clearing a space for Kate to get to the bar.

'Thanks,' she says, forcing her way into the space he's created.

'Not a problem.'

He smiles at her, and she takes in his features. He's around her age, his hair an unusual mixture of dark blonde and brown, short at the sides and longer on top. It looks freshly cut, and his face is clean-shaven.

'You might have to wait a while,' he warns, gesturing to the two harried bar staff. 'I've been trying to get their attention for ages. It's packed in here tonight.'

'I'm not in a rush,' Kate says. She imagines Aleena's already lost in conversation with Heidi.

'Well, enjoy your Friday night.' He smiles, and when he turns away to re-join his friends, the jolt of disappointment Kate feels takes her by surprise.

She spends some time downstairs with Aleena and her friends, then when they're engrossed in conversation she slips upstairs again, planning to leave. But the man from the bar catches her eye and he beckons her over. 'Going already?' he asks.

'I'm debating it. It means abandoning my friend, though, and I'm not sure my conscience will let me.'

'Come and sit for a bit, then,' he says. 'Don't tell the guys I came with, but I could really do with some quiet conversation. I didn't really want to come out tonight.' He glances back at the bar, where his friends don't seem to have noticed he's drifted away to talk to Kate. 'My bed is calling me. Plus, I've just started Harlan Coben's new book. That man is a writing machine, I don't know how he does it.' He pauses. 'You didn't want to be here either, did you?' he asks.

Kate doesn't answer.

'Sorry.' He holds up his glass. 'Nosiness is a side effect of this. And speaking of being nosy' – he points to Kate's glass – 'you've barely touched that.'

'I'm on lemonade now, so who cares?'

He holds up his hand and smiles. 'Sorry. It's none of my business how much you do or don't drink. But... there's something about you—'

Kate rolls her eyes. 'Oh, please. I'm beautiful, right? Breathtaking? You can't take your eyes off me? Give me a break.'

Briefly, he looks taken aback and his cheeks flushed, but then he smiles. 'Actually, I was about to say that you look sad.'

For a moment, she's unsure how to respond. She's misjudged him, and now he's thrown her off course. She studies his face, trying to work him out, but comes up with nothing.

'I'm sorry,' he continues. 'Just ignore me.' He holds up his glass. 'Can I blame this stuff?'

'Seems to me you're blaming the drink for a lot of things.' Kate surprises herself by smiling. 'Drowning your sorrows? Maybe you're the one who's sad?'

'Something like that, yeah.'

His words sound so plaintive that she regrets being so intrusive. 'Sorry. Not my business.'

'You're right, though,' he says. 'Messy separation. It's been hard. Trying to sort out all the financial stuff. Childcare arrangements. We have a son. Anyway, you don't want to hear about that. What's your story? Are you married?' He glances at Kate's hand and she instinctively pulls back, even though her wedding ring sits abandoned in her jewellery box at home; the only evidence of her marriage to Ellis is a pale line around her finger.

Something stops her explaining that she's going through something similar; the less she gives of herself, the better, even though she'll never see this man again. 'Nope. Not married. Anyway, if we're going to share a table then at least tell me your name so I can stop thinking of you as annoying chatty guy.'

He laughs and offers his hand. 'Jamie Archer. Nice to meet you.'

Kate shakes his hand, surprised to find his skin so cool in the cloying humidity. 'Kate Mason.'

'I like that name,' he says. 'No nonsense. Means business. Assertive.'

'Don't forget breathtaking and beautiful!' Kate laughs again.

'Actually, I was going to say it sounds like an author's name. Or a detective's.'

'I can assure you I'm neither of those things. I'm a vet.'

Jamie smiles. 'Ah. I don't think I've ever met a vet before. Except when I was a kid and we found an injured bird in our garden. I made my mum rush it straight to the vet, even though she insisted there'd be nothing they could do to save him.' He frowns. 'I actually have no idea if it was a *him*, but in my mind it was.'

Now he's got Kate's full attention – anyone who cares about an injured bird is someone she's happy to give her time to. And for the next hour they become so engrossed in conversation that neither of them notices when their glasses are empty.

'I have a dull job,' Jamie tells her. 'Economist for the Financial Conduct Authority. I'd only just moved to London when my wife and I decided to separate.'

'Was it amicable?' Kate asks, thinking of Ellis.

'No, sadly. She's having trouble accepting that our marriage is over. I think I've been more ready to move on than she has. She just became really difficult to live with. Neither of us cheated or anything; there was just nothing left of us together, other than our son. And it feels lonelier to be in a broken relationship than it does being single.' He looks away.

'New beginnings,' Kate says, burying her burning questions.

He smiles. 'Yeah, you're right. New beginnings. Speaking of new beginnings, I think I could do with another.' He lifts his glass. 'Can I get you another lemonade?' he asks, gesturing to her full glass. 'Not that I want you to overdo it or anything.'

They both laugh. 'No, thanks – I think I'm ready to head off.' Kate stands and holds out her hand. 'Nice to meet you, Jamie Archer.' As much as she's enjoyed talking to him, she's ready to leave now. She can't bear the thought of making her way through the swarm of bodies on the dancefloor downstairs, so instead Kate messages Aleena to tell her she's leaving.

Jamie smiles. 'You too, Kate Mason, veterinary surgeon.' He winks as she walks away, and she smothers the temptation to call him back and tell him she's changed her mind about that drink.

Outside, it's raining, and Kate shivers, pulling her scarf on. She takes out her phone again to order an Uber, trying to ignore her disappointment that Ellis hasn't replied. Why does she care? She's let him go.

'Well, this is a coincidence!'

She spins around and Jamie Archer is walking towards her, zipping his coat. 'Bloody cold, isn't it? And I'm sure it wasn't supposed to rain. Are you waiting for an Uber too?'

Kate nods and turns back to her phone, but she can feel his gaze on her. The app freezes again, and she has to reload it before it works.

'How long will yours be?' she asks.

'No idea – can't get the app to work. Think I'm going to have to walk.'

'Not exactly the weather for a nice walk – I hope you don't live far.'

'Richmond.' He laughs. 'Might be home for breakfast. Well, nice to meet you, Kate.'

Normally she's on guard, never taking reckless chances with anything, but there's something about the sight of Jamie walking off in the pelting rain that makes her throw caution aside. 'Wait!' she calls. 'Maybe you can share mine. Supposedly it's only three minutes away.'

He turns around. 'Are you sure?'

She's not sure, but what harm can it do to share an Uber? 'I'm going to Wimbledon – he could drop you off first then straight on to me. I'll have to change the booking. What's your address?'

Thanking her again, he tells her his postcode. 'I'm really grateful for this. The kindness of strangers, eh?'

'It's fine.'

By the time they reach Jamie's home – a luxury block of flats in a gated community – Kate's been laughing so much her stomach hurts. The Uber driver glares at them, making no attempt to hide his annoyance that they're being so loud.

Jamie thanks the driver and opens the door. 'Wimbledon next for my friend.'

The driver frowns and glances at Kate. 'No, it was one stop she booked. Only one.'

'Actually, it was two,' Jamie insists.

Kate checks her phone. 'Um, it might not have gone through. It's just showing your address.'

'Can't you just drop my friend home?' Jamie insists. 'Wimbledon's not too far.'

'No can do. There's somewhere else I have to be now.'

'Oh, come on.'

Kate closes her eyes. This driver won't give in, and through the haze of a few drinks, she hardly cares what happens.

'Sorry, can't,' the driver protests. 'Booking didn't come through. Not my fault.'

'It doesn't matter,' Kate says, opening her eyes and clambering out of the car. 'I'll just get out here and book another one.'

On the pavement, they watch as the car screeches off into the night. Kate clicks on the Uber app. 'It's saying the nearest car is forty minutes away!'

'I'm so sorry.' Jamie glances at his building. 'Want to come in for coffee? At least you'll be dry while you wait.'

'I'm not going in your house – I don't even know you.'

'Actually, it's a flat. Does that make a difference?' Jamie laughs, and Kate can't help but smile. 'My wife and son kept the family home,' Jamie explains. 'It was the right thing to do.' He points towards his building. 'Can't complain – I have a three-bed penthouse apartment all to myself. And Dex is here every weekend. It's our father–son time together. It makes it all the more special knowing he can't annoy me during the week.' He smiles. 'Just kidding. I love my kid really.'

His words disassemble her carefully constructed barriers. What's the harm in having a quick coffee with Jamie? All she has to go home to is an empty house, devoid of life because Thomas is with Ellis. She's never done anything like this, too afraid of the consequences, of what has already happened to her. 'Show me some ID,' she says.

'What?'

'If I'm going inside there with you, I need to know I can trust you.'

'Fair play.' Jamie reaches into his pocket and fishes out his wallet. 'Here you go,' he says, handing her his driving licence. 'Just ignore the mugshot.'

It turns out that Jamie looks nice in his photo, his mouth on the verge of a smile. He's got neatly trimmed facial hair in the picture but it's clearly him.

'Is madam satisfied?' he asks. Anything else you need before we go in?'

'Nope. Let's go.' Kate memorises his address before handing back his licence. She debates sending another message to Aleena, telling her exactly where she is, but doesn't want to explain herself over a text message.

Inside, Jamie's flat is even more luxurious than she'd expected. It's open plan, with bright white walls that look freshly painted, and the furniture is minimal but it still somehow feels homely and welcoming. 'Now you see why I was happy to give up my house,' he says, watching Kate take in her surroundings.

They walk into the spacious kitchen area, where on the fridge Kate sees a photo of Jamie and a young boy who must be his son.

'I don't have many photos up,' Jamie explains. 'My wife has them all and I keep meaning to get some printed from my phone but haven't got around to it.'

He makes coffee, while Kate stares out of the window at the huge communal garden, lit up with stake lights spaced around the circumference. 'Your son must love it here in summer,' she says.

'I hope so. He doesn't talk about the separation much so it's hard to know how he feels about it all. He just throws himself into his sports and we don't know how he's feeling unless we push him to talk.' He sighs. 'Guess it's a taste of what's to come in a few years when he hits those teen years. And he's just started at a new school so that can't be easy. Not really sure yet how well he's settling in.'

'I have a son, too. Thomas.'

Jamie's eyes widen. 'Ah, I didn't want to be rude and ask if you had kids. How old is he?'

'Ten. He's in Year 5.'

'Same as Dex. Let's sit on the balcony,' Jamie says, handing her a coffee.

'Isn't it a bit cold?'

'Not when I've got fleece blankets to keep us warm. Come on – it's so peaceful out there. Trust me, you'll love it.'

He goes to find the blankets, allowing time for doubts to set in and urge Kate to run for the door. She's in a stranger's house late at night, something so far removed from her normal life, and the buzz of alcohol is wearing off. But by staying right where she is, she's conquering her fears. She will see this through because it will heal her. This thought makes her smile.

'What's so amusing?' Jamie says, coming back with the blankets and handing one to Kate.

'Nothing. Just all this. Me being here with you. A few hours ago, we didn't even know each other.'

'Come on,' Jamie says, holding out his hand to her. 'Let me show you the views outside.'

On the balcony, she realises Jamie was right – as soon as they sit on the sun loungers, wrapped in blankets, a sense of serenity sweeps over her. She tells Jamie about Ellis, and how close they'd been until infidelity had ruptured their marriage.

'That must have been hard,' Jamie says. 'I was cheated on by an ex and it destroyed my faith in people.'

Kate nods, choking up. There is so much she could say to Jamie, so much of her pain she could shed but she has Rowan Hess, her therapist, for that.

'We need music,' Jamie says, when Kate doesn't speak. He jumps up and reaches for her hand again. 'Something chilled.'

In the living room, Jamie asks his smart speaker to play jazz, and even though it's a genre of music Kate's never understood, his passion is infectious, and she can't help smiling. When he asks her to dance with him, though, she hesitates. 'You're kidding?'

'Nope. Deadly serious. Come on, let go of your inhibitions.'

Her cheeks flush when he takes her hand and pulls her from the sofa, and within seconds, dancing with Jamie in the living room of his penthouse apartment feels like the most natural thing she could do.

And when he kisses her, Kate's body responds, even though her mind questions whether this is sensible. She lets herself get lost in Jamie, and when after a long moment, he gently eases back, about to say something, she pulls him back towards her, searching for his mouth again, tugging hard at his clothes until she feels his skin against hers.

And she forgets all about ordering her Uber.

TWO

Rowan is silent while Kate recounts meeting Jamie last Friday, and although his expression is impossible to read, his mind must be whirring with all the fresh judgements he'll be making about her.

'Do you think badly of me?' Kate asks.

'You're perfectly entitled to spend the night with anyone you wish to,' Rowan says. 'You're separated, and this man is too. It only matters how *you* feel about it.' He frowns, leaning forward. 'But I'm concerned about this woman you think wants to kill you. Can you tell me more?'

The way Rowan says this makes it sound farcical, as though there is nothing threatening and it's all a figment of Kate's distorted imagination. She needs to find a way to make him believe her, without having to tell him the whole truth. This is not just about Jamie. Kate's life has taken a detour and she needs to find her way back.

'I'm a little confused,' Rowan says. 'Who is this woman?'

His lips are moving but Kate can no longer hear him. Now there is only Jamie filling her head.

. . .

She parks on the road opposite Jamie's building. What if he doesn't remember asking her to come back today? What if he's changed his mind? They'd exchanged numbers last night but neither of them has sent a message to confirm. But his invitation had been clear, as he kissed her goodbye when her Uber turned up that morning. He'd said it would be nice to spend the afternoon together, that he didn't want it to just be about last night.

A car pulls up as she approaches the gate, and the driver inserts a code into the panel, the gate easing open after a few seconds. Kate slips behind him as he drives through, hoping he doesn't challenge her.

Before she can change her mind, she rushes up to the main door and presses the buzzer for the penthouse apartment. Seconds tick by with no answer. Glancing around, she sees a middle-aged couple walking towards her, their arms linked together. They're talking animatedly and don't notice Kate until they reach the door. And even when they acknowledge her with a brief glance, they don't try to stop her entering the building.

Again, Kate hesitates, but just before the door closes, she reaches out to stop it, and steps inside. The hallway looks different with daylight seeping through the large windows. The oak flooring and stairs match the banisters, and pots of flowers sit in each corner of the lobby, above them a large framed print of an autumn forest.

Instead of taking the lift, she walks up the three flights to Jamie's floor, and with every step her doubts grow stronger. But she's here now so feels compelled to see what will happen.

At his door, she knocks, surprised to find that the door eases open. Jamie must have left it open for her. 'Hello?' She pushes the door further and waits. Kate doesn't want to step inside until Jamie invites her in.

But he doesn't answer, and silence crashes around her. Immediately she knows something is wrong. She calls again, this time stepping inside.

'Jamie? It's Kate. From last night.'

Nothing.

Heading through the hallway, she enters the living room, stopping short when she sees him lying on the floor. 'Jamie?'

But he's not moving, and as Kate gets closer, she realises the contorted position he's in is all wrong. Arms outstretched, legs splayed, one of them twisted behind his body. And then her eyes fix on the large pool of crimson surrounding him.

It's happening again. Just like before.

All the air is sucked from Kate's lungs and her gasp echoes through the room. Doubling over, her legs almost give way and she can't seem to move. She stares at Jamie's body, unable to compute that this is real; it feels like something she's watching on television.

Then it hits her, and a surge of adrenalin kicks in. She needs to help him. She rushes to him and kneels on the floor, praying that he's still breathing. 'Come on, Jamie,' Kate whispers into the silent apartment. She needs to save him. He can't be dead. She won't let him die. But when she leans in, no breath comes from his open mouth, and when she clutches his wrist, there is no hint of a pulse.

Jamie is dead.

A tsunami of panic rises in Kate's body; she can't be here, not after last time. No one will ever believe she's innocent. She jumps up and runs.

Outside on the road, Kate scrambles in her bag for her car fob and opens the car door. She shoves her phone in the charger underneath the dashboard, and then she realises her house keys aren't in her bag. She hunts in the glove compartment and under the seats, but they're not there. She would never leave them in the car – she had them with her, she knows she did. Glancing back at the apartment block, Kate realises she must have lost them on her way up to Jamie's flat, or even worse, inside it.

Nausea swirls in her stomach as she gets back out of the car, *looking around to see if there are any CCTV cameras. There's no sign of any, but this does little to alleviate her anxiety. And now she has no choice but to go back up there and face Jamie's dead body again.*

The bitter chill wraps itself around Kate as she hurries to the door. Then she remembers she can't get inside unless someone buzzes her in. Frantically, she looks around but there's no one in the car park, and no sign of anyone coming out. Taking her chances, she presses the button for flat nine.

'Hello?' a female voice asks, after a few seconds.

'Delivery,' Kate says, steadying her voice so it won't betray her lie.

The door buzzes open, and she pushes through it, racing up the stairs to the top floor. As she approaches Jamie's door, Kate slows down. It terrifies her to have to go in there again, but she has no choice – her keys are in there and she can't leave behind evidence that she's been in his flat. She's sickened that it's too late for her to help Jamie, but she can't get tied up in this. She's only just met him and she has Thomas to think of. When this all comes out, how will she ever explain to her son that she spent the night with a stranger? One who is now dead.

Taking a deep breath, Kate reaches out to push the door, and it doesn't budge. It's shut now. And there's no way for her to get inside.

For the second time this morning, she runs from Jamie's flat.

'Kate?'

She snaps back to the present, focusing her attention on Rowan. Kate needs to tell him that Jamie is dead, but she can't let Rowan know she's the one who found him. He would immediately be on the phone to the police and Kate can't deal with that – not after last time. And Rowan would never risk his career by staying silent. Kate could never ask that of him.

'The man I slept with died,' Kate says.

'Oh,' Rowan says. 'I'm sorry to hear that. Can I ask how he died?'

'It was natural causes. An issue with his heart.'

'That's very sad,' Rowan says. 'I imagine that's affecting you.'

Kate nods. It's possible he can still help her, even if she can't tell him the whole truth. 'The woman who wants to kill me... it's Jamie's wife. And I think she knows I slept with him.'

Rowan's eyes widen. In all the time Kate's been coming here to this mews house in Kensington, she's never seen him taken by surprise, no matter what she's disclosed to him.

'Okay. I can understand how that can be alarming. Has she said something or done something to make you believe this? Has she approached you?'

Kate nods. 'Yes, a few days ago.'

'And she's told you that she knows about you and her husband?'

'Not exactly. But it's all too much of a coincidence.'

Rowan clears his throat. 'Then what makes you think she wants to harm you?'

Kate ignores Rowan's question, her mind is already steps ahead. 'What if all this with Jamie is to do with *him*?'

There's no hint of judgement on Rowan's face – no hint of anything other than eagerness to explore this further. 'Okay,' he says. 'You think this is about what happened when you were fifteen?'

'When it all comes down to it – everything is about him, isn't it?

THREE
JULY 2003

Kate and Mona sit on the hard red plastic seats at the bus stop, swinging their legs, glancing at the sign that tells them the bus should have been here four minutes ago. 'Come on, then,' Mona says. ''Fess up – you like Kian, don't you?' She nudges Kate and giggles. 'He is kind of cute.'

'No... no way.' But Kate feels her cheeks flame. Does she like him? Yes, he's an attractive boy, but everyone at school likes him and she finds that off-putting. He's not arrogant, though – Kian is surprisingly modest considering how many girls fawn over him.

'Maybe today is your lucky day,' Mona says. 'Got to pop that cherry some time!'

'I'm fifteen – it's not even legal,' Kate protests, half mockingly. But to be fair, her birthday is seven weeks and three days away so it barely makes a difference.

'Don't be such a prude,' Mona responds. 'I've seen the way he looks at you. It's a bit gross, actually.' She laughs, but it feels too forced, reminding Kate how much Mona has changed recently. She is usually cheerful, exuberant, and Kate's often in awe of her. Mona's home life has been difficult for years, since her dad left them, and her mum hardly knows she exists. As much as Kate wishes her own mum would give her some breathing space sometimes, she'd rather her mum worry about her than be too preoccupied to care.

'Will Robbie be there?' Kate asks.

Mona rolls her eyes. 'Oh, I'm so over him. He's actually really boring when you're alone with him. How is that possible? In front of his friends he's the life and soul, but get him away from them and it's like watching paint dry. No, scrap that – watching paint dry is way more exciting.'

Kate forces a laugh, but silently feels sorry for Robbie. He clearly adores Mona, and she lets him believe she feels the same – hanging all over him when they're around the others. It's cruel. As much as Kate likes Mona – they've been friends since primary school – sometimes it's hard to make excuses for her, even though Kate knows the darkness that is probably the cause of it.

Kate didn't want to come with Mona this afternoon. Not with her friend's strange, distant behaviour, barely talking and avoiding everyone until today. It's like a switch has flicked and Mona is back – eradicating the imposter who's taken her place. School has just finished for the summer and they're heading to the canal to hang out with Robbie and his friends. Mona had ambushed Kate when she was slipping out of the gates, grabbing Kate's arm and telling her she had to come, that they could spend the whole afternoon lazing around, eating and laughing. 'Robbie's stolen some of his dad's gin,' she'd whispered, as if that would entice Kate. But not being a big drinker like others in her year, Kate couldn't think of anything worse to pour down her throat. Still, she's glad Mona is happy, and saying no might have sent her spiralling.

'This bloody bus,' Mona says, glancing at her watch. 'Shall we walk?'

No, no no. Just go home, Kate. This day is bound to end in trouble if everyone is drinking.

Sweat coats the backs of her knees by the time they've reached the canal. The boys are sitting on the grass, their roars of laughter drifting to the far side of the grassland. Robbie races over when he spots them, heading straight for Mona. Like a scene from an old movie, he wraps his arms around her and kisses her as if he hasn't seen her for years.

'Get a room,' Kate jokes.

'Yeah,' says Kian, winking at her.

A frisson of excitement shoots through Kate's body and she smiles and quickly turns away. She can't bear to look at Kian; he's painfully beautiful, too perfect, and it makes her ache for him.

'Hey, Kate,' Kian calls. 'Come and sit with me.' He pats the grass beside him and her stomach flips. She needs to get a grip – he's just a boy; she can handle sitting next to him. She's not going to fall for Kian Roberts.

She makes her way over to him, her leg brushing against his as she sits beside him.

'Want one of these?' Kian asks, offering her a can of Budweiser.

Kate scrunches her nose. 'No, thanks. I don't drink. Seen what it does to people – my uncle's an alcoholic. It's not pretty.' She's offering too much information but she doesn't care. People need to know what that stuff can do.

Kian raises his eyebrows. 'Sorry about that. But you do know that most people can have a drink and not turn into alcoholics, right?'

'We're fifteen!' she protests. 'You *do* know it's not actually legal to drink until we're eighteen?'

'Hmm. I don't follow the rules,' Kian says, smiling. 'I feel like I have enough sense to know what's good for me and my body.'

Kate's unsure how to respond to that, and she's beginning to think perhaps she doesn't actually like Kian after all, and that sometimes people are better admired from a distance, but then the atmosphere shifts, as if suddenly Kian is stripping away layers of himself.

'I'm being a dick,' he admits, pulling his legs up to his chin. 'Sorry. I was just trying to impress you.' He gestures towards the canal, where Robbie and the others have picked Mona up, teasing that they're about to throw her in. She erupts into shrieks, pleading with the boys to put her down. Kate's pleased to see Mona enjoying herself after how withdrawn she's been the last few months.

'It's hard, you know,' Kian says.

'What is?'

He sighs. 'Living up to people's expectations of me. I'm supposed to be this... I dunno... popular, funny, cool dude. And everyone's watching me all the time. Like, *all* the time. Following my every move...' He reaches for his can and swigs his beer.

Kate stares at him, half expecting him to say *Just kidding, I love my life – it sure is great being the centre of attention.* But the frown on his face shows her he means every word.

'There's a lot of pressure on me,' he continues. 'And sometimes I get sick of it.' He lifts his can, which surely must be empty by now, and stares at it. 'So, yeah, I don't need to drink this, but I do it anyway, because that's what everyone expects me to do.'

'I don't care about any of that stuff people expect you to be,' Kate says. 'You just have to be yourself – whoever that is. It's not your job to keep other people happy. To be their leader. Is it?'

He tilts his head and appraises her, raising his eyebrows again. Kate expects him to laugh, to dismiss what she's said, but instead he says, 'Thank you, Kate Mason. That's just what I needed to hear today.'

While the others continue messing around by the canal, she and Kian talk for the next hour, shutting out the rest of the group, the rest of the world. Kian gets through another two beers, while Kate slowly sips her third Coke.

With no warning, Kian leans in to kiss her, and despite how much she wants him to, her bladder feels heavy and uncomfortable. 'I'll be right back,' she says, jumping up.

He looks disappointed.

'I just need to find a toilet,' she explains.

'Can't you go behind a tree or something?'

'Not that easy for girls. I'm sure you know that.' Kate places her hand on his shoulder to reassure him. In the last hour she's learned that Kian isn't as confident as everyone thinks. Just like everyone else, he has his own insecurities.

'Hurry, then,' Kian says. 'I like talking to you, Kate.'

There are no toilets near the canal, so she ends up walking to the high street, practically running because she doesn't know how much longer her bladder will hold out, and because she's desperate to get back to Kian. He was about to kiss her and she wants that so badly.

She dashes into the customer toilets in Marks & Spencer.

As she's washing her hands, someone taps her shoulder.

'Excuse me – can you help me?'

Kate turns around to see an elderly lady smiling at her. 'I've lost my daughter and I don't know what to do.'

Kate's no expert, but she's heard stories about elderly people with dementia getting lost. 'Don't worry. I'll help you find her,' she says. 'Let's go and see if we can talk to someone who works here.'

. . .

It's nearly an hour before Kate gets back to the path leading to the canal. Luke appears, walking towards her.

'What's going on?' she asks.

'I'm out of here,' he mumbles. 'You should probably go too.'

'Why? What's happened?'

But he ignores her and continues on. Kate's always found Luke a bit strange, so she shrugs and puts it down to him and Robbie having fallen out again – they are always arguing.

When she reaches the canal, she can't see Kian, or Mona, or any of the others. She scans the area but there's no one familiar in sight, and when Kate checks her phone, there's no message from Mona telling her they've gone somewhere else. Not even a message asking where she was.

Furiously typing a message to Mona, she continues towards the wooded area. *Where are you?*

Before she can send it, she hears voices. She stands still and scans the woods, and there in the distance is Mona. She's sitting down, and Kate is about to call out until she realises what her friend is doing. And who she's doing it with.

Mona and Kian, his hands all over her, pulling up her top, exposing tanned skin.

Nausea lurches in her stomach as Kate turns away and makes her way back towards the canal path. She ignores Kian's shouts for her to wait, and instead she runs until she's far away from them.

She holds it together until she reaches the main road, but then her tears fall fast, burning her flushed red cheeks.

Intense anger is burning inside Kate. She's seething, and she's never felt this hollow before, as if she's been gutted like a fish. She's aware of noise all around her – the heavy thrum of traffic, and voices, but she can't make out any words. She reaches her road and remembers that her mum is at work, and normally she'd be the person Kate turns to for anything. Her mum listens without judgement, and Kate always feels better after sharing things with her. But today her mum is on a twelve-hour shift at the hospital, caring for sick people who need her far more than Kate does.

Kate barely registers the white van that pulls up on the other side of the road, as consumed as she is by rage. Nor does she pay any attention to the man crossing the road.

Until she's forced to acknowledge what's happening. There's an arm around her chest, a damp hand covering her mouth. She's being dragged backwards and thrown into a van, her body smashing against the hard floor, rattling her bones. And then a heavy fist slams into her face.

And then nothing but darkness.

NOW, FRIDAY 24 JANUARY

Salty tears pool in Kate's eyes as she stares at Rowan.

Without a word, he gets up from his chair and hands her a tissue. 'I know this is difficult for you,' he says. His voice is so warm and tender, which only intensifies her tears. 'You don't have to talk about it all again. If it's too distressing.

'No,' she says. 'I need to. I need to tell it again.'

'Okay. If you're sure.'

'I've never told you all the details,' she says. 'I think I should.'

'I'm listening,' Rowan says, folding his hands together.

Kate takes a deep breath. 'I remember opening my eyes and the van was moving. I had no idea where he was taking me, but the roads were bumpy and I kept sliding along the floor. It was filthy and dusty.' She closes her eyes; she's back there once more. 'But the dirt was the least of my worries.

'I just kept thinking that I'd never see my mum again. Never finish school and begin living. And even though I was scared, I knew I couldn't let that be a possibility. I had to fight to survive, no matter what.'

Rowans tilts his head. 'I imagine you must have felt terrified.'

Kate nods. 'He hadn't tied my hands, so I tried the doors, but they were locked. And there were no windows in that van. He must have taken my phone – or I dropped it when he forced me in there. That drive felt endless. The only thing I could do was use the time to plan what to do the second he opened those doors. I figured I had to be quick, to be ready the second that door opened so I could kick out at him and run. I knew I couldn't overpower him, so I had to make sure I was at least faster than him.' Kate feels the burn of tears in the corners of her eyes.

Rowan offers her the tissue box.

'When the van stopped and the engine cut out, I was ready for him,' Kate continues, reaching for a tissue. 'Like some feral creature ready to lash out.' She dabs her eyes. 'But he antici-pated my move, and he grabbed me by the neck before I could do anything. He dragged me out of the van towards what looked like an abandoned building. I found out later it was an old disused farmhouse. I tried to kick out but it was pointless. No amount of kicking could stop him. I kept asking him what he wanted from me, but he wouldn't answer. And then...' Kate stops; the pain of reliving this is overwhelming.

'You don't have to tell me any more,' Rowan says.

'I want to,' Kate insists. Now she's started, she will see this through. 'He... he kept punching me, and I fell back, smashing onto the ground. But somehow I managed to kick out again, and then then I scrambled to my feet and ran. He ran after me, but I rammed my body into him and he flew backwards. He shrieked when he hit the ground. I carried on running, expecting him to follow, but he didn't.' Kate stares at the grey carpet. 'There was only silence. I was torn between wanting to run and needing to check him. I don't know how long I stood there, but eventually I went back to him. That's when I saw the huge pool of blood under his head. He was dead. And I was the one who killed him.'

FOUR

FRIDAY 24 JANUARY

Rowan pours Kate a glass of water. Her hand trembles as she takes it, and she hopes he doesn't notice. He observes everything, though – that's his job. She gulps it so fast it hurts her throat.

'Kate – you did what you had to do to stop him. You were a child. I know it still haunts you but that's in the past.'

'Graham White will never be in the past,' Kate says. 'He's made me the person I am today, don't you see that? Everything in my life has been determined by what happened.'

Rowan bites his lip. She's offended him with her acerbic tone and she needs to rein it in. She can't turn him against her, not when he's the one person who can help her.

'I mistrust everyone because of him. I've put up barriers to protect myself that stop me living my life fully. That man might be dead, but he's won. He broke me.'

'Remember what I told you before? Focus on the good in your life. You have a wonderful son. A career you've worked hard for. Don't lose sight of that.' Rowan pauses. 'Can I tell you what I think?'

'Yes. Please do.'

'I think your guilt over what happened when you were fifteen has carried over to this night you spent with this married man. And now that he's dead, it's exacerbated your feelings of guilt. But you had nothing to do with this man's death. It was just terribly unfortunate.'

'Graham White's death was different, though,' Kate says. 'I killed him.' And she hasn't told Rowan that she found Jamie dead. He would never believe that she had nothing to do with it.

'In self-defence. You didn't know he'd die. You were just trying to get away from him.'

This doesn't matter to Kate. She has become the person people think she is, the label they have foisted upon her. And the reality of what happened when she was fifteen doesn't stop the nightmares. Or the devastating pain that has been stirred up again because she found Jamie Archer's body. Is it just paranoia, or is he, too, dead because of her?

'And you were never charged with Graham White's death,' Rowan continues. 'As far as the police were concerned, there was no crime. Can we get back to why you think you're in danger?'

He won't say this, but he knows Kate is holding back. Perhaps he doesn't truly want to know any more gritty details of her life. 'Shall we talk about this woman?' He leans forward, again. It's starting to annoy her that he always does this. 'Do you need to call the police?' he says.

'No! Not the police. Not after last time. I can't... I can't deal with that. The interrogation. No. I can't go back there.'

Rowan sighs. 'This isn't like last time,' he assures her. 'You haven't done anything. You won't be in any trouble.'

But he has no idea. And I can't tell him because he'd be legally obliged to inform the police that I'm a witness in Jamie Archer's murder.

'I slept with a stranger,' Kate says.

'I think you know that's not a crime.'

She places her glass on the table by her chair.

'Kate. I really think you should tell me about this woman. It's understandable you'd worry she's upset about you and her ex, but why do you think she wants to kill you?'

Kate takes a deep breath and begins.

THREE DAYS AGO, TUESDAY 21 JANUARY

Kate is early picking up Thomas. It had been quiet at the surgery so David had ushered her out, assuring her he'd cover on his own. She'd been reluctant to leave – she's been avoiding Aleena at the school gates all week because it's an easier pill to swallow than lying to her closest friend about what happened after she left the bar on Friday night. Kate's already done enough of that – Aleena knows nothing of her past with Graham White – and now she's somehow involved in another death. *Jamie Archer*.

She's tried to search for a connection between the two men, but there's nothing online. Jamie isn't some relative of Graham's – distant or otherwise. Kate stops and sits on a low wall outside the Sainsbury's Local near the school, and googles Graham White again. She again pores over articles written at the time, even though she doesn't need to – she knows every detail of Graham White's life – thirty-nine years old when he died – only two years older than she is now. A partner called Jennifer Seagrove, who'd left him the day before he'd thrown Kate in the van and abducted her. At the time, police concluded that the end of his relationship had sent him spiralling out of control, and that he'd seen Kate walking home and full of rage had acted impulsively. There'd been nothing in the van to suggest premeditation. There is no excuse for what he did to Kate – for what he would have done to her. The man was sick in the head. Kate stares at the photo of Jennifer, smiling for the camera, her head resting on Graham White's shoulder. How can a man who looks so innocent, so in love with his partner, have been such a monster?

Jennifer shut down after talking to the police, refusing to speak about Graham, insisting their relationship was over so it was nothing to do with her. Kate always wondered why this didn't strike people as odd; Jennifer and Graham White had been together for three years and then suddenly she cut him off and never looked back, even when he died.

Even though she's done it before, Kate types Jennifer's name into Google, once again coming up with no match for the woman who was seeing Graham White. Anything could have happened to her – it's been over twenty years so she may not even be alive.

Graham had no children or siblings. Parents who were now both dead. Nobody who would be seeking vengeance for his death. And even if there was someone out there, why would they wait twenty-two years?

Slipping her phone back in her pocket, Kate assures herself it's just coincidence. That she has just been unlucky twice in her life. Wrong place, wrong time. Jamie could have gone home with anyone the other night – it just happened to be her.

She walks towards the café near the school, pausing outside; she's still too early to turn up at the school gates.

Stepping inside, a blast of warm air envelops her, and she unzips her coat. It's too warm in here, and she considers ordering her coffee in a takeaway cup and sitting outside where she'll be able to breathe.

Kate places her order and hears someone call her name. She scans the coffee shop and sees Aleena sitting in the corner, at the table the two of them always try to commandeer whenever they're here. Aleena beckons her over, and with no choice, Kate forces a smile and makes her way towards her friend.

'Where have you been?' Aleena asks, standing up to hug Kate. 'I haven't seen you since you abandoned me at the bar. I can't believe you went home so early.' She sits again and taps something on her laptop before closing it.

'Work's been so busy,' Kate says. 'You know how it is. Anyway, it's only been a few days.'

Aleena frowns. 'Yep, a few days of silence.' She pauses. 'Well, at least you're alive. Hope you don't mind me saying this, but you look exhausted.'

'I haven't been sleeping too well.'

'You know what that could be, don't you?' Aleena lowers her voice. 'Perimenopause. I read about it – it can start in your thirties. Did you know that? And sleep disruption is definitely a symptom.'

'Yeah, it must be that,' Kate says, assuring Aleena she'll make an appointment with the doctor.

While Aleena catches her up on what's been happening with her this week, a woman in a quilted coat and baseball cap walks in, her reddish-brown ponytail protruding from the gap at the back. She keeps her head down and speaks softly to order her drink, as if she's trying to avoid being noticed.

Aleena stops talking and looks up, staring at the woman for a moment. 'There's that new mum whose son's just started Year 5,' she whispers. 'Her name's Harper Nolan. I wonder if Theo has played with him today.' She turns back to Kate. 'I mean, what do you say?' Aleena continues. 'Poor kid. I can't even imagine what it must feel like.'

Kate turns back to the woman. 'I didn't know a new boy had started. And what do you mean? What's happened?' She takes a sip of coffee, ready to switch off when Aleena tells her whatever rumours she's heard. Kate wants no part of it.

Aleena frowns. 'He started after the October half term. Didn't Thomas say anything? Theo always tells me when there's a new kid starting. He thinks it's exciting or something.'

'But what's happened to this boy?'

'You really haven't heard? I thought everyone knew. Well, I

suppose you've had a lot going on. It was mentioned in the WhatsApp group.' Her eyes narrow. 'Oh, I forgot – you haven't been checking your phone.'

Guilt wedges in Kate's throat. 'Aleena, I have no idea what you're talking about.'

Aleena glances at Harper Nolan again, and when she speaks her voice is barely audible. 'Her husband was the man who was found murdered at the weekend in his apartment. His name was Jamie.'

FIVE

THREE MONTHS AGO, 19 OCTOBER

Harper stares out of the window at the tree-lined street. She feels claustrophobic here, in this Victorian terraced house that has plenty of square footage but is hemmed in by the houses either side of it, and the identical homes opposite. She'd told Jamie moving here was a bad idea; they would have been fine in Southend, and at least Harper had been near the sea. She needs that. To be close to the vast ocean that extends further than she can see. Moving to Wimbledon has been a huge mistake.

All of it's a mistake. And she wants out.

Jamie appears behind her and puts his arms around her waist, nuzzling her neck.

'That won't win me around,' Harper says, shrugging him off. She pulls the black hair tie from her wrist and fixes her hair into a ponytail. 'I still hate it here. I need sea air, Jamie. Not this.' She flaps her arms. 'And it's not fair on Dexter.'

'He will be fine. He's resilient,' Jamie says, pulling back. 'You know this is for the best. A fresh start for us. We couldn't stay in Southend. Too many...' He trails off, leaving his unspoken words to cast darkness over them.

'Always running,' she says. 'When will it stop. I still don't see why—'

'You *know* why. How could we have a fresh start when we were still in the same place. With everything that happened.'

'We didn't have to come to Wimbledon. I've never liked London. It's too busy. Too many people. How can that be good for us? We could have—'

He places his finger on her lips and kisses her forehead. 'Do you trust me?'

No! she wants to scream. Instead, she nods. She's learned that in order to exert any control over Jamie, she needs him to believe that she will go along with what he wants, however reluctantly.

'I'll never like it here.' She looks around. 'It will never feel like home.'

He sighs. 'We'll make it a home. Dex loves it already. He'll make friends at his new school and... everything will be fine.'

'Until it's not.' Because Jamie is trouble, and nothing will change that. 'How do I know it won't happen again?'

He pulls her towards him. 'I love you, Harper. Never forget that. No matter what happens. Okay?'

'What do you mean? What's going to happen? I don't like this, Jamie. Nothing about it feels right.' Harper has always had an instinct for knowing when something awful is about to happen. This will not end well.

Jamie strokes her hair. 'It's all under control. Let me do the worrying. All you have to do is keep being my beautiful wife. Mother to our son. Okay?' He strokes her cheek. 'Think I'll go and have a shower. Want to join me?'

But Jamie is underestimating her if he thinks there isn't more to her than being a mother and a wife. 'No,' she says, too quickly.

His eyes widen. 'Maybe next time, then.'

She watches him leave, then checks on Dexter in the play

room. It's crammed full of boxes, yet Harper has no urge to unpack, to make this place their home.

Harper shivers, and she's sure it's not from the cold. Does the heating even work here? The house is immaculate, but they'd never thought to check the running water or boiler. It didn't matter. Jamie would have taken any house if it meant they could leave Southend quickly.

'I can't believe there's a climbing wall in here!' Dexter says, walking into the living room.

'I think it's for toddlers,' Harper says. 'You're too big, Dexter.'

'Doesn't matter,' he insists. 'I can still do it. Look!'

Harper watches as Dexter climbs the wall. She gives it one day before he's bored of it and they're left with the task of removing it. She and Jamie won't be having any more kids. Not when there'd be such a huge age gap between any baby and Dexter. That ship has sailed. Jamie still mentions it now and again, telling her she's not even forty yet so they could still try.

But there's no way she'll bring another baby into this... whatever it is they're doing.

When Dexter pulls out his Harry Potter Lego from one of the packing boxes and sits down to build it, Harper leaves him to it and heads upstairs.

She can hear the shower on so she slips into their bedroom and sits on the bed, taking in the unfamiliar and unwanted surroundings. At least up here the walls are white, a blank canvas waiting for her to add character to. But she won't do that. They will stay white until they can get out of here – and she prays that time will come, like it did before.

On the bedside table, Jamie's phone catches her eye. She glances into the hall at the closed bathroom door, tuning into the sound of the shower. Jamie has no idea she knows his passcode and she feels no guilt as she taps it in and his home screen appears. She checks through his WhatsApp messages, relieved when she finds there's nothing to worry about. Mostly he deletes his messages, preferring to keep his app clear. She understands this – it's the way Jamie has to live. She's known that about him for years. There's one message on there, though, from his sister Annie in New Zealand, asking how he is, urging him to keep in touch. Annie knows nothing about Jamie's life here. Nothing about Jamie. His sister lives in her flawless home with her perfect kids, and shuts her eyes to the harsh realities of life. It's as if she thinks that ignoring pain and death and horror will make those things non-existent.

Holding her breath, Harper checks Jamie's camera roll. There she is with Jamie, their arms around each other, picture-perfect smiles for the camera. Then there's Dex, with a shy grin because he hates having his photo taken.

She's about to stop scrolling when a face she doesn't recognise fills the screen. A woman with long dark hair and large brown eyes. Long eyelashes that don't even look like they have mascara on them. She's pretty, but there's ferocity in her eyes. Something that screams *don't mess with me*.

Harper stares at the photo for a few moments and wonders what it's doing on Jamie's phone. She should ask him. She won't jump to conclusions – she's done that before and ended up with egg on her face. She's sure there's a rational explanation for this woman's photo being there, whoever she is.

But by the time the shower stops, Harper can't stop thinking about her. Has she been wrong and this woman is the real reason Jamie has uprooted them from their home? Harper needs to find out.

But something tells her that digging too deep will be the beginning of the end.

SIX

A flash of heat burns through Kate's body as she turns back to Harper, who's still waiting at the counter for her coffee, leaning on it as if she needs the support to keep her upright. This time Kate takes in the woman's appearance fully: dark reddish-brown hair, shiny and smooth, a wide mouth and thin lips, large green eyes.

'Are you sure?' she asks Aleena, horror spreading over her like a disease. The woman at the counter can't be Jamie's ex-wife. 'How do you know?'

'Jen told me. She knows everything, doesn't she? Working in the school office has to have its perks. But please don't tell anyone you know – I don't want Jen to get in trouble.'

'What's her son's name?'

'Dex.'

Kate's breath is sucked from her lungs. It's true, then. Jamie had said his son was called Dex.

'But...' Kate struggles to form words. She has to be careful. 'How come her son's back at school? Shouldn't he have taken some time off? I read about it and wasn't it only a few days ago?'

'I thought that too,' Aleena whispers. 'But maybe it helps him to be at school. Takes his mind off it?'

Before Kate can respond, Aleena calls out to Harper, beckoning her over.

'What are you doing?' Kate hisses. 'We have to go – we'll be late.'

'I feel bad for her,' Aleen replies. 'She can't know many people yet so I think we should talk to her. I met her yesterday but I should introduce you so there are at least two parents she knows.' Aleena is oblivious to Kate's torment, and she smiles at Harper as she reaches their table. 'Hi, we met at the school – I'm Aleena, Theo's mum, and this is Kate – her son Thomas is in Year 5 too. I'm so sorry for your loss.'

Harper nods. 'Thank you.' She turns to Kate. 'Hello,' she says. Her voice is strained, as if she's trying to force her words out. And she looks uncomfortable, as if talking to other school mums is the last thing she wants to do. Unsmiling, she doesn't even hold out her hand. 'Dexter told me he's been playing with a boy called Thomas. Unless there's another Thomas in Year 5? It's a big school, isn't it?'

'Only one Thomas,' Aleena says. 'And, yep, it's definitely a big school. That put me off at first. Three classes in each year. Impossible to keep up with everyone.'

Which is why Kate failed to notice that a boy called Dex had started in Thomas's year.

Harper doesn't look at Aleena, but keeps her eyes fixed on Kate. 'We should get the boys together,' she says. 'As they've been playing together. It's hard to start at a new school when friendships are already established, isn't it?'

'Totally,' Aleena agrees. 'And yes, getting the boys together sounds like a great idea. Anything to help, you know, after what you're both going through.'

'Actually, I meant just with Thomas, if you don't mind.' Harper smiles at Aleena. 'Dexter finds it a bit overwhelming being in a crowd. Probably best if he gets to know one child at a time.'

Aleena's smile fades and she folds her arms. 'Oh. Yes, of course. Whatever's best for him.'

The atmosphere has shifted and Kate feels like Harper Nolan is homing in on her. 'So when are you free?' Harper asks, pulling out her phone.

Kate glances at Aleena. 'I, um, I'm not sure. Afraid I never use my phone calendar. Still write things on the paper one in my kitchen. But I can find you on the WhatsApp group and message you some dates.'

'I'm not in that group,' Harper says. 'Bad experience in Dexter's last school. I find it much better to stay off things like that. All that endless pinging. It's all a bit much. How about we just exchange numbers?'

While Aleena turns away to pack up her laptop, mouthing something behind Harper's back, Kate has no choice but to recite her mobile number, listening to the click of Harper's fingernails as she taps on her phone.

'Shall we all go, then?' Aleena says, hoisting her bag onto her shoulder.

Harper nods, looking at Kate instead of Aleena. 'Thank you, yes, I'll walk with you. It feels a bit weird being the new parent. Everyone hangs around in groups and it's hard to get to know anyone.'

'Just stick with us,' Aleena says. 'We'll look out for you, won't we, Kate?'

'Yes,' Kate says, swallowing the heavy lump in her throat. 'Of course.'

At home, while Thomas watches football on TV, Kate sits on the sofa and scrolls through the local news, once again hunting for any mention of Jamie's murder. Before meeting Jamie, she'd avoided the news; reading anything only served as a reminder of Graham White's murder being plastered all over the news. She'd been a minor so they'd never mentioned Kate's name, and she'd pore over every article, forming a picture of the man whose life ended that summer night. The man who had without a doubt intended to kill her that same night.

The police have no leads in Jamie's murder investigation, but they believe the person was someone known to him. There was no sign of a break-in, so it appears he let the person into his apartment. Guilt churns in her stomach when she reads that they're still appealing for witnesses, anyone who might know anything about what happened to him. She closes the app and considers calling the police. But it's been days, and her keys are somewhere in Jamie's flat – how could she possibly explain why she hasn't come forward until now? And when they found out about Graham White – which they would – the police would never believe she's innocent of Jamie's murder. The whole truth will come out – and then what?

There's barely any information about Jamie other than he was a thirty-five-year-old dad of one, who worked for the financial conduct authority. Jamie had been telling the truth about that, then. Kate replays the conversations they had that night in his flat; despite her tendency to mistrust people, she'd never once doubted that he was being authentic and honest.

Kate glances at Thomas then slips her phone in her pocket. Whatever she does, protecting her son at all costs is her priority.

'What's Dexter like?' she asks.

'It's Dex, Mum. No one calls him Dexter.' Thomas keeps his eyes fixed on the TV. 'He's okay. He doesn't like football, though.'

'Well, everyone's different, aren't they?' Her son is obsessed with football, and silently Kate hopes this means a bond won't develop between the two boys.

'Yeah, I know,' Thomas says. Dex is okay, though. I like him.' He glances at Kate then turns back to the TV.

'Remember your dad's taking you to football training tomorrow,' Kate says.

'Is Maddy coming?'

Kate flinches. It took a few weeks, but Thomas seems to be accepting his father's new partner, and Kate is proud of how respectful he is about her, despite his initial protests that it was Maddy's fault that his parents' marriage ended. It had been a shock when the two of them had ended up together after Ellis and Kate separated, after what had started as a one-night mistake.

Kate isn't bitter about this; even though it's hard to hear Maddy's name mentioned, she's glad that Thomas is at peace with it all. And she'd never had to have a difficult conversation and explain that things happen sometimes between adults. They make mistakes. And one day, when he's older, she hopes Thomas will understand about the mistakes she has made herself.

'I don't know if Maddy will be there,' Kate says. 'But I'm glad you like her.'

'She's quite nice,' Thomas says. 'And I just want Dad and you to be happy.' He smiles. 'Do you think you'll ever meet anyone, Mum?'

Jamie Archer's face flashes into her head: alive with passion and longing, then quickly morphing into pale and lifeless. 'I don't need anyone,' Kate says. 'I've got all I need right here.' She hugs Thomas, and tears he can't see fall softly onto his hair.

Kate's in the bath when her phone buzzes by the sink. She wants to ignore it, but the warm water and bubbles are doing little to relax her mind. She steps out of the bath and grabs her phone, getting back in to keep warm.

Instantly she regrets her decision. It's a text message from Harper Nolan. She stares at the name, tempted to drop her phone to the bathmat and ignore it, but she's compelled to read it.

It was lovely to meet you this afternoon. Are you and Thomas free to come over tomorrow after school? I know the boys are old enough for a non-supervised playdate, but I thought it would be great for us both to get to know the two of you.

This is too much, too soon. How can Kate possibly start a friendship with a woman whose ex-husband she slept with?

Kate types a reply: *Sorry, I have plans tomorrow. Another time, though.* And then she hesitates. Rather than avoiding Harper, it could work in Kate's favour to get closer to her. There is scant information about Jamie online, so befriending Harper might be the only way she can keep up with the investigation.

Deleting the message, she replies that she and Thomas can come over after school.

A wave of regret hits her the moment she's sent it.

She's playing with fire. And she's starting to believe that it's no coincidence Harper Nolan has come into her life.

Downstairs, Thomas sits at the kitchen table, his homework book open in front of him. 'Need any help?' Kate asks.

'No thanks. I'm fine.'

The doorbell rings just as Kate pulls out a chair to sit with Thomas. She pulls her dressing gown tighter around her and heads to the door.

'Who's that?' Thomas asks. 'It's really late.' His words echo Kate's thoughts.

She checks the peephole, as Thomas rushes up to her. Outside their house, a white van drives off. 'Just a delivery,' Kate says. 'I haven't ordered anything, though.'

Frowning, Kate opens the door, and stares at the long cardboard box on their doorstep. 'They're flowers,' she says, noticing the Bloom & Wild Logo.

'Maybe they're from Dad?' Thomas says, smiling.

'No. They won't be from him.' Kate picks up the box, peering once more into the street, even though the white van is long gone.

At the kitchen table, she carefully opens the box. 'Maybe they're from a customer at work,' Kate says.

'Well, you do save animals, Mum.'

But Kate freezes when she sees what's inside. A bunch of dead lilies, crumbling and withered, coated in something black that makes them look more haunting. She gasps, shutting the box.

'What's happened?' Thomas asks, his eyes wide.

'Oh... don't worry. I think they must have needed water and died in transit.'

'That's a shame,' Thomas says, turning back to his homework.

But Kate knows this was deliberate. She just doesn't want to think about what it means.

Harper waits by the window, as daggers of rain pelt against the glass and dark clouds loom in the sky. Every bone in her body aches for Jamie; for the person he was before everything changed. A few weeks ago, he'd discussed moving to Portugal. Starting over. Just the three of them. She'd quickly dismissed it, of course, and put it down to Jamie trying to run away from things again, and she wasn't going to let him do that.

She shouldn't be nervous – she is the one who is in control here – Kate Mason has no idea what she's walked into. She will have worked out who Harper is by now, so she'll be on her guard. Harper just has to make sure she doesn't slip up. Jamie has taught her that it's all about being one step ahead of your opponent, knowing things they don't know.

But none of that explains why Jamie spent the night with Kate. And that's what Harper can't wrap her head around. Jamie and that woman, his hands all over her. It sickens her. She needs to find out why it happened, why Jamie veered off course. Kate is not someone he should have become involved with. What the hell was he doing?

Through the window, Kate walks up the path with Thomas.

She hesitates briefly at the gate; no doubt she's taking in the air of neglect in the small front garden, the overgrown grass and flowerbeds full of weeds. Everything dying. Just like Harper feels she is. Just like Jamie did. But let Kate judge her; neglecting her garden pales in comparison to what Kate has done. And Harper has no concern for the garden – how can she care about such a trivial thing now?

Thomas walks in front as they make their way to the door, and Harper is certain he's the one who has led the charge to come here today. 'Dexter?' she calls, as she makes her way to the kitchen, just as the doorbell rings. 'Would you mind answering the door? I need to get the cakes out of the oven.'

Harper hates baking – she only did it to create the impression that she's welcoming Kate into her home, and her life, but then she discovered that it was a good distraction from thinking about Jamie. How senseless his death is, yet so significant.

She hears Dexter thundering down the stairs and pulling open the door. Then muffled voices. 'Come through,' Harper calls, as she places the baking tray on the worktop. She walks to the kitchen door and waits.

'Come up,' Dexter says to Thomas. 'I can show you my Harry Potter Lego.'

The boys rush upstairs, as if they've known each other for years, and Kate watches after them, as if she wants to call her son back and drag him home.

'Hi,' Harper says, forcing a smile, mustering the energy to propel her legs towards Kate. 'Thanks for coming. This really means a lot to Dexter.'

Kate returns her smile. 'You have a lovely home.'

'Oh, it's not really. Not yet. We've only just moved in and I've hardly done a thing to it.' Harper gestures to the long, narrow kitchen. She loathes the Farrow & Ball Hague Blue walls, but at least the skylight in the ceiling brightens the room.

Kate's wearing jeans and a loose cream blouse, while she's

dressed in black leggings and a dark grey jumper. The colours of mourning.

'I hope these are okay,' Harper says, pointing to the tray of cupcakes. 'You're not dairy or gluten intolerant, are you? I should have checked. Seems like these days everyone has something they can't eat.'

'No, I eat everything,' Kate says, glancing at the cakes. 'They look lovely. You really didn't have to do this, not when...' Kate's words evaporate.

Harper knows exactly what she's talking about but wants to hear the words from Kate's mouth. 'When what?' she asks.

'I just meant you must be really busy, moving here and settling Dex into school. And... losing your husband.'

'School has been no problem. And I actually like baking. Don't often get the chance. Coffee?'

'That would be lovely, thanks,' Kate says, her eyes darting around the room. She must feel threatened here, and that right now she's probably wishing she was anywhere else but in this house.

They sit with mugs of coffee at the kitchen table, while above them the boys thunder around.

'Thanks so much for coming,' Harper says. 'It really means a lot. It's not easy making new friends at the best of times, but... I'm sure you've heard the details about what happened to my husband? Everyone must be talking about it.'

Kate shakes her head and sips her coffee. 'No.'

Liar! Harper turns away and stares through the kitchen doors. The lawn, just like at the front of the house, needs mowing and the flowerbeds surrounding it are full of rampant weeds. 'He was murdered.'

'I'm so sorry.'

Kate is so believable – her words, her body language. Everything about her. It's a shame, perhaps if they'd met under different circumstances, Harper might have quite liked her. But

Harper has seen Kate's hands all over Jamie, and she will never remove that image from her head. *And what happened afterwards.* Bile edges along her throat. 'I'm surprised you didn't know,' Harper manages to say. If she keeps probing then Kate is bound to slip up. 'The other parents must be talking about it.'

Kate twists her mouth. 'I try to stay out of other people's business,' she says.

'I know what they're all saying.' Harper fixes her eyes on Kate. 'Or thinking, at least. And you probably are too now. How could I send Dexter to school so soon after his dad's murder? How can I arrange a playdate for him as if nothing's happened? But he wanted to keep going to school. He insisted. He needs... everything to feel normal.' Harper wills her tears to stay behind her eyes. As broken as she feels, she won't let this woman sense any weakness. 'He's a very conscientious child. Couldn't bear the thought of missing out on his learning. I even told him I could get him a tutor but he wouldn't have any of it.'

'I can understand that,' Kate says. 'I'm sure having the distraction of school is helping him.'

But Kate has no idea what it's like when Dexter gets home. The silence that's becoming too familiar, the nods and grunts that Dexter is using to communicate. The sense of helplessness. And Kate sits there as if she's had no part in this.

'That's what I've been telling myself,' Harper says. 'And it's the reason I invited you both here. Dexter's not the only one who needs some normality. I do too. But I'm sure you know what mum guilt is like – how do we ever know if we're actually doing the right thing for them? I feel so numb. I've only just managed to tidy the house this morning because you and Thomas were coming after school.'

Kate nods. 'It must be so hard for you,' she says. 'I'm separated from my husband now but I can't imagine what it would feel like if anything happened to him. He's still very much a part of our lives.'

Harper's eyes narrow. 'Yes, hard under any circumstances,' she says, lifting her mug. 'But it's remarkable what devastation humans can live with. What other choice do we have? We just pick ourselves up, or sometimes drag ourselves, and carry on somehow.'

'You're right,' Kate says, smiling as if they're close friends. 'And how is Dex doing?'

'Dexter's just... Dexter. He's a remarkable boy, really. His strength has astounded me. But I do worry he's in shock and the grief is bound to catch up with him.' *My own too.*

Another thud reverberates upstairs.

'Sorry about that,' Harper says. 'Dexter's room is just above us.'

'I hope Thomas isn't destroying your house.'

'I'm just happy that Dexter's found someone to play with. It's important, isn't it? Connections with people. Jamie was always saying that.' She smiles, scrutinising Kate's face. Mentioning Jamie must surely unnerve her. 'I don't know about you, but I'm more of a lone wolf myself. Sometimes I find dealing with people... hard work. Shall we go in the living room?' she says, standing and tucking her chair in. 'It's more comfortable on the sofa. And the boys could be upstairs playing for quite a while.'

Harper leads the way into the large lounge, where the two huge bay windows still don't have curtains. The walls are dark red – Florentine red, the estate agent had informed them – and filled with family photos, that Harper only put up this morning. She can barely look at them, but notices Kate staring at the largest one in the middle – a wedding day canvas of Harper and Jamie, confetti floating around their heads. Blessing them. Cursing them.

'That's Jamie,' Harper says. 'He was a special man. That's why I married him. In it for the long haul, until he was so cruelly taken away.'

'I'm so sorry,' Kate says. Her skin seems paler since they came into the lounge. Then her eyes seem to fix on the vase of white lilies over the fireplace, and her face drains even more.

Harper wonders what Kate is apologising for. Sleeping with Jamie? What else did she do to him?

'I can't even imagine what you're going through,' Kate continues. 'And I know that getting divorced doesn't mean there isn't still a special bond there.'

Harper stares at her. 'Divorced? Oh, no – Jamie and I were very much together. I kept my maiden name because I don't believe women should have to take their husband's name. And Jamie didn't mind Dexter having my surname.'

Kate's face pales. 'Sorry, I... I don't know why I thought you were divorced. I must be thinking of someone else. Work's been so hectic lately, my mind's all over the place.'

Silence surrounds them. Is this some game she's playing or did Kate really believe Jamie was divorced? Either way, Harper can't underestimate this woman. 'I can assure you that Jamie and I were very much together. I'm not saying it was perfect – what relationship is? – but Jamie was my... soulmate.' She bites her lip. 'I know that's cringy, but that's honestly how we felt about each other.' No one will understand the things that tied them together.

Kate points to the large canvas wedding picture on the wall, effortless smiles stretched across Harper and Jamie's faces. 'He clearly felt the same,' she says, her voice too animated.

Harper glances at the photo, tries to ignore the wrench in her gut. 'I believe so.'

'I'm so sorry about what happened. I... I read about it.'

'I thought you didn't know?'

Kate hesitates. 'I didn't know the man I'd read about was your husband. But I'd read about what happened.'

'There hasn't been much written has there?' Harper says. Kate is tying herself in knots and sooner or later she'll slip up.

'Not that newsworthy unless it's a young woman or child. Who cares about a man in his thirties? Someone who's not considered vulnerable.' A single tear snakes down Harper's cheek.

Reaching into her bag, Kate pulls out a small packet of tissues and hands one to Harper. She almost doesn't take it – she doesn't want anything from this woman. 'I read that he was found in a flat in Richmond,' Kate says.

Harper nods. She knew it was only a matter of time before Kate would begin to ask questions. Harper will play along for now. 'Yes. It's a property we rent out. We were between tenants and had just done up the flat. It needed a lot of work. Jamie sometimes stayed there if he'd been out and didn't want to disturb us coming home in the middle of the night.' She dabs her eyes with the tissue. 'I don't sleep well. Never have. The slightest noise wakes me and then I'm up for the day. Now, though, I'd give anything to change that night – so that he'd come home instead. He'd still be here, then.'

'I can't imagine what life's been like for you over the last week. I hope the police find who did that to him.'

'The police have no clues. Nothing was taken. There was no break in, so it must have been someone he'd let in the flat.' Harper studies Kate's face. 'Someone he knew or was expecting. But why would someone target Jamie? There's no reason for it. He was a good person. He didn't have enemies.'

When Kate reaches for Harper's hand, Harper notices her glance at the platinum and diamond wedding band Jamie had given her.

'It's been a nightmare with the police here all the time. I had to tell the family liaison officer to please give us some space. But she still turns up every day. I haven't been able to work since it happened,' Harper continues. 'I'm an HR manager for a hospital trust. They need me, and I've let everyone down. Without me there, the team will be struggling with the heavy workload.'

'You're grieving,' Kate says. 'It's only been a few days.'

'Suddenly work doesn't seem important any more.' Harper presses her fingertips to her eyes to stem the tears. 'Maybe I won't even go back. This is all really making me think I need to make some changes.' She leans forward and clutches her stomach, groaning softly. Kate Mason is the last person who should be here, witnessing Harper's despair, but Harper needs to see this through. Raucous laughter drifts down from upstairs.

'They're getting on really well, aren't they?' Harper says, pulling herself straighter. 'That makes me so happy. Dexter really misses all his old friends.'

'Thomas really likes him,' Kate says. She finishes her coffee. 'Have you thought about therapy?' Kate asks. 'It could help you through this... this awful time.'

Harper looks up. 'No, I don't think so.' She pauses. 'I tried to convince Jamie to go when he was having some issues, but he wouldn't listen. Have you ever had it?'

'No,' Kate says, too quickly, too defensively. There's something there that Harper needs to dig into. 'But I've heard you can do it online now, if you don't want to see someone in person. That works better for some people.'

Harper scrunches the damp tissue in her hand. 'The thing is, I'm a very private person. The idea of sharing such personal thoughts and feelings makes me shudder. Jamie was the only one I spoke to about personal things.'

'I understand,' Kate says. 'But—'

'Let's change the subject,' Harper says. 'I'm finding it hard to talk about Jamie right now.' She forces a smile. 'Tell me about you, Kate. Do you work?'

'I'm a vet.'

Of course Harper already knows this – she's made it her business to find out who Kate Mason is. 'I've never met a vet before.'

Kate shifts in her seat, then forces a smile.

'I'm not really a cat or dog person,' Harper continues. 'Too much mess. Dexter's often asking for a dog but... well, we are who we are, and I'm not going to apologise for that. It's not that I don't care about animals or what happens to them – I'm vegetarian and don't even eat meat. I'm just not keen on sharing my home with one. And we moved a lot and that's not fair to animals, is it?'

Kate nods. 'It's hard when one of you is an animal person and the other isn't. My ex didn't want pets, but I convinced him to let Thomas have a cat.'

Harper stares at her. 'We didn't have that problem – Jamie wasn't an animal person either.'

Kate raises her eyebrows. 'Sounds like you were a good match, then.'

For two hours, Harper sits listening to Kate make small talk about the school and the other parents, as if that's the most important thing in her life. But Harper knows it isn't – there is so much more to Kate Mason than the school community. And she's going to find out what that is.

She's relieved when Kate finally announces that she needs to get Thomas back for dinner.

'I'll go and tell the boys,' Harper says, leaving Kate alone in her living room. She can guess what Kate will do in her absence: stare at the endless photos of Jamie that Harper has deliberately plastered everywhere.

Upstairs, instead of finding the boys, who she can hear are on the top floor in the spare room, Harper goes to her bedroom. She stares out of the window at Kate's blue Mini Countryman and pictures herself throwing cans of paint over it. Blood red. To remind her about what happened to Jamie. What she set in motion. Silently she begins to count; Kate will be getting anxious when there's no sign of Thomas and all is silent upstairs. Just a fleeting glimpse of what's to come.

When she gets to one hundred, she leaves the bedroom and goes up to find the boys.

Kate is at the bottom of the stairs, peering up when Harper herds Thomas and Dexter down. She's already in her coat and has her phone in her hand. Kate won't call the police, though, not when she's the one they will be most interested in talking to about Jamie's murder.

'Come on, Thomas, we need to get going,' Kate says, handing him his coat. 'I need to feed Lula.' There's urgency in her tone, and it pleases Harper.

At the door, while Thomas and Dex say goodbye to each other, Harper grabs Kate's arm, startling her. 'Thanks for coming,' she says. 'Let's get together again. It's been so good for me – you've really taken my mind off everything.'

Before Kate can answer, Thomas tugs the sleeve of her coat. 'Can Dex come to our house? I want to show him the new football goal Dad's just bought me.

'That would be lovely,' Harper says, answering for Kate. 'How about Friday? We could order in pizza for dinner?'

'Yeah!' Thomas says, and beside him Dexter nods.

'Um, maybe another day,' Kate says. 'Dad's picking you up after school on Friday.'

'Please, Mum?' Thomas pleads. 'He won't mind coming later. Or I'll just see him on Saturday before football.'

All eyes are on Kate, and surely she will cave. Seconds tick by.

'Please, Kate,' Dexter adds.

'Okay,' Kate finally says. I guess it's fine if Thomas's dad doesn't mind.'

Harper hugs her, a gesture that turns her body cold. 'Send me your address. And I'll see you then if I don't catch you at school.'

When Harper closes the door, Dexter rushes upstairs. She'll speak to him later and make sure he had a nice time. They're going to be seeing a lot of Harper and Thomas, so she wants to make sure that Dexter will be happy about that. Despite everything she needs to do, she won't risk her son's happiness and wellbeing; if he and Thomas don't bond then Harper will find other ways to get to Kate. She rushes to the window in the living room and watches Kate drive off.

Things have been set in motion now, and there's no turning back.

EIGHT

FRIDAY 24 JANUARY

Kate finishes speaking and waits for Rowan to say something. She's just told him about being in Harper's house, under the woman's scrutinising gaze, surrounded by photos of Jamie. And somehow Kate has been forced to agree to see her again this afternoon.

Rowan's hands form a steeple in front of his chin. 'It doesn't sound like you to give in to anyone, if you don't mind me saying so. From what I've learned of you over the years – you don't let people control you.'

'I was sent some flowers,' Kate says. 'Dead lilies in a box. Covered in a sticky black substance – I don't know what it was.'

'I see. That's troubling. And you think it was this woman who sent them?'

'I don't know, but when I was at her house she had some beautiful white lilies in a vase on her mantelpiece. And I know what you're about to say. Lilies are often sent to people when someone dies. But... it had to have been Harper who sent me those flowers. She's letting me know that she's aware I spent the night with her husband.'

Rowan contemplates her words. 'It's possible. Did she make you feel angry?'

Kate's head jolts up. She should have known Rowan would refer to her anger issues. 'No. Not angry. Of course not – I feel sorry for her. Her husband has died.'

'Then what did you feel?'

Rowan's pushing her and Kate can feel anger bubbling. She must keep it at bay. Especially here with Rowan. 'I just felt... anxious, I suppose. Being in her house like that only days after I've slept with her husband. And that's the other thing – according to her they were very much together.'

'So this man lied to you.'

'Yes, I suppose. Or she's lying.'

'I can totally understand why this troubles you,' Rowan says. 'It must feel very unnerving, and perhaps she's having trouble accepting that her marriage is over if she's still got wedding photos up. But I hope you'll trust me when I say that stranger coincidences have happened.' He pauses. 'In a sense, everyone's connected in some way, through the people we know. So coincidences are only to be expected.'

'If she's lying about them being together then that's disturbing,' Kate says. 'What does she want with me?'

'Kate, the dead flowers aren't evidence that she knows you spent the night with her husband. I think this is a problem you're creating that hasn't even happened yet. That's what anxiety does.'

Kate knows this – but she also trusts her instinct. Rowan will never understand that, though.

'But if you're worried, you could lie low for a while. Let the dust settle. You don't have to have anything to do with this woman if you don't want to – you could cancel the arrangement for this afternoon.'

'I'll work it out,' Kate says. 'I always do.'

Rowan nods. 'It does trouble me that you think this woman

wants to harm you. Even if she did send those flowers, she could just be tormenting you. You haven't said how you know she wants to hurt you.'

Kate doesn't answer. *Because Harper knows I slept with Jamie – she must do. And if she's the one who killed him then there's a chance she could do the same to me.*

'And I'm worried,' Rowan continues, 'that even if you believe this, you're still inviting her into your home.'

Kate can't tell Rowan that she's doing this to keep Harper close, so she can find out what happened to Jamie. 'The truth is, I don't know which one of them lied to me. Harper or Jamie? There were wedding photos in her house, and wouldn't her son have said something if they were divorced?' *And Jamie had been so convincing.* 'And I went to her house for Thomas's sake,' Kate explains. 'He seems to really like her son, and I'm sure she wouldn't do anything when her son is there. The boys really get on.'

Frown lines crease Rowan's forehead, like tracks in sand. 'I'm just not sure how healthy this is.'

'They all talked me into it. I would never have agreed otherwise.'

'This doesn't sound like you, Kate. You've never struck me as someone who can be manipulated.' He frowns again. 'Which makes me wonder if there's more to this story.'

'You don't believe that she wants to harm me – do you?' she asks Rowan.

His mouth twists. 'I think it must feel like that to you. But it's all a bit messy. Especially if she's grieving now. We can't be sure what state their relationship was in. You and Ellis have worked hard to have an amicable split, but not everyone can manage that. And when people are hurt, they can act out of character. If you're worried about this woman, then I'd stay clear of her. And if she does anything at all that threatens you in any way then—'

'Call the police.'

Rowan nods. 'Please, Kate. I know you'd find it hard, but—'

'I think that's time up,' Kate says, pointing to the clock on the wall.

'Oh, yes.' Rowan stands and walks her to the door. He doesn't look happy, and Kate knows it's because he won't feel that he's been professional in this session. Handing advice out to her instead of allowing her to talk things through and come to her own conclusions. 'Look after yourself, Kate. I'll see you next week. Have you booked in with Frieda?'

'Definitely,' she assures him.

Outside in the reception area, Rowan's secretary sits behind her desk talking to a tall woman in a long, belted wool coat and knee-high boots. She seems overdressed for a therapy session, and when the woman laughs, a deep, hearty laugh, and says Rowan's name – Kate knows for sure she must be Rowan's wife. Kate's been coming here for two years now and has never set eyes on her.

'Thanks, Frieda,' the woman says. 'I'll pop in now, then.' She smiles at Kate as she walks past, flashing bright white teeth.

Kate smiles back and watches the woman make her way to Rowan's office, opening the door without knocking. Rowan seems so down to earth, so immune to money and material things that Kate would never have pictured him to have such a glamourous wife, so perfectly made up. So confident.

'Would you like to rebook?' Frieda asks.

Kate turns to her and considers telling her she'll call on the phone and book, but Rowan's appointment slots fill quickly and she needs him now more than ever. 'Yes, please. Friday again. My usual time, please.'

'Of course.' Frieda smiles then taps on her keyboard.

Kate thanks her and walks out into the icy cold air, her thoughts a jumbled amalgamation of too many things, none of which make sense.

Ellis calls when she's walking to the station, asking if they can talk.

'I can't now,' she says. 'I'm on my way to pick up Thomas.'

'It's important, Kate.'

'Is this to do with Thomas?'

There's a pause. 'Um, no. But—'

'Then it can wait. I'll call you later.' She hangs up and shoves her phone in her bag before disappearing into the Tube station.

NINE

FRIDAY 24 JANUARY

No matter how prepared she'd thought she was for this moment, now that Harper is in her house, a cyclone of nausea twists around Kate's stomach.

'The other mums at the school don't like being around me,' Harper tells her. She's sitting on the sofa, her back ramrod straight and her legs crossed. Today she's wearing a long, black ribbed jumper dress with a turtle neck, and her hair hangs in loose red waves around her shoulders. And even though her skin looks paler than before, almost translucent, it's clear that she's made an effort for this visit, despite her grief.

'Why do you say that?' Kate asks, sipping bitter green tea she doesn't want.

'Because they don't know what to say to the grieving widow.' She smiles. 'But you're different. You seem... comfortable around me.'

This couldn't be further from the truth. Harper has wormed her way into Kate's life, and Kate's only allowing her in so that she can find out what Harper wants, and what happened to Jamie.

Upstairs, Thomas and Dexter are playing with Thomas's

Harry Potter Lego, their muffled voices drifting down to the living room. 'Maybe you just need to give people time to get to know you?' Kate suggests. 'You've only been at the school a couple of months. How about I call Aleena?' she says. 'She could come over too so you could get to know her. I'm sure Dex would love Theo. He's a lovely boy.'

Harper raises her eyebrows. 'Bit short notice, don't you think? I'm sure she's busy, so maybe another time? I'm still getting to know you, aren't I?' She smiles, placing her mug on the coffee table. 'Have you been at work today?'

'Yes.' The lie falls easily from Kate's mouth. She doesn't work on Fridays; they are her days for therapy with Rowan, and because she works every Saturday, she needs this day off in the week.

The cat prowls into the room, making her way straight to Kate. Harper reaches out to beckon her but Lula arches her back, scurrying to Kate and nestling against her leg. 'Sorry, she's a bit wary of strangers,' Kate explains. 'She was a rescue cat. Barely alive when someone brought her into the surgery. I knew the second I saw her I had to give her a home.'

'How lovely,' Harper says, but her gaze feels heavy. 'And no need to apologise. I don't take offence easily.' She studies Kate. 'I spoke to your ex-husband yesterday. He was lovely.'

Her words thunder around the room, even though she's speaking softly.

Kate stares at her. 'What?'

'About football. He runs the junior's team, doesn't he? I only realised when I noticed his surname. And Ellis isn't a common name, is it?'

Kate's mind whirs. Did she mention Ellis's name to Harper?

'I'm trying to get Dexter signed up. He told me they were full, but said he'd see what he could do.'

It takes her a moment to process what Harper is telling her. Usually with Ellis it's very cut and dried – either there's space or there isn't. He's never been known to negotiate. There's nothing he can do if they're full to capacity. 'I thought Dex didn't like football,' Kate says, recalling Thomas's words.

'Of course he does,' Harper says. 'What boy their age doesn't like football?'

'It's a very popular club,' Kate says.

Harper nods. 'Yes, that's what he said.' She reaches for her mug again. 'What's Ellis like?' she asks. 'He sounded so... kind.'

'He's... he's a good dad. And you're right – he *is* kind. He's the kind of man who's always got things under control. Never flustered. Just kind of... calm under pressure, I guess.' Kate's not sure why she's providing Harper with so much detail about Ellis.

'He sounds like a catch,' Harper says. 'Forgive me for asking this, but what happened?'

Despite not wanting to talk about any of this to Harper, Kate's glad she's asked; it will help her work this woman out. 'He had an affair.'

Harper's eyes widen. 'Oh. That's awful. I'm sorry. Wow. That must be really painful.'

'It was, but... people make mistakes, don't they? We're human – we don't always get it right.' Kate's breath catches in her throat. Graham White's face plasters itself in her head, quickly blending into Jamie's.

'Sounds like you've forgiven him?' Harper says.

'I have. But that doesn't mean our marriage could ever work. I had to walk away; I'm just not going to be bitter about it. He's Thomas's dad, and despite what he did, he's always been there for me. Still is.'

Harper sips her coffee, studying Kate. 'That's very big of you. Not sure I could do the same.'

'We all have to do what's right for us, don't we?' Kate says, turning away from Harper's loaded gaze.

'I would never have forgiven Jamie if he'd had an affair.

Never. Oh, I know it's not healthy and blah, blah, blah, but what goes around comes around, doesn't it? Justice should always be served.'

Harper's words turn Kate's blood cold, and she puts down her cup, unable to trust her hands to continue holding it.

'But I wouldn't *just* blame him,' Harper continues. 'It's the woman's fault too. And I'd definitely never forgive her either.' She studies Kate. 'You're very blessed.' Harper turns away, glancing through the window. 'And you have a lovely home.'

Before Kate can respond, Thomas and Dexter fly into the room, asking if they can play on the green opposite the house.

'If Harper doesn't mind?' Kate says.

'How lovely to have all that green space out there.' Harper stands and peers out of the window. 'We just have a view of houses.' She sighs. 'You're so lucky, Kate. You have everything.'

'Except my husband,' Kate says, without forethought.

'Well, it seems like you're dealing with your divorce remarkably well.'

Unsure how to respond, Kate ignores her comment. 'It's very safe,' Kate says. 'In case you're worried. All the kids on the road play out there, and the parents can watch from their windows.'

'I'm fine with them going out there,' Harper says, but the way her eyes flit to the window every few seconds tells a different story.

They both watch the boys for a moment, and Kate notices that Dex hangs back, unsure of what he's doing, barely managing to kick the ball in the right direction. Harper was definitely lying.

For the next hour, Harper doesn't mention Jamie or Ellis, or anything else that puts Kate on edge, and she begins to wonder if Rowan is right and she's being paranoid, if guilt has skewed her view of what's going on. *No. It's not paranoia. There is defi-*

nitely something off about this woman. How she's fixated on me so quickly.

Harper talks about growing up in Cornwall, and how being by the sea is her happy place, and Kate hangs on to every detail, hoping for something she can use to catch her out in a lie.

Despite the way their conversation flows, Kate's relieved when Harper finally says it's time she got Dexter home.

At the door, they call across to the boys, who are deep in conversation, sitting on makeshift swings one of the neighbours erected for the neighbourhood kids, their football game abandoned.

'How lovely to see that,' Harper says, lightly placing her hand on Kate's arm. 'What a blessing.'

Once again, Kate has no idea how to respond. She's in the dark about what Harper is doing, and only knows she needs to put an end to it.

'Thank you so much for having us,' Harper says, wrapping her thin arms around Kate.

Kate's smiles, but doesn't suggest they do it again.

A red Renault Clio pulls up outside, stopping right in front of the house. 'Expecting anyone?' Harper says, turning back to Kate.

'No,' Kate says as she watches Maddy climb out of the car. She glances at Harper. 'That's the woman Ellis cheated on me with. They got together properly a couple of months ago.' Kate recalls the first time she saw Maddy – at Ellis's work Christmas party two years ago. That night, she hadn't taken any notice of Maddy, hadn't spotted a single sign that something might happen between her and Ellis.

'Oh,' Harper says, staring at Maddy as she makes her way towards them.

'Hi,' Maddy says, briefly glancing at Harper before focusing back on Kate. Sorry, am I interrupting?'

'Not at all,' Harper says. 'I was just leaving. The boys have just had a playdate.'

'Sorry,' Maddy says again, turning to Harper. 'Do we know each other? You look very familiar.'

Harper frowns. 'I don't think so. I'm sure I'd remember – I'm quite good with faces.'

Maddy inclines her head. 'Oh, okay. Sorry. I'm just sure I recognise you.' Maddy continues to stare at Harper.

Before Harper can respond, the boys walk back to the house, Dexter hanging back when he realises there's someone he doesn't know there.

'This is Maddy,' Thomas says. 'My dad's girlfriend.'

Maddy's cheeks redden. 'Hi, Thomas,' Maddy says, smiling.

'Is something wrong? Is Dad okay?'

'He's fine,' Maddy assures him. 'I was just dropping off this. Thought you might need it.' She hands Thomas a plastic bag. 'It's your school library book. You left it at your dad's.'

'Oh, thanks.' Thomas takes the bag.

Harper takes Dexter's arm. 'Come on, time to go. Thanks again, Kate. See you soon.'

Maddy turns to watch as Harper gets into her car. 'I've definitely seen her before.'

'She didn't seem to remember that.' Kate says.

'I know she *said* that, but I definitely know her. I'm sure of it. I don't forget faces, Kate. I just can't think where I remember her from.' She sighs. 'Oh, well. It will come to me.'

Maddy glances back as she drives off, and her words ring in Kate's ears. As much as Kate wants it to be a coincidence that Maddy recognised Harper, she knows it can't be.

Kate's eyes snap open as she's woken by a noise, something that doesn't belong in their house. She sits up in bed and glances at the time on her Echo Dot. Two fifty-seven. It must have been the cat, but when she turns on the torch on her phone, she sees Lula curled up at the end of her bed.

Kate slips out of bed and steps into the hall, where she can see the light from Thomas's room seeping through the gap in his door. She rushes over and opens it wider, relieved to find him sleeping soundly.

She makes her way downstairs, checking everything's as it should be. There's nothing out of the ordinary until she approaches the kitchen and hears a tap running. 'Thomas?' she calls, though she knows there's no way he could have come down without her noticing.

Holding her breath, she makes her way into the kitchen, and sees the tap on full, water cascading into the sink. Kate rushes over to it and turns it off, scanning the room. She is alone. The windows and doors are locked.

Rushing upstairs, she opens Thomas's door; he's fast asleep, snoring gently. Kate nudges him awake. 'Thomas?'

He mumbles and turns over, but his eyes stay closed.

'Sorry to wake you. Did you leave the tap running in the kitchen? Did you get up for water?' Even as she asks this, she knows it's not likely. Once Thomas is asleep nothing stirs him, and Kate always has to force him up in the morning.

Thomas rubs his eyes. 'No. I've been sleeping.'

'And you didn't get up for anything at all?'

'No. Why?'

'Don't worry. Go back to sleep.'

Back downstairs, Kate checks the front door again and the windows. She'd left her keys in Jamie's flat, and now someone has been in her house.

Someone is sending her a message. And Kate's sure this is only just the beginning.

TEN

SATURDAY 25 JANUARY

The moment dawn breaks, Kate is up, checking every room in the house again, making sure nothing else has been disturbed.

'What are you doing, Mum?' Thomas stands on the stairs, watching her.

'Nothing. Just tidying,' Kate says, affecting a casual tone, determined to hide her fear and anxiety. She will do whatever it takes to protect her son. But how long will she be able to do that when someone's been in their house?

He shrugs and doesn't question her, heading to the kitchen for breakfast.

They sit together at the table, even though Kate can't stomach any food, and has to force herself to drink the coffee she'd normally relish in the morning. If she didn't know before, then now it's clear: someone knows she was with Jamie the night he died. And the fact that they're not going to the police means there's something worse they want for her.

Changing the locks is the first thing she needs to do.

The doorbell rings when Kate's loading the dishwasher after breakfast. Cold fear slivers through her body; after the dead lilies and the tap left running, Kate knows there will be more. Plus it's been exactly a week since she found Jamie's body – is this the day the police will come for her?

She rushes to the living room window, but it's Ellis's car in the drive, not a police vehicle. With a mixture of relief and confusion, and dread because surely it's only a matter of time, she heads to the door.

'Hey,' Ellis says. Dressed casually in jeans and a dark green hooded top, he leans in as if he's about to hug her but Kate pulls back. She's not going there. Any kind of physical contact with Ellis would be dangerous. 'Everything okay?' he asks.

'You're early.'

'Is that a problem? I thought you appreciated my punctuality?'

But these are not normal times, and Kate doesn't have the patience for this. 'Have you got any keys to this house?'

Ellis frowns. 'Only the ones I gave back to you. Why?'

'And you never got another set cut? For Thomas?'

'No, I'd have told you. What's going on, Kate?'

'Nothing. I'll go and make sure Thomas is getting ready.'

'It's still strange coming in here when I don't live here any more,' Ellis says. 'And I'm worried about you. You don't seem okay.'

Kate turns back, opening her mouth to tell him what's been going on, but she thinks better of it. Like Rowan, he will tell her to go to the police. 'I'm fine,' she says, disappearing upstairs before he can question her further.

At the door, Kate hugs Thomas, clutching him tighter than usual, reluctant to let go. 'Good luck today,' she says, as Thomas pulls away.

Ellis pauses and looks back at her. Whatever it is he wants to say, he changes his mind and ushers Thomas outside.

Once they've gone, Kate grabs her laptop and sits on the sofa, googling locksmiths. She manages to get someone to come in the afternoon, but the promise of new locks does little to ease her anxiety.

Before shutting down her laptop, Kate googles Jamie Archer again, as she's done countless times over the last week. There's still barely any mention of him, and the police haven't made any arrests. And there's no mention of him having a wife or son, which leads Kate to believe Jamie when he said he and Harper were separated. Kate's a good judge of character – she didn't detect at all that Jamie was lying. In contrast to this, everything Harper says feels laced with lies. And there's still no trace of Harper online.

Who would want Jamie dead? A disgruntled ex-wife? Kate might have been able to accept and move on from her husband's affair with dignity, but not everyone can do that.

Kate's walks to the kitchen to stretch her legs. Standing by the kitchen doors, watching the pattering of rain on the patio, she pulls her phone from her pocket and makes a call she never thought she'd make. A call she doesn't want to make.

There's no answer, only a computerised voice telling her the person she's calling isn't available. Kate takes a deep breath. 'It's me. We need to talk.'

Her heart pounds in her chest as she ends the call. Has she just made a huge mistake?

Just before lunch, Aleena messages, asking if they can meet this afternoon, telling Kate she won't take no for an answer. Kate politely fobs her off, telling her friend that it's her weekend with Thomas, and there's no reply – there is a limit to what Aleena will put up with.

The locksmith arrives and Kate watches him as he works. She feels safer being in the presence of this stranger, someone who has nothing to do with Jamie, or Kate's past. But while he makes small talk, asking her how she came to lose her keys, she silently urges him to hurry up and finish.

Once he's handed her two sets of new keys and she shuts

the door behind him, relief floods over her. Whoever was in her house last night won't be able to get in again. She needs to get a burglar alarm. And a doorbell camera. Whatever it takes to protect her home, and her son.

In the kitchen, Kate glances at the calendar to check the week ahead. Her blood runs cold at the sight of the unfamiliar entry marked on Monday's date:

Jamie's 36th birthday.

ELEVEN

2013

It's past one a.m. and Jamie hasn't come home. Harper paces their tiny flat, listening for the sound of his key in the door. Her swollen stomach feels heavy and tight, ready to thrust her baby out any day now. Her due date is a month away but the baby will never hold on until then, she's sure of it. And she'd told Jamie that morning that she felt the baby might come any day; he'd hardly paid attention, consumed with something else that's been clouding his mind for months now.

Rubbing her stomach, she grabs her phone and calls Jamie again. Straight away she gets his voicemail: *Hi, this is Jamie. Leave a message and I promise I'll get back to you.*

With a sickening lurch in her stomach, Harper ends the call, immediately texting him again. *Where are you? Getting worried. The baby feels weird.*

He'd said he was going for drinks after work with a few colleagues, but even if he stayed until closing, he should have been back by now. And Jamie never turns off his phone. The baby kicks so forcefully that Harper has to sit. 'You're sensing my anxiety, aren't you?' she says aloud, rubbing her stomach again as the baby thrashes beneath her hand. She's read every book she could find about what to expect during pregnancy, and how to nurture and care for her unborn child, so she knows she needs to get a grip on her fear. 'I am calm,' she says, taking a deep breath. 'I am calm.' But the bubbles in her stomach are still there, ignoring the messages her mind is attempting to send.

She flicks through her phone until she finds Sam's number. She's not sure if he'll know anything about Jamie's whereabouts, but he's the only one of his friends whose number she knows.

'Hello?' Sam's voice is heavy with sleep.

'Jamie hasn't come home,' she says without preamble.

'Oh.' There's a brief pause. 'Jamie?'

'Yes. Jamie. This is Harper. He went out with friends after work and he hasn't come home. I'm worried – he's never done this before.'

'Oh, look, um, I don't know what to tell you.' Sam's voice fades, as if he's holding the phone away from his ear.

'Have you heard from him today?' Harper asks. 'I know how close you are. Did he mention anything?' Harper's words are gushing out of her; she's not convinced she's making sense. And all the while her stomach stretches and throbs.

Silence again, so intense that Harper is sure she can hear her own heartbeat.

'This is awkward,' Sam says. 'I actually haven't spoken to Jamie for about a year now.' His words echo around the room.

Harper's chest tightens and she struggles to catch her breath. She thinks of all the times Jamie has said he's meeting up with Sam, all the times he's been glued to his phone, messaging his closest friend. They're in contact daily. See each other every week, at least. 'But... I don't understand. He met up with you last week.'

There's a deep exhalation before Sam speaks. 'Look, I don't know what he's been telling you, but Jamie and I haven't communicated at all over the past year. Our friendship... let's just say there hasn't been one for a long time. I'm sorry.'

Harper's breath catches in her throat; she can't find any words, despite a thousand thoughts stampeding through her head.

'I need to go now,' Sam says.

'Wait! What happened?'

'I really think you need to talk to Jamie about that,' he says.

'I'm eight months pregnant!' she shrieks. But it's too late, Sam has already ended the call.

An intense burst of pain erupts in her body. She clutches her stomach, groaning, as a gush of liquid trickles down her legs. She looks down, and finds herself staring at a river of blood.

Harper opens her eyes, and for a brief moment she doesn't know where she is. And then, with sickening clarity, it all comes back to her.

Beneath the crisp hospital sheet, she feels her stomach – flatter now, devoid of life. And then she turns to see Jamie sitting by her bed, his eyes red and swollen.

'The baby,' Harper says, though she already knows from the aching emptiness in her body.

Jamie shakes his head. 'She's... she's gone, Harper.' And then his tears come thick and fast.

Watching him, it all floods back to Harper. How she couldn't find Jamie. The lies he's sold her. 'How long was I there before they found me?'

Jamie hangs his head. 'I don't know. They think not long. I got back around two and found you. But they said even if I'd been at home and could have got you to the hospital sooner, she wouldn't have survived the birth.

Harper shakes her head. 'No!' she screams. 'I don't believe that. She would have been fine! You did this!'

And in that moment, she knows she will never forgive Jamie for their daughter's death.

TWELVE

MONDAY 27 JANUARY

The weekend has crawled past, and Kate feels as though she's been holding her breath, waiting for something else to happen. The calendar entry has unsettled her. She had no idea when Jamie's birthday was, and she would never have written it on the calendar. It has to be Harper's doing.

Kate has expected Harper to message her, but her phone has been eerily silent. Even Aleena hasn't responded, despite Kate sending a message to apologise for letting her down again. All of this makes Kate even more uneasy.

And she still hasn't heard back from the one person she needs to speak to. She tries again now, but again it goes to voice-mail. 'We really need to talk. Now. I'll keep calling until you answer me. I don't have any choice.'

After walking Thomas to school, stepping into the surgery feels unfamiliar this morning, as if Kate no longer belongs there. She thinks about Brighton, where her mother moved them after Graham White, and part of her aches for it. Her safe place, away from everything that's happened to her. She should never have come back to London it was insanity to think that coming back here in her twenties could heal her, that she could confront the city where something so heinous had begun. And now it's happening all over again.

She and Thomas could start a new life by the coast, away from all of this. Before it's too late.

She switches on the lights, bathing the reception area in a warm, golden glow. Her eyes are drawn to the photos of pets adorning the walls, the adverts for pet food and the insurance the surgery offers, the reminders for pet owners to keep up to date with their inoculations. A flood of defiance surges through her. This is her surgery – hers and her business partner David's – and she won't let anything drive her away.

The cleaners have already been, leaving behind the faint odour of bleach and gleaming floors that will be patterned with muddy paw prints by the end of the day.

Alone in the surgery – it will be an hour before Lara the receptionist arrives – Kate makes green tea and takes it to her office at the back of the building, turning on the computer to check today's bookings. There are no surgeries, but a long list of consultations in the morning.

Kate looks up to see David standing in the doorway. 'Hey,' he says. 'You okay? Are you sure you don't need to take some time off?'

Last Monday she'd let David believe that if she didn't seem herself, it was because of her impending divorce. Nothing to do with her sleeping with a man one night only to find him dead the next day.

'I really don't need to take time off,' Kate says. 'I'm fine. Being here is good for me.'

David smiles. 'Just don't forget you hardly used any leave last year. And you covered for me loads so I owe you.'

'You had your daughter's wedding – it was the least I could do.'

'Still. Just think about taking a break once in a while.'

Kate had met David eight years ago when they'd both

worked for a large veterinary practice in Hammersmith. She'd immediately liked his strong work ethic, and the way he cared for the animals, and they'd hit it off. She'd kept that wall around her though, meaning he would never know the whole of her, but she felt as comfortable as she could around him. As long as they didn't talk about anything personal, which thankfully David never did. Sometimes he'd look at her as if he wanted to ask her something, but he'd always refrain. At forty-nine, with a wife and three grown-up children, their lives never crossed outside of work.

When he'd asked her if she wanted to start a practice with him, Kate had initially said no. Being tied to something that she couldn't easily walk away from terrified her. But he wouldn't take no for an answer, and two years ago The Pet Clinic opened. At the same time as the podcast about Graham White. Kate shudders to think of this, of how it triggered memories she'd thought she'd managed to bury. All of this – owning the surgery, and having to confront her past – is what led Kate to seek help from Rowan.

'Being at work is like a break,' Kate tells David.

'Oh, I almost forgot,' David says, pulling off his coat. His cheeks are red from the cold and he rubs his hands together. 'A man came in asking for you the other week. It must have been a Friday as you were off.'

'Oh?'

'Yeah, sorry I forgot to mention it last week. It's been a busy week.'

Kate looks up from her computer. 'What did he want? Did he leave his name?'

'No, don't think he did. He just said his dog didn't respond well to male vets so he wanted a female. Told me you'd been recommended to him. He said he'd come back on Monday but he never did. I'd forgotten all about it. Thought it was a bit weird to be honest.'

'Maybe he'll come back,' Kate says. 'Or maybe he found somewhere else.'

'That's the thing,' David says, pulling out his phone. 'I don't think he will.'

Kate stares at him. 'Why?'

'Because I'm sure it's this guy.' David holds out his phone to Kate, and she finds herself staring at a photo of Jamie Archer. The only one she's found of him online when she's checked each day. 'And he was found dead last Saturday.'

Focusing on the animals forces away all the disturbing thoughts clouding Kate's mind, masking the sense that her life is rapidly imploding. But when the morning consultations are over, once again darkness spreads over her. She'd let herself believe that meeting Jamie had been nothing more than a chance encounter, but David's revelation is proof that he knew who Kate was before they met at the bar that evening.

Kate can't wrap her head around how he could have known she'd be at Tequila Mockingbird – only she and Aleena knew where they were going. And they'd only decided on that bar earlier that week. It had been Aleena's recommendation, and nobody else's... Kate realises that Ellis also knew – she'd mentioned it to him when he'd picked up Thomas that evening. They'd laughed at the name. *Tequila Mockingbird.* Now she can't see how they ever found it funny. Kate considers messaging Aleena to ask her if she'd mentioned to anyone where they were going that night, but how would she ever explain why she was asking?

Questions burn in Kate's head as she finally sits down and pulls out the salad she brought from home. What did Jamie want with her? Since the incident with Graham White, Kate's kept her head down, minded her own business and never had any trouble with anyone. Whenever she's felt her temper rising, she's walked away, stifled emotions that must be trapped inside her, ready to erupt.

Graham White is the only enemy she's made, but whenever Kate's checked online, there's been nothing to suggest any connection between Jamie and Graham White. So what is she missing?

Her phone buzzes in her bag and she checks her messages. Three from Harper, all sent within the same hour earlier this morning. One asking how Kate is, another suggesting they go for a coffee after school today, and the last one telling Kate she's worried she hasn't had a reply from her.

Kate stares at her phone and considers switching it off, but she needs it on in case the school need to contact her about Thomas for any reason. Though Harper's obsessiveness is really unsettling her.

In a couple of hours Harper will be at the school gates – they both live too far from school for their children to walk on their own – and Kate is sure Harper intends to look for her. There's nowhere to hide. She pulls out her phone and sends a message to Ellis. *Could you pick Thomas up from school? Emergency at work.*

Within seconds his reply comes. *Working from home today so fine with me. Everything okay?*

Kate hastily replies, telling him she needs to stay later at work.

As soon as Ellis's response comes – a thumbs up and two kisses – she slips her phone in her bag and shoves it in her drawer. 'I'll do the surgery on the Taylors' cat,' she tells David when she finds him in the reception area, sorting out a problem with the booking system with their receptionist Lara.

'Are you sure?'

'Yes. You leave early. I'm happy to stay late and monitor Lucky.'

'Thanks, Kate,' David says, turning back to the computer. 'I could actually do with getting home early today.'

Envying their normality, she watches David and Lara for a moment, engrossed in their task, their minds free of turmoil. And with her stomach twisting into knots, Kate slips out to her office.

She attempts to reason with herself: It's been nine days since Jamie was murdered; if the police had any idea that Kate was in his flat, they would have knocked on her door by now. Her keyring had nothing personal on it that could lead them to her. Yes, her DNA will be all over Jamie's sheets, and the glass she drank from, but they'd have to know about Kate to link her to it. If Harper or anyone else had any evidence, then it would be in the hands of the police. But now it seems likely that Jamie sought her out and made sure he bumped into her that Friday night. He couldn't have predicted that she'd go back to that flat with him, or that she'd sleep with him. She casts her mind back and finds nothing predatory in the way Jamie acted towards her. He never once pushed her to do anything – Kate had done what she wanted to do.

With nothing online to help her, it can only be Harper who will lead her to the truth. Kate won't stop until she finds out what Jamie wanted with her, and why he ended up dead. And who is targeting her because of it.

Chatter greets her the moment she steps into her house – Ellis's throaty laugh followed by Thomas's chuckle – and for the briefest moment it feels like it did before the separation, as if time has been erased. But Kate's thrown back to reality when her phone pings and she sees Harper's name. A voicemail this time. Once again, she ignores it and goes to the kitchen, where she finds Ellis and Thomas playing Uno.

'Hi,' she says, forcing a smile and hugging Thomas. She turns to Ellis. 'Thanks for doing pick-up, Ellis.'

'You're welcome.'

'Dad! You'll lose again if you don't concentrate,' Thomas warns.

Ellis studies his cards before placing one down.

'Don't you need to get back?' Kate asks.

'Nope. All done for the day.' He smiles at Thomas. 'Pick up two!'

'Great,' Thomas moans. 'Mum, can Dad stay for dinner?' He places a card on the table. 'Please?'

Kate glances at Ellis. 'I don't think so. Maybe another time?'

Ellis nods and turns back to his cards, masking his disappointment, she's sure. And when Kate looks at Thomas, the sadness on his face is too much to bear.

'Maybe it's okay,' she says. 'We're only having pasta, though.'

'My favourite,' Ellis says, even though they all know he'd rather avoid it.

After they eat – all of them pretending it's a regular family dinner – Ellis helps Kate clear away while Thomas goes upstairs to have his bath. 'What happened to the calendar?' he asks, nodding his head towards the fridge.'

'It got ruined. I spilled milk all over it so had to throw it out.'

'Oh.' He smiles. 'Make sure you don't forget anything.'

Kate doesn't respond, and focuses on rinsing the plates.

'Are you okay?' Ellis asks. 'You seem... quiet.'

'Just tired. Work's been busy this week. I operated on a cat today. She's twenty-one – that's a hundred in human years. She's an amazing animal.'

He nods, but Kate can tell he's not listening, even though he's looking right at her. Behind his eyes is something unspoken.

'What is it?' she asks. 'Something's wrong.'

Ellis smiles. 'You know me so well.'

'Just spit it out.'

'Maddy wants us to move in together.'

Kate's breath catches in her throat for a moment, before she recovers herself. 'Do it then.'

'But we've only been together properly for a couple of months. I don't count that one night a couple of years ago. Or the few times we've met up and tried to make it work. How do I know it will even work this time?'

'Do you love her?' Kate asks.

He hesitates, and in that brief silence she has her answer. 'Please tell me this isn't about me. Our marriage is over, Ellis.'

'It doesn't have to be,' he says, reaching for her hand.

Kate pulls away; she can't let Ellis drag her back in, especially now. 'We're separated. There's no going back, you know that.'

'Kate, I know you inside out. You don't have to start again with someone else. And have to explain your past all over again. You know I get it all, and I've supported you one hundred per cent.'

A vision of Jamie flashes into her mind. 'What makes you think I want to start again? I'm happy for it to be just me and Thomas. I don't need anyone or anything else.'

'You never have needed anyone, have you? So determined to do it all yourself. But Kate – we all need people to help us get through stuff.'

Kate knows this – as independent as she is, she's come to rely on Rowan Hess. She doesn't mention this to Ellis. He knows she has therapy sessions – he'd encouraged it when she'd told him she thought it was time she faced her past – but Kate's aware that Ellis thinks she shouldn't still need them after two years.

'I think you should stop this,' she says. 'Stop even entertaining ideas of us. It's not fair to Maddy. She... she loves you.'

'And you're my wife.'

'Not any more.' She turns away. 'Can you just go?'

There's a long pause, but still she doesn't turn around to face him.

'I'm sorry,' he says eventually. 'I should never have said all this. I'll say goodbye to Thomas.'

Kate watches Ellis leave, surprised that she has no tears left to cry.

Later, she sits in Thomas's room, listening as he talks about his day. Kate lets his words soak in, forcing all other thoughts from her head. 'Can I go to Dex's house again?' he asks. 'He's really cool. Even though he's not that good at football. How about after school on Friday?'

Kate freezes. She'd been hoping that their friendship would fizzle out before having a chance to fully form. 'But it's your weekend with me. You've been with your dad the last two so it would be nice if we did something together.'

'I know, but maybe you could come too? You like Dex's mum, don't you? Please, Mum?'

Kate won't leave her son in Harper's care, and nor does she want to spend any time there. 'Um, I'll have to think about it. I was planning some things for us to do. I know I've been a bit distracted with work lately.'

'Please, Mum? It would still be us doing something together.'

'I suppose I can ask his mum,' Kate says, praying that they already have plans on Friday.

Thomas's face brightens. 'Actually, Dex said it was his mum's idea and they're not doing anything on Friday.'

Heat rushes to Kate's cheeks, burning her skin. 'You've seen a lot of him this week,' she says. 'Maybe Dex needs to make some other friends too? Otherwise how will he get to know any other kids?' Thomas has no shortage of friends; it's one thing she and Ellis never had to worry about.

Thomas shrugs. 'Yeah, but I like Dex. I feel bad for him. He lost his dad and he's new to the school – he must feel a bit lonely.'

'You're a kind boy,' Kate says, smiling, despite the stabbing pains in her stomach.

'But you will ask his mum, wont' you? You won't forget? Dex said she's getting him a pet gecko. How cool is that? They're getting him on Thursday after school. So if we go on Friday we can see it. That's why she said I should go over – so I can see it. They're calling him Dumbledore – you know, from Harry Potter.'

More lies. Harper made it clear that she doesn't like pets, so why would she get Dex a gecko? 'Are you sure they're getting a pet? You have to feed geckos live insects.'

Thomas squints at her; he knows there's more to Kate's questioning – he's always been able to read her. Because she hasn't yet found a way to tell him about Graham White, Kate has vowed that she will never lie to Thomas about anything – big or small. Yet now she's having to keep things from him. To protect him, she reminds herself. One day she will tell him the truth, but she has to know that he'll be ready to hear it first.

'Don't you like Dex?' Thomas asks.

'I don't really know him,' Kate says. 'But he seems nice.'

'His mum's a bit weird, though, isn't she?'

'What makes you say that?'

He shrugs. 'Dunno. She's always just... staring at me. And then when I look at her, she turns away and pretends she hasn't been looking. But I still want to go to their house. It's not Dex who's weird.'

'It's late,' she says. 'Let's get some sleep and talk about this tomorrow.'

Downstairs in the hallway, Kate tidies away the shoes, coats and bags. She checks Thomas's school bag, where she always finds notes he's forgotten to tell her about. A white A5 envelope falls out of his reading book, bearing a printed label with Thomas's name and class on it.

Kate rips it open and pulls out the folded sheet of paper, freezing when she sees the photo printed on it.

Smiling back at her, his blue eyes gleaming in the light of the camera lens, is Jamie Archer.

THIRTEEN

TUESDAY 28 JANUARY

After another night devoid of sleep, Kate wakes Thomas earlier than usual. He rolls over and stretches, taking his time to open his eyes.

'Thomas, I need to ask you something,' Kate says, sitting on the side of his bed while slowly her son becomes alert. 'I found a white envelope in your school bag. Did you see who put it in there?'

Rubbing his eyes, he frowns and pulls himself up. 'No. Why? What is it?'

Kate's already prepared her answer – a harmless lie she must tell to shield Thomas from this. 'Nothing important. It was for another parent in a different year. I just wondered how it got in your bag. It wasn't for you. Are you sure you didn't see anyone put it in there?'

'No. I don't know why it was in my bag. Why are you being weird, Mum?'

Kate takes a deep breath. 'Sorry. I just wondered how it could have got in your bag. 'So you definitely didn't see anything? None of the teachers put it in there? None of your school friends?'

'No.' He pulls the duvet back and stretches again. 'You're still being weird.'

'Sorry.' Kate stands up. 'I'll let you get ready.'

Downstairs, she boils the kettle, trying to organise her thoughts so she can work out what to do. It could only have been Harper, and she could have got Dex to put the envelope in Thomas's bag – no one other than the teachers would have access to it during the school day. Ignoring the kettle, to quell her nausea Kate quickly drinks the water that's been sitting on the worktop since last night.

Thomas could have opened the envelope – it had his name and class on it after all, not hers – and how would she be able to answer the questions he'd have? He might even tell Ellis. Thinking of her ex-husband reminds Kate that he picked Thomas up from school yesterday – so he might have looked in the bag himself.

'Mum? Are you okay? You look worried.'

Thomas's voice startles her – she hadn't heard him come downstairs. 'Sorry, just work stuff on my mind. Nothing for you to worry about.'

Kate drops Thomas at the school breakfast club, relieved that Harper doesn't send Dex to it – at least not yet. Then she walks to the surgery, preparing herself to tell more lies.

David's already in when she gets there, sitting in his office, frowning as he stares at his computer. He doesn't look up but waves his hand.

'Everything okay?' Kate asks.

'Yeah. All good with you?'

'Actually, I need a favour.'

David stops tapping on the keyboard and looks up.

'Could you cover for me this morning and then I'll return

the favour in the afternoon? There's something I have to take care of and it really can't wait.'

'Yeah, of course.' He frowns. 'Is everything okay?'

'Just stuff going on at school with Thomas.' She winces at her lie.

'I hope he's okay?'

'He's fine. I just need to go in and sort something out.'

David offers a thin smile. 'We've actually got a quiet morning for once, so don't worry. Take as long as you need.'

Kate thanks him, offering to make him coffee before she leaves, and as she makes her way to the kitchen, she can feel David's questioning glance on her. He knows something is wrong. How long can she keep it hidden?

Standing across from the school, Kate waits for Harper and Dex to arrive. A steady flow of parents come and go, and with one minute to go until the gates are locked, Kate wonders if Harper has chosen to keep Dex at home today. If Harper is the one who put that photo in Thomas's bag, she'll assume that Kate's found it by now, and she'll have no way to know how Kate will react.

Just as the head teacher Mrs Finnigan pulls out her keys, Kate sees Harper and Dex rushing towards the gates – Harper in Adidas leggings and trainers, her long hair tied back in a ponytail that swings as she runs. At the gate, she stops and says something to the head, then watches Dex as he races in.

When Harper turns and walks towards the park, Kate is confident that she must be going home via the shortcut through the park. Kate follows.

Harper walks fast, never once looking behind, and when she reaches her front door and pulls her keys from her bag, Kate calls out to her. 'Wait!'

Harper turns around and there's a flicker of shock in her

eyes before she smiles. 'Kate! This is a surprise. What are you doing here?'

'Can we talk?'

Harper's brief hesitation is barely perceptible, but Kate is tuned in to every detail. 'Of course. Come in. I'm sorry the house is a bit of a mess. We both overslept this morning so Dex was late for school. Thankfully Mrs Finnigan was very kind about it. She knows how hard things are for Dexter right now.' Harper sighs. 'For both of us.'

Taking a deep breath, Kate follows her inside, forcing away panic when Harper closes the door. Kate has no idea who this woman is, or what she's capable of, but clearly that photo, the dead flowers, and that calendar entry were all sent as a warning.

'Can I take your coat?' Harper offers, hanging her own on a coat hook.

'I'll leave it on. I won't be staying long.'

Harper's eyes widen. 'Okay. Come through – I'm gasping for a coffee. Would you like one?'

'When's Jamie's birthday?'

Harper stares at her. 'What? Why are you asking me that?'

'When is it?'

'It was actually yesterday. Or it should have been. Why do you want to know? Has something happened?'

Kate follows Harper into the kitchen.

'Sorry, Kate, but you just seem a bit... I don't know. Off? Have I done something? You haven't replied to any of my messages.'

Kate reaches into her bag and pulls out the envelope, a flash of heat exploding in her body. 'I found this in Thomas's school bag yesterday.' She hands it to Harper.

Harper's fingers barely grasp it as Kate pushes it into her hand. 'What is it?'

'Open it.'

Harper frowns, staring at the envelope. 'This is for Thomas.

What is this about, Kate? I don't understand. And I have to be honest, you're starting to freak me out.'

'Just open it,' Kate repeats, trying to remain calm.

Finally, Harper pulls out the picture of Jamie. Kate watches her face, unreadable as always. Harper stares at it for a moment, then tuns to Kate. 'Why have you got this picture?'

'Someone put it in Thomas's bag, addressed to him. Was it you?'

Her mouth hangs open. 'Why would I do that? This is a picture of my dead husband!'

'I know that.'

Something passes across Harper's face. 'Then I'll repeat my question. Why would I put that in your son's bag?'

'You tell me!'

'I don't know anything about this. It's absurd! Why on earth would I do this? And why are you asking about Jamie's birthday?' Harper stares at the picture again, then clutches it to her chest. 'My Jamie.' But not a single tear falls from her eyes. 'Is this why you've been ignoring my calls and messages?'

'There's no one else it could be,' Kate says, but she's wavering, less certain now. Harper looks so distraught – what if Kate's got this wrong? 'And you sent me dead flowers. Lilies, like the ones in your living room. You've been in my house too. Writing on my calendar – I know it was you. There's no one else it could have been!' Her eyes narrow. 'I won't let this lie, Harper.'

Harper shakes her head. 'I don't know what's going on, but I think you should go.'

It's only when Kate's outside, breathing in the chilly air, that she realises she's left the photo and envelope with Harper. And with it, any hope of proving it was Harper who planted it.

FOURTEEN

Harper has spent the morning trying to make sense of what's happened. Kate appearing on her doorstep has thrown her off course, and she hates surprises.

A printed photo of Jamie in Thomas's school bag. Dead lilies. None of it makes sense. She and Kate are the only ones who know that Kate spent the night with Jamie, but she hasn't done any of these things Kate's accused her of. It troubles Harper that she can't work it out. Did Kate do it herself? For what purpose? Either way, it's disturbing. She hadn't figured that Kate wasn't of sound mind, but now she's beginning to wonder.

Harper places her phone in the pocket of her leggings. She needs to run – to clear her mind and help her work out her next move. She hasn't run since Jamie died, but she desperately needs to feel adrenalin firing through her body. It will help her think. She puts on her trainers and thermal running jacket and leaves the house.

Up ahead, she spots Kate's friend Aleena walking on the other side of the road, heading towards the parade of shops.

Harper had spoken to her yesterday when they were waiting for the kids to come out, and Aleena had seemed kind and friendly. People's loyalties can be turned, Harper knows – if you approach them in the right way.

Aleena is on her phone, paying no attention to anything around her, so doesn't notice Harper walking up behind her just as she finishes her call.

'Hi,' Harper says, coming up beside her.

'Oh, hi. Sorry – I didn't see you. My boss was on the phone harassing me for something I can't actually do until she sends me the right documents. Which she's been promising to do for around a week.' She rolls her eyes. 'Honestly – some people!'

This is Harper's chance to make a connection with Aleena. 'Tell me about it – my manager is dreadful. We're in human resources so you'd think he'd know a bit about managing staff, but he doesn't have a clue. I feel your pain. Sometimes it makes me want to resign,' Harper adds.

Aleena nods. 'I have that thought most days.' She pauses, studying Harper. 'How are you doing, anyway? Having to meet new parents at the school gate can't be easy with everything you're going through.'

'It's definitely hard to make friends. And I thought I had, but ...'

Aleena stops walking. 'But what?'

'Actually, do you have a few minutes? Maybe we could grab a quick coffee?'

Aleena checks her phone. 'Yeah, sure. I'm in no rush to get back to my laptop. The joys of working from home! I just popped out to get milk before we run out.'

Harper smiles as they make their way to the coffee shop. This will get her back on track.

'Is everything okay?' Aleena asks, when they're sitting with their coffee.

Harper takes her time to answer. 'Actually – there is something, and I was hoping I could talk to you about it. I know we've only just met but... you seem like a kind person.'

'I try to be,' Aleena says, smiling. 'Not always easy!'

Harper mirrors her smile. 'This might be a bit awkward, but I'm a bit worried about Kate.'

'Kate as in Thomas's mum? Why?'

'I really don't know how to say this, but I've found out some things. And I don't think Kate is who she says she is.' There – Harper has done it now, unleashed words she can't take back or mould into something else.

Aleena shifts back in her seat, frowning. 'What do you mean?'

She's getting ready to defend her friend, but Harper is sure that won't last long. 'It's better if I show you,' Harper says, reaching for her phone. She pulls up the local news story and hands it to Aleena. 'Read this first.'

As she reads, Aleena's mouth twitches, and Harper feels a flood of guilt for having to involve her. Aleena is innocent – she's not the one who is responsible for Jamie's death. But this is a means to an end, and now she's started it, Harper needs to see this through.

'I don't understand,' Aleena says. 'What's this Graham White got to do with Kate?'

'That's what I wondered,' Harper says, her words carefully rehearsed. 'So I did some digging and I found out that the fifteen-year-old girl it's talking about was Kate.'

Aleen's jaw drops. 'No. It can't be. That's not Kate. She wouldn't—'

'That's what I was hoping. But... it's her. I know someone who works for the crown prosecution service and they verified it was Kate Mason, and her address was in South Norwood. Does that ring a bell? Did Kate ever tell you she grew up there?'

With a sigh, Aleena nods. 'Yes. I have cousins close by in Thornton Heath so we've talked about it before.' She looks up to the ceiling, her shoulders drooping. 'Jesus. Why wouldn't she tell me?'

Harper lowers her voice. 'But you can never share that I told you how I found out. My friend's job would be on the line.'

There's a moment of silence before Aleena responds. 'I won't say anything. Of course not.' She points to Harper's phone. 'But that says it was an accident. The police didn't even press charges. It says this Graham White had attacked her and she was just trying to defend herself. He could have killed her.'

'That's what I thought,' Harper says. 'But then I looked into it more. There's a podcaster who investigates old cases that are a bit ambiguous. Faye Held. She did a podcast on this case a couple of years ago and the reaction was disturbing. People who knew Kate came forward to say that Kate had deliberately killed him. That maybe she'd had some kind of relationship with him and killed him in a jealous rage. Who knows?'

The disbelief in Aleena's eyes is a warning that Harper needs to rein it in. But it's all there online, Aleena will be able to find it for herself, and then she'll know that there is another side to this story. And if Kate is guilty of one murder, it's not too much of a jump to assume she could be guilty of another.

'People will say anything, though,' Aleena says, but her voice is quiet, uncertain. 'Especially to get listeners.'

'I know. But this goes way beyond what a podcaster is suggesting.' Harper sighs. 'I don't want to believe it,' she says. 'Kate's been so kind to me and Dexter. But why wouldn't she have told you – her closest friend – if she was innocent? You've been friends for years now. Haven't you shared things with her?'

Aleena stares at Harper, then slowly nods. 'Yeah, course. We talk about lots of things. Our kids. Work.' She falls silent.

'But has she ever shared anything really personal with you? Anything at all?'

Aleena takes a moment to answer. 'Just her divorce. But even then she doesn't say much about their break-up. But she doesn't have to, does she? It's nobody else's business.'

'It just makes me uneasy,' Harper says. 'Friendships are based on trust and vulnerability. Showing how you truly are. I've already done a lot of that with Kate – shared things about my marriage, and Jamie's death. And, yes, it's understandable that she wouldn't confide in me about her past when we've only just met. But you're her closest friend. I'm just worried about Dexter if he's going to be spending a lot of time in Kate's house. I was actually hoping you'd tell me you already knew, and back up her story. But the fact she didn't tell you—'

'You said you were worried about her.' Aleena pushes her unfinished coffee aside.

'Yes, I am.' Harper takes a deep breath. The lie she's about to tell needs to be convincing. 'When I was at her house the other day, there was a pile of papers on her coffee table. When Kate went to the bathroom, I accidentally knocked them off when I reached for my bag. They fell on the floor, and I was just sorting them out when I found a picture of Graham White, printed from an article. That's when I looked it up. I wouldn't have found out anything otherwise.'

'This is just... I don't really know what to say.' Aleena pushes her cup away. Her distress makes Harper feel a jolt of guilt, until she reminds herself that this is Kate's doing. 'Why would she have a picture of the man who attacked her?'

'I don't know. But... it's a bit worrying. I don't know if she's... spiralling in some way. If she never dealt with her trauma then it's likely it will still be inside her, waiting to explode.'

'Sorry,' Aleena says. 'This is a huge shock.'

Silence sits between them, drowning out the clinking of cutlery and the hiss of the coffee machine.

'I think I should go.' Aleena stands up and pulls her bag

onto her shoulder. 'Thanks for telling me this, though. And for looking out for Kate.'

Harper watches Aleena leave, crossing the road with barely a glance left or right. There's no way of telling what Aleena will do next – but at least it sends a message to Kate just how easily Harper can disrupt her life.

FIFTEEN

TUESDAY 28 JANUARY

Kate leaves the surgery and makes her way to South Kensington. The Tube is packed with rush-hour commuters, hot bodies crammed together, vying for space. She wants to scream, but wills her mind to be silent. Harper had been so convincing, so believable, but Kate won't let herself be fooled. Nobody else could know she spent that night with Jamie.

Relieved to finally breathe in the cool outside air, Kate rushes towards Rowan's practice. It's nearly six p.m., but she's sure that Rowan won't have left yet. He's told her before that he doesn't leave until all his paperwork for the day is done, and neatly filed away, and Kate knows each of his work days is booked solid with appointments.

Once again, Kate has had to call on Ellis to pick up Thomas, but at least he did it without asking questions, other than to check she was okay. He still cares about her – although it's more than that – but she can't give headspace to that now.

The door is open when Kate reaches the mews house, and she steps inside, expecting to see Frieda at her desk, but instead her chair sits empty. Feeling like an intruder, Kate makes her way to Rowan's door and listens for a moment before knocking, just to make sure he's not still with a patient. Or his wife again.

'Come in,' Rowan calls, when she finally raps on his door. He looks up as she enters the room, his eyes widening.

'I'm sorry,' Kate begins. 'The door was open so I came through.'

'I thought you were Frieda,' he says. 'Coming back because she's forgotten something. I let her go a bit early today. Are you okay? Has something happened?'

Kate hovers by the door; this will be a defining moment and she wants to be able to run if she needs to. 'You said if I needed to, I could talk to you any time.'

He nods. 'Yes, I tell all my patients that. I want to be available whenever anyone needs me. If it's urgent, of course. I do need some boundaries.'

'This *is* urgent. Someone put a photo of the man I slept with in my son's school bag. Addressed to him. Thankfully I found it before Thomas saw it and opened it. And there are things I haven't told you.'

Rowan stands. 'You'd better sit down.' He walks to the door, leaving it slightly ajar.

'Do you mind if I stand?' Kate says. 'I really can't sit right now.'

'Whatever makes you comfortable. Just start from the beginning.' He sits down, showing her he's ready to listen.

Kate tells him how she found the photo, and how when confronted, Harper denied all knowledge of it. 'I know it was her – it had to be. Nobody else could have put that envelope in Thomas's bag. What I don't get is why she'd do that? Why not just confront me? What is she hoping to achieve?'

For a moment, Rowan considers everything she's said. 'I agree this is troubling,' he says. 'And I'm happy to talk through any of it with you, but you know I can't tell you what to do, Kate. I can help you work it out, though.'

As frustrating as this is, Kate understands. 'I know. I'm not looking for you to tell me what to do. I just...' She takes a deep breath. 'There's more to this. And telling you will change everything.'

Rowan shifts in his seat. 'Okay. But again, we can work through that together.'

'I wasn't exactly honest with you about the man I slept with.'

'Okay.' Rowan's forehead creases.

'I'm sorry. I just wasn't ready to talk about it. It was too painful. But now I have no choice, because things are escalating and I need you to believe that this woman is targeting me.'

'Go on,' Rowan says.'

'The man I slept with was called Jamie Archer. And I... I lied about how he died. It wasn't natural causes... it looks like he was murdered.'

Silence descends on them as Rowan grapples with the bombshell she's dropped. 'I'm very sorry to hear that,' he says, after a moment. 'That must have brought up all kinds of feelings. And I can see that this makes everything with his wife so much harder. When did he die?'

Kate pauses. Part of her still can't believe she's telling Rowan all of this. But what choice does she have? It's all catching up with her. 'The day after I slept with him.'

Silence again – deafening and excruciating. Kate hadn't wanted to do this, but now she has there's no going back.

'How dreadful,' Rowan says, sitting straighter. 'What happened?'

'I don't know. I don't know anything. All I know is that I left him in the early hours of that morning and he was fine. I spoke to him. We said goodbye to each other and arranged for me to go back the next afternoon.'

Rowan's mouth hangs open as he stares at her and his body seems to freeze. Kate's never seen him stunned speechless, and for a second he feels like a stranger, until finally he composes himself. 'Kate, have you told the police that you were with him?' he says, glancing at the clock above her head.

'No. And please don't tell me to.'

'But you would have been one of the last people to see him. You must go to the police. Right away. And you can tell them what you believe his wife is doing too.'

Slowly, Kate shakes her head. 'I can't.'

Rowan sighs. 'Because of Graham White?'

She doesn't answer.

'That's got *nothing* to do with this,' Rowan continues. 'Kate, please listen to me. You need to tell the police. Now. It's already been several days, hasn't it?'

'Nearly ten.'

'Can I ask what's made you tell me this now?' Rowan asks. 'You must have known that I'm duty-bound to inform the police. Why tell me at all?'

'Because I need your help. That photo was a warning from Harper. And she's done other stuff too. Sending me dead lilies. Writing Jamie's birthday in my calendar.'

Rowan stares at her. He doesn't believe her – and even Kate, now that she's said it aloud – wonders if she's losing her mind.

'I'm not sure how she knows I was with Jamie,' she continues, 'but clearly she does. And I've been thinking about this a lot – if she believes I had an affair with him, why doesn't she confront me? That's what most people would do? It scares me that she's trying to make friends, to have me in her life. It can only mean she's got something else in mind. I told you she wanted to kill me and now this is proof.'

Rowan stands and walks over to her. 'Kate, I'm urging you to go to the police. None of this sounds like it will end well.' He glances at the clock again. 'I'll even come with you. Will that help? I'll just have to call my wife – we have a dinner reservation at seven.'

Kate shakes her head. 'Thank you but you don't need to do that. I'll go to the police.'

Rowan sighs. 'I'm relieved to hear that. You're innocent, Kate – you've got nothing to hide.'

But these words offer her no comfort. 'Harper thinks I had something to do with Jamie's murder.' Although Kate's had this thought in her head, saying it aloud breathes life into it.

For the first time since she met Rowan there is stark fear in his eyes. 'But... I'm sure she can't think that. Why would she? You left in the middle of the night, didn't you?'

Now Kate has reached another crossroads. If she says out loud the thing she's tried to suppress, there'll be no going back.

'There's something else, isn't there?' Rowan says, his shoulders sagging. Seconds tick by while he waits patiently for her to answer. 'I really think you need to talk about this, Kate,' he urges.

'There's nothing else,' she says, forcing herself to maintain eye contact.

But she can tell from his silence that Rowan doesn't believe her.

SIXTEEN

TUESDAY 28 JANUARY

With adrenalin coursing through her body, Kate makes her way home from South Kensington. It's still busy on the underground, but she manages to find a seat this time, next to a woman with a crying toddler in her arms.

There's a silent clock ticking now – Rowan has promised to give her until the end of tomorrow to go to the police, otherwise he will do it himself. But Kate will make sure it never comes to that.

Ellis opens the door before she turns the key, immediately pulling her inside. 'Where have you been? I've been trying to call you for the last hour. Why haven't you checked your phone? You said you were working late but I called and David said you'd left ages ago.'

Kate stomach twists. 'Is Thomas okay? Where is he?'

'He's fine. It's not that. But we need to talk.' He takes her arm and leads her into the kitchen.

'Let go.' She pulls away. 'What's going on?' This can only be about Jamie; she's never known Ellis to be agitated.

'Sorry. It's just... what did you say to Maddy?'

'Maddy?' Kate's been so sure that Ellis was about to confront her about Jamie that she's momentarily stunned.

'She's left me. For no reason. She said you'd called her and had a long chat about me. Warned her that I'll never love her. You told her I still have feelings for you! Why would you do that, Kate?' He shakes his head.

Stunned silent, Kate struggles to comprehend his words. 'I... but I didn't call Maddy!'

'So you're saying Maddy's lying?' Why would she do that? I don't believe you, Kate. You've been acting really strangely lately and I don't know what's going on with you. Is this because of the other day? When I told you it doesn't have to be over between us? Why are you punishing me?' In all the time Ellis and Kate were married he'd rarely raised his voice, and Kate has never experienced this level of anger coming from him.

'I've already told you – I didn't call Maddy! Why would I interfere in your relationship?'

'I don't know! To get back at me for having an affair?'

'How long have you known me? You know I'm not vindictive!'

With a heavy sigh, Ellis looks up to the ceiling. 'So you haven't spoken to Maddy at all?'

'Only when she stopped by here to drop off Thomas's homework book. I swear. We barely spoke for more than a minute and Thomas was right there. He heard it all – you can ask him.' This is Harper's doing, Kate knows it.

His looks her straight in the eyes. 'She said we weren't working and there was no future for us. It doesn't make sense. It's only been a couple of days since she said we should move in together! She sounded so upset. I've never heard her like that before.'

'I'm sorry,' Kate says. 'But I honestly had nothing to do with that.'

Thomas strolls in holding an empty glass. 'Hi, Mum. Didn't know you were back.'

Kate glances at his backpack on the floor in the hallway. 'How was school? Everything okay?'

'Yeah. Good.'

'And is... Dex all right?'

He shrugs. 'Yeah. Course. He's looking forward to Friday.'

Kate's stomach tightens. 'I haven't arranged it yet,' she says. 'Please don't get your hopes up.'

'Okay,' Thomas says, filling his glass and taking it back to the living room. 'But they *are* free, remember.'

'What's this about Friday?' Ellis asks.

'He wants a playdate with Dex. The one with the mum who called you about football.'

'Oh,' he says, wrinkling his nose. 'Not surprised you're not keen, then.' He glances at his phone. 'I'd better go. Maddy's got some stuff at my place and I'm sure she'll want it back. Better get it over with.' He looks at Kate then shakes his head. 'I hope you sort out whatever's going on with you, Kate. But you can talk to me – you know that, don't you?'

She nods. 'I'm fine. Really.'

At the door, Ellis picks up Thomas's backpack and hangs it on the peg. 'I checked his bag. Nothing from the school.'

And that's when it hits her – Ellis always checks Thomas's bag. He likes to know what's going on at school. 'Did you check Thomas's bag yesterday?'

He frowns. 'Can't remember. Why?'

'There was a letter in there. And you normally check it.'

'I guess I must have forgotten.' He shrugs. 'Was it something important?'

'No,' Kate says.

. . .

Kate has ignored her phone all day, and now she sits on her bed and picks it up, scrolling through the urgent messages Ellis sent earlier. There are no other messages from anyone, and Aleena hasn't replied to the voicemail Kate left, asking how she's doing. Kate sends her a message, telling Aleena she's worried she hasn't heard from her, then places her phone on the bedside table. Kate knows she didn't do anything to him, but the police will never believe her. Not unless there's another suspect.

Unless Jamie called Harper that night, after Kate had left, and admitted to sleeping with someone, how is it possible that she knew Kate had spent the night with him? He was dead the next day, so there was no time for Harper to have found out. Unless Harper saw them. Was she stalking Jamie and followed them from the club? But still, Harper would have no evidence that they actually slept together.

Kate doesn't want to believe that Harper killed Jamie out of revenge; it sickens her to her core, but it's possible. Though surely the police must have explored this line of enquiry?

Kate messages Maddy, asking if they can talk tomorrow. Kate needs proof that Harper was impersonating her on the phone, and she needs to know if Maddy can remember where she recognised Harper from. She's surprised when she gets an immediate reply.

I think you said everything you needed to say last night.

Please, Maddy. It's really important. It wasn't me who called you.

Tomorrow morning at mine. 10 a.m.

Relieved, Kate calls David, praying that he'll answer even though it's late.

'Kate? Is everything okay?'

'Actually no, it's not. You were right. I think I need to take a few days off. Sort things out in my head. The divorce has hit me harder than I thought. Could you manage without me until Monday?' By then this will all be over – Kate will make sure of that.

There's no hesitation in his response. 'Of course. We'll be fine. But Kate...'

'Yes?'

'Look after yourself.'

WEDNESDAY 29 JANUARY

Kate stands outside Maddy's apartment, anger and determination strengthening her resolve to put a stop to Harper. She rings the doorbell and scans the road, just in case Harper is watching her.

At the school this morning, Kate had walked right past Harper when she'd dropped Thomas off. Their eyes had locked, neither of them looking away until they'd walked past each other. Harper will never let this go – it will be a fight to the end. Graham White's face forces its way into her head. Ultimately, he lost, and Harper will too. Kate will do whatever is necessary.

Maddy answers the door, wearing a trouser suit and dark purple blouse. 'I can't be long,' she says. 'I'm due at work in just over an hour.'

'This won't take long,' Kate says, though the truth is she has no idea how long it will take to convince Maddy.

Inside, Maddy's flat is clean and bright, with a long corridor leading to the kitchen. Kate follows her into it, trying to picture Ellis here.

'I know why you're here,' Maddy says, flicking on the kettle. 'And I should have saved you the bother. I'm not changing my mind about Ellis. What makes it even worse is that he obviously went straight to you and told you I'd left him. That alone shows me I've done the right thing.' She blinks away tears.

'It wasn't me who called you, Maddy. I swear to you.'

'What are you talking about? I thought you were just saying that in your text to get me to see you.'

'No – it's the truth. I did not call you.'

Maddy stares at her, frowning.

'But I think I know who did. What number did the call come from?'

Maddy takes her phone from the kitchen worktop and scrolls through it. 'It was a landline. Local number. Here.' She shows the phone to Kate.'

'Can I call it?'

'Why? What the hell's going on, Kate?'

'Just humour me.'

'Fine.' Maddy hands Kate the phone.

Dialling the number, Kate puts it on speaker. It rings three time before someone answers.

'Good morning, Lucio's. How can I help you?'

'Sorry, wrong number.' Kate hangs up and turns to Maddy. 'That's the coffee shop near Thomas's school.'

'I don't get it.'

'Do you remember that woman who was at my house when you dropped off Thomas's homework book the other day?'

Maddy nods. 'Yeah. What about her?'

'She's been... doing some stuff. Stalking me is the best way I can describe it. She's trying to mess with my life.'

'But why would she do that? Your sons are friends.'

'She's disturbed, Maddy. That's all I know. But she must have called you and pretended to be me so she could mess with your head. She wanted you to leave Ellis.'

'But why would she do that? My relationship with Ellis doesn't affect you now.'

'No, but maybe she wanted to turn Ellis against me. And

she was right – he wasn't happy when he confronted me about it. I've never seen him that angry.'

'I'm surprised,' Maddy says, folding her arms. 'You're the one he really wants to be with – not me.'

'That's not true,' Kate says.

'Isn't it? I think you know the truth, Kate.'

Kate ignores that comment. 'Whatever she said about Ellis is not true. She doesn't even know him. And why would you listen to this woman? She's a stranger to you.'

'Not entirely. I remember her now.'

Kate's leans forward, her pulse racing. 'How do you know her?'

'I met her through Ellis.'

Horrified, Kate stares at Maddy. 'I don't understand.'

'It was a while ago now. In the summer. I'd randomly messaged Ellis the day before, just to see if he wanted to meet up. He seemed happy to hear from me and we arranged to meet the next day after work. It had been a while since I'd seen him. When I got to the bar, he was talking to a friend of his who he'd bumped into. They were deep in conversation so Ellis didn't notice me at first.'

'Who was this friend? Did you know him?'

Maddy shakes her head. 'Never seen him before. And now that I think about it, Ellis seemed a bit shocked that I was there, as if he didn't realise what the time was, and that he was supposed to be meeting me. Anyway, his friend quickly left, saying his wife was waiting for him outside.'

Kate gasps. Her body turns rigid. *His wife.* Ellis was meeting Jamie. She pulls her phone from her pocket and finds a photo of Jamie. 'Is this the friend Ellis was with?'

Maddy studies it. 'Yes, that was him. Who is—'

'What happened next?'

'I watched him leave and saw his wife through the window. It was Harper. Definitely. I told you I never forget a face.'

Kate struggles to make sense of what she's hearing. 'Are you sure it's her?'

'I'm one hundred per cent sure. But Harper never really saw me. Unless she looked through the window. That's why she was adamant that she didn't recognise me.'

'When exactly was this?' Kate asks.

'Why does that matter?'

'Please, can you just think when it might have been.'

Maddy sighs. 'I can't remember the exact date. But as I said, it was definitely during the summer – I remember she was wearing a red sundress and I thought it went really nicely with her hair.' She smiles thinly at Kate. 'What a small world it is. And now you know her.'

'Did Ellis see her?'

'I don't think he was looking out of the window. He was just asking what I wanted to drink and then we discussed where to go for dinner.' Maddy glances at her watch. 'Look, I need to leave for work now.'

'Listen, Maddy. That woman – Harper – is... not a good person. I think she was stalking her husband. They were separated but she's making out that they were still together when he died.'

'Well, they looked like they were still together to me,' Maddy says. 'When I saw them in that bar. Anyway, I don't want anything to do with this. Please can you just go?'

'We're just stopping by Dad's for a bit,' Kate tells Thomas when she picks him up from school.

'What? Both of us? You're coming in too?'

'Just for a bit, yeah.'

'Are you getting back together?' Thomas's face brightens and hope glints in his eyes.

'No, I'm sorry. It's not that. Your Dad's feeling really sad at the moment, and might need some company. He and Maddy have split up.'

'What? Oh. Why?'

'It's complicated adult stuff. But let's just go and see him. I've parked around the corner to save time.'

When Ellis opens the door, his hair is unruly and there are grey circles under his eyes. 'Don't ask how I am,' he says to Kate. 'Hey, Thomas. School okay?'

'Yeah, Dad. Sorry about Maddy.'

We need to talk, Kate mouths, while Thomas isn't looking.

'Okay,' Ellis says, ushering Thomas inside. 'Why don't you set up Mario Kart and I'll come in and play once I've had a quick chat with your mum.'

Thomas races to the living room, leaving Kate and Ellis alone. 'Let's go in the kitchen,' Kate suggests.

She closes the kitchen door. 'Don't get angry, but I went to see Maddy today.'

'What? Why are you interfering, Kate?'

'Because it wasn't me who called her. But I know who it was.'

'Who?'

'Do you remember that school mum who called you about the football.'

'Yeah.'

'It was her. She's been... doing some weird things. Messing with me.'

'Why would she do that?'

'I don't know. But I need your help proving what she's been doing to me. And to you now. She's messed with your relationship, Ellis. We can't sit by and do nothing.'

Ellis sits at the table and folds his arms. 'Hardly something we can go to the police with, is it?'

'I'm not talking about the police.'

'Then what?

'I've ordered some tiny cameras, and I need to hide them in her house. We might be able to catch her doing something. And then I can go to the police. She's not going to stop at this, Ellis.'

'Is this why you've been acting strangely lately? Do you realise how far-fetched it all sounds?' He lets out a deep sigh, then stands and paces the room. 'You're disturbing me, Kate. All this stuff about hidden cameras and spying on someone. It's not... normal. You need to stop.'

'I know exactly how it sounds, but everything I've told you is true and I need you to trust me. The thing is – I can't go to her house. She won't let me in. We've already had a confrontation, so even if she did let me in, she'd never leave me alone long enough to hide them anywhere.'

'Let me guess – you want *me* to do it.'

'You could go round there. Say a place has opened up on the football team or something. Anything that will get you through the door.'

Ellis shakes his head. 'Surely this is illegal, Kate.'

'So is what she's been doing. Please, Ellis.' Under the table, Kate crosses her fingers.

Minutes of silence tick by, and Kate can hear the sounds of Thomas's game in the living room.

'I don't like this,' Ellis says finally. 'But I'll do it.'

SEVENTEEN

2014

All the years she's spent with Jamie have been a mistake; Harper knows that now. Her baby girl is dead because of him, gone before she had a chance to take her first breath. And now their relationship has been shredded and Harper is moving on.

Despite her resolve, doubts descend on Harper as she approaches the restaurant. Why is she doing this? She's not lonely – she doesn't need a man to fulfil her. She's content with her career and the flat she's renting by the sea in Southend. And most of the time she can live with the aching hole the absence of her baby has left her with. But she won't forget that it's Jamie's fault Molly is dead.

Her work friend Coraline had arranged this date, ignoring Harper's protests that she doesn't want a relationship. Coraline had been so persistent that Harper agreed just to stop her going on about it. That's why she's here, making her way to a restaurant in Covent Garden she's never been to and probably won't like. The man she's meeting – Pierre – had seemed nice when Harper had spoken to him on the phone. But then so had Jamie when she'd first met him. People only show you what they want you to see – Harper has learned that the hard way.

Outside the restaurant, she's stopped short by an attack of nerves. This really isn't like her – Jamie has done this, shred every ounce of her that made her Harper Nolan. But beyond her nerves at being appraised by a man she doesn't know, lies something else. Jamie's the only man she's ever pictured herself settling down with – she'd rather be alone than with someone just for the sake of it. She should walk away now and send Pierre an apologetic message.

She's about to walk away when she glances through the window, doing a double take when she sees a man who looks like Jamie sitting in the corner with a dark-haired woman. Typical, she's seeing him everywhere, even though she knows it's highly unlikely he'd be at the same restaurant on the same evening that she's planned to go there.

But when Harper looks again, she realises it *is* Jamie, and her stomach lurches as she clamps her hand to her mouth. It's shock. Confusion. But what had Harper expected? She'd moved out of their flat, and she's here to meet a man for a date, so why shouldn't he be able to do the same?

Because it's his fault our baby is dead.

With a surge of defiance, Harper thrusts open the door and steps inside, praying that Pierre is already in there. She spots him on the opposite side of the restaurant, and he gives a small wave when he looks up. He will never know how close Harper came to not being there, or that his fate has been decided by the man who sits in the corner of this restaurant, engrossed in the conversation he's having with the dark-haired woman, who looks older than Harper had thought from outside.

Pierre stands up as she approaches their table, giving her a tight hug and beaming. He looks different to his photo – slightly larger than he'd appeared, his hair thinner. If she'd been at all invested in this date, then she'd be disappointed.

'I was beginning to think you weren't coming.' Pierre taps his expensive-looking watch. 'Ten minutes late usually means a no-show. But you're here now. I feel as if I know you so well already,' he says.

Harper stifles a sarcastic response. They've only spoken three times, and shared a few text messages. This man doesn't know her – and he never will. How strange it feels to have dinner with someone you know you will never see again.

'I was bit early,' Pierre continues when they sit. 'So I ordered a bottle of red. I hope that's okay. I hate to be presumptuous.'

'Red is fine.'

He pours her a glass and her eyes flick to Jamie in the corner, still captivated by the conversation he's having with his date. He looks nice. Jeans and a black shirt. And he's shaved his stubble. Harper can't remember the last time she saw him without it – she'd always told him she preferred him clean-shaven but Jamie had insisted his facial hair was his security blanket.

Rage bubbles inside her – how can he sit there laughing with someone when their baby is dead? Yes, he'd been crushed when it happened, but six months on and it barely seems to register with him any more. Their lives would be different if Molly had survived – a small part of Harper wants to believe becoming a father would have made Jamie a better man.

'The food is great here,' Pierre says, handing her a menu. 'Have you been here before? I think I'll go for the steak.'

Harper has no appetite, but she'll have to force some food down. She scans the menu, opting for a mushroom risotto that she hopes she'll be able to stomach.

And while Pierre talks without taking a breath, Harper's eyes drift back to Jamie. The sight of him sitting there makes her body burn, yet she can't pull her eyes away.

'That's crazy, isn't it?' Pierre's voice cuts through her reverie.

'Um, yeah. It is. Crazy.'

'This must be fate then – not many others agree with me about that.'

Their food arrives just as she notices Jamie standing up, flicking through his wallet to find money for a tip before pulling on his coat. She watches helplessly as he takes the arm of the dark-haired woman – who Harper sees now is clearly at least a decade older than Jamie – and leads her towards the door.

'I have to go,' Harper says, grabbing her bag and coat.

Pierre stares at her. 'What? But the food's just come!'

'I'm so sorry.' She forages in her purse and pulls out a twenty-pound note. 'Here,' she says, putting it on the table. 'I'm sorry, Pierre. I suddenly feel a bit sick. I think I need to go home.'

He continues gawping at her, but doesn't say anything.

'I'll call you,' she says. But they both know she won't.

Outside, Jamie and the woman have crossed the road, heading towards Tottenham Court Road Tube station. Buttoning her coat, Harper follows them at a safe distance.

And when she gets closer, neither of them pays her any attention; Harper is invisible. In the harsh light of the Northern line Tube train, she gets close enough to take in the woman's features: sharp, thin nose, eyelashes that are far too long to be the work of mascara alone. Faint lines on her forehead.

Harper is right by them, no longer caring if Jamie sees her, and she can hear their conversation – something about cocktails at the woman's place – and she sees her place her hand on Jamie's chest, her long, deep-red fingernails lingering too long.

Something crosses Jamie's face – is it fear? Does he really want to be with this woman? Is she the reason he hasn't checked up on Harper for months, since she threw him out the day she got out of hospital?

Jamie and the woman get off at Camden Town, and Harper follows them through bustling streets, until they turn onto a tree-lined street of Victorian terraces.

Only when they disappear into the woman's house does Harper wonder why she followed Jamie. It's clear what he's doing – she didn't need to torture herself. But still, she crosses the road to the bus stop opposite the house and sits.

For nearly an hour she sits there, thinking about her baby. And then, when fatigue weighs her down, she stands and heads back to the station.

'What the hell are you doing?'

Harper freezes. She doesn't need to turn around to know that it's Jamie.

There's no point answering him – they both know she shouldn't be here. She continues walking.

'Don't ignore me. Why are you following me? You shouldn't be here, Harper. You should never have come here. You've messed everything up! What the fuck have you done?'

Harper doesn't stop. His words don't make sense and questions swarm around her head. Questions she doesn't want to know the answer to.

And as she walks away amid Jamie's shouts, she takes her phone from her pocket, dialling the number before she can change her mind.

EIGHTEEN

THURSDAY 30 JANUARY

The tiny cameras Kate ordered arrive in the morning so things are nearly set. Ellis will need to get Harper's Wi-Fi password, and with no other choice, Kate is putting her faith in a man who has already let her down before.

At around lunchtime she walks to Aleena's house. She knows that Aleena works from home on Thursdays, and she's worried that she hasn't heard from her friend since Tuesday, despite Kate's persistent messages.

There's no answer when she knocks, but Aleena's silver Kia is in the drive. Kate tries her phone, but it rings until her voicemail kicks in. She tries again and presses her ear to the door – she can hear Aleena's mobile ringing inside. She peers through the window just as a figure disappears from view.

At least she knows her friend is okay. Aleena avoiding her is better than the alternative. Kate bangs on the door. 'Aleena! I'm worried about you. I'm calling the police!'

Within seconds, the door opens a fraction and Aleena peers out. She doesn't say anything but stares at Kate as if she doesn't recognise her.

'What's going on?' Kate asks.

'I'm working. I can't talk now.' Aleena tries to shut the door, but Kate thrusts out her arm to stop her.

'Hey!'

'We need to talk, Aleena. Please. Can I come in?'

'I told you – I'm working. This really isn't a good time, Kate.'

'Please can I just come in for a minute. We need to talk. Why are you being like this?'

Aleena sighs. 'You've lied to me, Kate. All these years.'

Kate's legs weaken beneath her. 'What do you mean? What have I lied about?'

'Just stop!' Aleena shouts. 'I know all about Graham White!'

Aleena's words seem to echo through the street, and Kate stares at her, wondering how this has come out now. It feels like long minutes pass before she can bring herself to say anything. 'Please let me come in – I can explain everything.'

'No. I don't want to know anything. I thought we were friends, Kate, but you've kept something so... so huge from me. I've shared everything with you – things I've never told my own husband! All you've done is prove that our friendship meant nothing to you.'

'Please, Aleena. Just let me explain. Two minutes. Can I just have my say?'

Aleena sighs, then without a word, holds the door open and heads into the living room.

Kate shuts the door and follows her, preparing herself to relive the nightmare of Graham White all over again.

'Aleena, I—' Kate stops short.

Sitting on the sofa watching her is Harper Nolan.

'Hi, Kate,' Harper says, standing up and walking over to her. She wraps her arms around Kate. 'How are you?'

Stunned, Kate can't find any words to respond

'Well, it looks like the two of you have got things to talk

about,' Harper says, smiling. 'I'll leave you to it.' She reaches for her bag and slips it over her shoulder, turning to Kate. 'Don't forget the boys have a playdate tomorrow.' She turns to Aleena, 'Thanks for the coffee – it was lovely chatting to you. We really have to do it again.'

'I'll see you out,' Aleena says, glancing at Kate.

Kate listens to their muffled voices drift from the hallway. Aleena telling Harper what a lovely morning she's had, then Harper suggesting they go for dinner. Kate's body stiffens. First, Harper got to Maddy, and now Aleena.

She walks to the window when she hears the door open, and watches Harper walk down the driveway. At the end, Harper glances back, smiling when she sees Kate; a smile full of menace.

'Well?' Aleena says, standing in the living room doorway with her hands on her hips. The tension between them is palpable, and Kate knows this conversation won't be easy. 'I'm sorry I didn't confide in you after everything you've told me. I... I've just tried to put it behind me. It was such a long time ago – I was *fifteen*. And that man tried to—'

'I know it must have been horrific,' Aleena says. 'It just hurts that I sat there telling you all about my experience with that man at college, but you didn't say a word about yours. I feel like our whole friendship has been a lie.'

Kate crosses to her. 'I promise you it hasn't. It's just... hard to talk about what happened.'

'I can understand that. But after all the things we've talked about. I told you about *my* attack. By a man I trusted. You could have told me about Graham White.'

'He's dead because of me.' Kate sinks to the sofa. 'Do you know how hard that is to live with?'

'I don't exactly know but I can imagine. You never gave me a chance to understand. Did you think I wouldn't support you?' She sits opposite Kate and folds her arms. 'I can understand why you wouldn't tell most people, but this is *me*.' She shakes her head.

'Graham White would have killed me. I know that for sure. I'd seen his face – he would never have let me live to tell the police he'd attacked me.'

Aleena listens silently.

'I'm still the person I've always been. Nothing has to change our friendship. In fact, you knowing the whole truth now can make it even stronger.'

Aleena shakes her head. 'It's not as simple as that, Kate. How do I know I can ever trust you to be honest? Isn't that the most important thing in friendship? Trust and honesty? That's why you left Ellis, isn't it? You couldn't trust him any more. He made a mistake but you didn't forgive him.'

'That was different.'

Aleena shakes her head. 'I want to be okay about this, but it's hard. I can't think straight right now. I need space.' She stands, signalling that she can't give Kate any more time. 'I have to get back to work.' She shakes her head. 'I don't think things can ever be the same between us. Please can you go now?'

Resigned that she won't be able to change Aleena's mind – at least not right now, Kate makes her way to the door, turning back when she gets there. 'What was Harper doing here?'

'We'd arranged to have coffee. Why? I'm allowed to have other friends, Kate.'

Kate could confide in Aleena, tell her everything that happened with Jamie, but the stony look on Aleena's face stops her. 'How did you find out?' Kate asks. 'About Graham White.'

Aleena hesitates. 'Oh, I came across an old podcast.'

Kate turns and walks away.

Now Aleena is the one who's lying.

. . .

Kate knows Ellis is working from home today, so she makes her way to the house he inherited from his dad a few weeks ago. It's not far from Kate's house, which makes things easier with co-parenting Thomas. The house is in need of modernising, but it's a good space for him, and Thomas when he's staying there.

'Kate,' Ellis says when he opens the door. 'I was hoping you'd changed your mind about the cameras.'

'No. We need to do this, Ellis.'

'We...' he says, letting the word float around them. 'It's not often you ask for my help with anything.'

'Well, now I am.'

He closes the front door. 'I'm not sure about this.'

'We're doing this for Thomas,' Kate says. 'I need to find out what Harper wants with our family.'

Ellis sighs. 'I'm sure she wouldn't—'

'We don't know that!'

'Where am I supposed to put it? I don't know anything about hidden cameras.'

'There are loads of photos hanging on her walls. With white frames. The cameras are white so there's every chance she won't notice them.' Kate pulls out the small package from her pocket. 'See how small they are. And then you'll just need to get her Wi-Fi code. Tell her you need it for your phone.'

Ellis stares at the package, but when she pushes it into his hand, he takes it without another word.

'I was having a late lunch – didn't have time earlier. Do you want to join me?'

'I can't. I need to go.'

Ellis looks hurt. 'Fine.'

'But there's something I need to ask you first.' Kate was going to wait, but she needs to get this over with. Pulling out her phone, she scrolls to a photo she found online of Jamie. 'Do you know this man?'

Ellis takes her phone and glances at the picture, handing it back to her immediately. 'No. Why?'

'Are you sure? Look properly. For longer than one second.' She thrusts the phone out.

This time he studies it more carefully. 'Nope. Still don't know him. Who is he? What's going on, Kate? Why are you asking me this?'

Her chest tightens, as if all the breath is being slowly sucked out of her. Ellis is lying to her, she can tell by the way he's firing questions at her. 'Are you sure you've never seen him before?'

'Positive. Are you going to tell me who he is?'

'It doesn't matter,' Kate says, snatching back her phone. 'I have to go.'

'Wait, we need a more solid plan about the cameras!'

But she's already at the front door, throwing it open and rushing outside into the foggy air.

Now she knows there is no one she can trust.

NINETEEN

THURSDAY 30 JANUARY

'Thanks for meeting up with me.'

'I'm intrigued,' Faye Held says, holding out her hand to Harper. They're in a bar in Covent Garden – Faye is due to have dinner with friends in a couple of hours so it was the only place she could meet this evening. It should be more than enough time for Harper to plant the seed.

Faye's an attractive woman in her late twenties; her smooth dark skin seems to shimmer, matching the sparkle in her large brown eyes. The mojito she ordered sits in front of her and she taps on her phone, her long, burgundy manicured fingernails clack-clacking on the screen. Harper tries to stifle her annoyance; she needs this woman's full attention.

'Sorry,' she says, her eyes still fixed on her phone. 'Work email. You wouldn't believe how many messages I get every day from people requesting specific cases on *Beneath the Surface*. But there are only so many that hold my interest. I have to choose carefully. One – I've got to be excited about it, and two – I need to know there's more to it than just what people see on the outside.'

'Like the Graham White case,' Harper says. She's got a still water in front of her.

'Exactly. That one certainly piqued my interest.' Faye stops tapping on her phone and places it on the table. 'I'm obsessed with true crime. Scares a lot of people. But I look at it like this – I'm doing a service to society. I'm the voice for people who can't speak for themselves. Have to be impartial, though. I pride myself on that. I really can see things from all perspectives. But there can be only one truth.'

Harper smiles. In some ways she admires Faye Held – who at such a young age already has the confidence and wisdom of someone far older.

'So what is it you wanted to see me about?' Faye asks. 'You said it relates to the Graham White case, but what is it exactly?'

'I need to know everything you know about the Graham White case.'

Faye frowns. 'No offence, but that's not why we're here. You said you have new information.'

'I do,' Harper says. 'But I need to check a few things with you first. I need to know what you know about the case.'

Faye eyes her suspiciously. 'Have you tried actually listening to my podcast?'

'I did. Every word. But there must be stuff you couldn't fit into the episode. Or any thoughts you've had since then. It's been two years since you recorded it. Has anything changed?'

Faye clasps her hands together, resting her chin on them. 'Hmm. And what's in it for me? How do I know what you're going to tell me will interest me?'

Harper's been anticipating this. 'I know Kate Mason.'

Faye's eyes widen. 'Interesting. Tell me more.'

'And I think she's killed someone again.'

For a brief moment, Faye's mouth hangs open, before she composes herself again and once again becomes laid back and calm. 'If that's true, then shouldn't it be the police you're talking to, not a true crime podcaster?'

Harper has expected this question. 'This woman is too clever. She's already got away with it before, and I'm sure she's covered her tracks this time. She was fifteen then – now she's a grown woman.'

'I'm going to need more than that,' Faye says.

'Wouldn't you like to break this story on *Beneath the Surface*?' Harper asks. 'Imagine how many subscribers you'd get if you had an exclusive.'

Faye rolls her eyes. 'I'm not a tabloid journalist.' She pauses. 'But you do have a point. What's in it for you?'

'Nothing but justice,' Harper replies. 'That's all I care about.'

Faye takes a long sip of her cocktail. 'Okay. I'll tell you my thoughts on Graham White and then you can fill me in on what you know about Kate Mason.' She raises her head, appraising Harper. 'And I really hope you're not wasting my time. I get a lot of that, I'm sure you can understand. Time is precious.'

Harper nods. 'I assure you, this will be totally worth your while.

'Okay. At first glance, it seems like an open and shut case, right? Man tries to attack young girl. Girl fights back. Accidentally kills him. Police are happy with that conclusion. But upon further examination – I don't think it happened quite like that.' Faye rests her elbows on the table.

'What do you mean?'

'Kate Mason had a best friend – Mona Shaw. She wouldn't come on my podcast but I managed to convince her to speak to me off the record. To give me some background that I wouldn't use in the podcast. Believe me, it took a lot of convincing.'

Harper's pulse races. 'What did she tell you?'

'Mona said that on the afternoon Kate claims she was attacked, she and Kate had had a huge argument. Apparently,

Kate said some vile things to Mona and really lost it with her. She even lashed out and punched her.'

'Why?'

'She wouldn't tell me. But then Mona broke down and said she didn't believe that man was trying to attack Kate.' Faye sighs. 'Then she shut down and wouldn't tell me anything more. She seemed nervous. Actually, it was more like scared. She said she'd already told me too much.' Faye rolls her eyes. 'Which was hardly anything, really. At least, nothing I could use in my podcast. But her words stayed with me, and made me mistrust Kate. Don't get me wrong – I don't just believe everything I'm told – definitely not. But there was something about Mona and I felt the pain and honesty in her words, especially when she broke down.'

Harper nods. 'What happened after that?'

'She said she'd moved on with her life, put all that behind her. She said the church was a huge part of her life now and she didn't want to think about anything that came before. Then she told me she had to cut Kate out of her life straight after it happened and she wants to keep it that way.'

Harper understands this. The sooner Kate Mason is out of her own life, the better. 'What's your take on it all?'

Faye taps her fingers together, her shiny nails glinting in the light. 'I've done extensive research on Graham White and I can't find anything to suggest he was a bad person. He'd never hurt a woman before. All his work colleagues said he was extremely respectful to all the female employees in his office. So you tell me – how does that fit with this idea that he wanted to attack Kate?'

Harper ponders this for a moment. 'You're right, it does seem odd. To suddenly become someone who would attack a teenage girl doesn't make sense.'

'And the police found nothing suspicious on his computer.'

Harper nods. 'Did you ever speak to Graham White's ex-partner?'

'Jennifer Seagrove. Yes – and she found it hard to believe that he would be violent. She said they'd broken up but he didn't go crazy or anything like the media suggested. She thought he handled it well. Although she'd only left him the day before he was killed, so there's no telling what he might have done. Who knows what goes on in people's minds? But my take is this – the dead can't speak for themselves, so someone has to do it for them. And that's me.'

Harper thinks of Jamie, how she has become his voice. 'Can you give me the contact details for Mona and Jennifer? I'd really like to talk to them.'

Faye frowns. 'Why? I've told you everything they said.'

'I know. But I'd still like to speak to them.'

'Hmm.' Faye studies her with narrow eyes full of mistrust. 'I can't give you their details. Data protection – you know how it is. But I'll tell you what I'll do. I can contact them both and give them your info. You'll just have to hope they respond.'

That will have to do; this is as far as Harper can push Faye Held, and she's already got more than she'd expected. 'Great. Thanks.'

'First things first, though. Tell me what Kate Mason has done.'

Harper takes a deep breath, forcing away an image of Jamie lying dead on the floor. 'She killed my husband.'

Faye's mouth drops, her eyes widening with shock and something else. Glee.

'I need to know exactly why you're saying this. And why you haven't gone to the police if it's true. Over to you.'

Harper is ready for this moment, because if she can get Faye Held onside, then Kate's life will be over. Even if the police never prosecute her, a podcast reaching hundreds of thousands of people will be enough to wreak havoc on her life. A lump catches in Harper's throat – poor Thomas; he's a nice kid and doesn't deserve this. But he also doesn't deserve a murderer for a mother.

'I know for a fact that Kate Mason slept with my husband the night before he was killed.'

'How could you know that? Did he tell you?'

'No. But I saw them. There was a... a camera in the bedroom of the flat we normally rent out. I saw them together. They were in bed. They... they slept together.' Harper's surprised she's able to get these words out with no emotion. She's never uttered them aloud but somehow manages to bury her feelings because she just needs this done – she needs Faye Held to believe her.

'You were filming them? That's hardly ethical.'

'I know... but it wasn't like that. I didn't watch – I just had to know what Jamie was doing with her.'

Faye raises her eyebrows. 'Show me,' she says, beckoning with her hand. 'Not the whole video, just a still of it.'

'I don't have the video any more. I wasn't able to save it, but I took a screen shot.' Harper reaches into her bag and pulls out her phone. 'Here.'

The picture is blurry but it's clearly Kate Mason with Jamie, her lips caressing his chest.

'Jesus!' Faye says, her eyes glistening. 'That's... I have no words. Why haven't you shown this to the police?'

'Because I can't prove when it was taken.' And the truth is, if the police know Harper knew Jamie was having an affair, then they'd start to look into her. She can't have that – not even for a second. She is all Dexter has left. Jamie was estranged from his parents and Harper's both died before Dexter was born. Before she'd even been pregnant with Molly. Her mum never got to see Harper become a mum.

Harper will never admit her fear to Faye – she doesn't want

the woman to start investigating her instead. What destruction that would cause.

'The police would be able to ascertain that it's legit,' Faye says, leaning back and folding her arms.

'Do you have kids yet?' Harper asks.

'Well, that's rude. But no – not yet. I'm only twenty-seven. Plenty of time for that. I've got a podcasting goal to reach. One million followers by next summer.'

'And you'll get there,' Harper says, meaning every word. Even the one episode she listened to of Faye's was enough to show her that this woman is compelling, and that *Beneath the Surface* has more potential than maybe even Faye realises. 'The reason I'm doing this,' Harper continues, 'is for my son. He lost his dad and I need to make sure that justice is served. But I need to be sure. And you investigating this for your podcast will prove that I'm right. Then the police will have to listen.

Faye's expression is inscrutable.

'Please, Faye. You're the only person who can help me.'

Faye purses her lips and drums her fingers on the table, and Harper focuses on the click-clack of her burgundy nails, willing her to agree.

'Sod it – what have I got to lose?' Faye says, finally. 'But if you're lying to me about anything I will make sure this ends up in court – got it?'

'I wouldn't expect anything else,' Harper says, holding out her hand.

Faye takes her hand. 'You've got a deal.' She loosens her grip and rubs her hands together. 'I knew there was something about Kate Mason when I investigated the Graham White death. Let's make sure that this time, she doesn't get away with taking someone's life.'

TWENTY

Rowan is running late. It's three minutes past ten and he's never overrun before. Behind the reception desk, Frieda shifts her glasses down and looks at Kate. 'I do apologise. He had to fit someone in as an emergency this morning. He shouldn't be too long.' She smiles before turning back to her computer.

It's nearly twenty past by the time his door opens and a tall, thin woman steps out. She's wearing a fitted black dress and knee-high leather boots, and looks more as though she's been to a party than a therapy session. She catches Kate's eye and smiles, looking her up and down, probably making judgements about Kate's casual attire: loose joggers and trainers.

For a moment Kate watches her, intrigued by what has brought her here to Rowan. 'I'm so sorry for the delay,' Rowan says, standing at his door. 'An emergency, I'm afraid.'

'The woman who just left looked fine,' Kate says. 'You must have helped her.' Of course Rowan will detect the annoyance in her voice; once again Kate needs to suppress her anger. 'It's fine,' she says.

'Of course, you'll have your full hour,' he explains, closing the door.

Kate sinks onto the sofa.

'So, how did it go with the police?' Rowan asks. 'It must have been hard.'

'I haven't been to the police. Yet. I made a promise to do it, and I'll keep my promise, but I need to do it on my own terms.'

'Okay.'

'I found something out, and I don't know what to feel about it. Ellis knew Jamie.'

Rowan raises his eyebrows. 'I see. And how do you know this?'

'It doesn't matter. But Ellis is denying it.'

'Is there a chance you've got it wrong and he's telling the truth?'

'Of course there's a chance. But I can tell when Ellis is lying, and he definitely was. He's seen Jamie before. I know it. And it's just more evidence that Jamie didn't come into my life by chance.'

Rowan considers what she's said. 'So... you think Ellis had something to do with it?'

'I don't want to believe that. He's the father of my child. I've trusted him with my past. With everything. And if it was anything to do with him, then this is far worse than his affair.'

'Remember when we talked before about coincidences. How they're much more common than people believe. Perhaps they met briefly through work? It doesn't mean that it's got anything to do with you meeting Jamie or spending the night with him. If it were me – I'd want definitive proof. Speculation serves no purpose. It does no good.'

'There's more that's happened,' Kate says. 'My closest friend found out about Graham White. She says it was from that podcast a couple of years ago. I thought I didn't have to worry about that any more. But that podcaster has grown massively in the last year or so. And all her podcasts are online for anyone to listen to any time. This will never go away.'

Rowan nods. 'Okay, but I'll remind you again – you did nothing wrong, Kate. Even if people find out, you have nothing to worry about.'

'Except condemnation. Being labelled a murderer. Like I was back then.'

'Oh, Kate. The labels people inflict on us don't make them real. Only what we believe about ourselves holds any weight. Tell me how I can help you – what do you need me to do? It's not to tell you what to do, is it? Because I have. Go to the police. Let them work it all out. That's the only thing that will help you.'

'I... I need you to believe me. Not just tell me you do. I need you to believe I'm not a murderer.'

Rowan takes so long to answer that Kate pictures herself running from here and never coming back.

'Oh, Kate, there is no question in my mind that you're innocent. None whatsoever.'

Weight lifts from her shoulders at his words.

'But,' he continues, 'this is the last time I can see you. I'm so sorry, but I think we're treading an ethical line here. I don't think I'm the person who can help you, even if you go to the police. I'm going to have to refer you to someone else.'

She's numb as she makes her way to Thomas's school. With all the things that have happened to her over the last two weeks, Rowan's bombshell shouldn't have hit her this hard. She'd been hoping she could persuade him to give her more time before she had to go to the police – just enough to prove that it was Harper who killed Jamie out of rage, and that Kate had nothing to do with it.

Kate scans the school playground, looking for Harper. As far as she knows, Dex isn't in any after-school clubs. There are a few parents she knows chatting by the gate, so she pulls out her phone and holds it to her ear, to deter anyone from approaching her.

It works, and she's left in peace until the gates open and the basketball coaches begin dismissing the kids one by one. Kate searches the line – Thomas is usually near the back, but she can't see him. Moving closer so that she can see all the kids, her stomach tightens when she sees he's not there. The line gets shorter and soon there is only one child left, who quickly points to his mum and heads towards her.

Kate rushes up to one of the coaches. 'Where's Thomas?' she asks.

He frowns. 'Um, Thomas didn't come today. We got a message from the office saying he was missing basketball today.'

'No,' Kate says. 'Thomas was meant to be here.' Turning away, she pulls out her phone and calls Ellis. 'Have you got Thomas?' she asks, the second he answers.

'No. It's your weekend. What's going on?'

'I'll call you back.' Kate hangs up and rushes to the office, pressing the buzzer and peering through the glass doors.

The door clicks open and Ruth comes out of the office, strolling over and smiling. 'Everything okay, Mrs Mason?' she asks.

'No! Thomas wasn't at basketball and I don't know where he is!'

Ruth frowns. 'Oh, but you called this morning and said Dexter Nolan's mum was picking him up after school for a play-date. Nancy took the call and let the basketball coaches know.'

Kate stares at her as she processes Ruth's words. She hadn't heard from Harper and assumed there was no way she'd believe the playdate was still on. Kate's about to tell Ruth that she's wrong, that it wasn't Kate who called, and this is a dreadful safe-guarding incident, but it would take too long. 'Yeah. Sorry, I've been busy at work and completely forgot. Sorry.' She rushes off without giving Ruth a chance to respond, but before the door closes Ruth calls out, asking if everything is okay. Kate ignores her; she needs to find her son.

Harper answers the door with a smirk on her face. 'How lovely to see you, Kate,' she says, glancing behind her.

'Where's my son? Where's Thomas?' Kate pushes past Harper and stands in the hallway. 'Thomas!' she shouts.

'He's fine, Kate. He's upstairs with Dexter. They're having a great time. I hope you don't mind – I've given the boys some biscuits and I've got pizza for dinner. Oh, I know it's not the healthiest thing, but what harm does the odd treat do? Actually, you're a bit early for picking Thomas up. Didn't we say seven?'

'What the hell are you doing?' Kate hisses. 'You abducted my son from school!'

Harper's eyes widen. 'Don't tell me you forgot!' she exclaims. 'Oh, I know you've had such a lot on your mind lately, but we had this planned, didn't we, and Dexter reminded Thomas at school. I had a feeling you might have forgotten. And Thomas said you wouldn't mind if he missed basketball just this once. Otherwise I would have had to make two trips to school.'

'I've been wondering what it is about you that just isn't right,' Kate says. 'And now I think I've finally worked it out. You act nothing like a grieving wife who's just lost her husband. Why is that, Harper?'

The smile on Harper's face disappears. 'What exactly are you saying, Kate?'

'That I don't trust you. Or believe a word that comes from your mouth.'

Thomas appears at the top of the stairs. 'Hi, Mum,' he says. 'But it's not time to go yet. I've only just got here! We're about to watch the fourth Harry Potter.'

Seeing that Thomas is okay calms Kate. Harper hasn't done

anything to him. 'Can you get your things? We need to get home. Now.'

'Why? We haven't had dinner yet. We're having pizza.'

'No, I'm sorry but we have to go. I can do pizza at home. Sorry, Thomas. Quick, go now. Get your stuff.' She fails to keep the urgency from her voice.

With a huff, Thomas marches back upstairs and Kate waits until he's disappeared before turning back to Harper. 'Pull a stunt like that again and—'

'And you'll what? Call the police? I doubt that very much. You're the last person who'll want the police involved. In fact, you're lucky I haven't called them myself. It's still an option, of course. But I prefer to deal with things myself. Can't rely on other people, can you? Too many loopholes. Too much bureaucracy.' She smiles. 'At least I know I can get things done. Make things happen. You've just had a taste of that today. Of how easy it is for me to manipulate things.' Her eyes bore into Kate.

But Kate refuses to be intimidated. 'Maybe there's another reason you haven't told the police,' she says, stepping closer to Harper so that there's no chance either of the boys will hear.

'And what's that supposed to mean?'

Before Kate can answer, Thomas and Dex thunder down the stairs, laughing with their heads together as if they've known each for years rather than a couple of weeks.

'Why does Thomas have to go?' Dex says to Harper. 'It's not fair, Mum.'

'I know it's disappointing,' Harper says, fixing her eyes on Kate. 'But we'll see Thomas again soon – I promise you that.'

'Bye, Thomas,' Dex says. 'Thanks for coming.'

'Let's definitely do it again soon,' Harper says, ruffling Thomas's hair. 'Now that you two are such good friends, we'll have to make sure you see lots of each other, isn't that right, Kate?'

Ignoring her, Kate ushers Thomas out to the car, holding

her breath until they're driving away, and Harper's road disappears in the rear-view mirror.

Harper has crossed a line, dragged Kate's son into this, and the only way to win against her, to make sure she can't harm Thomas in any way, is to bring her down.

TWENTY-ONE

SATURDAY 1 FEBRUARY

Rain splatters around them, making Harper wish she hadn't worn jeans today. They're already sticking to her legs, the denim feeling like cardboard against her skin. And beside her, Dexter is miserable.

'Why are we here, Mum?' he asks again, as if he expects the answer to be different each time. It's a reasonable question, but one she can't truthfully answer.

'I just need to check with Thomas's dad if there could be a space for you. I'm not giving up, Dexter,' she'd says. 'Plus, we get to support Thomas, don't we?'

'But it's so boring,' Dexter moans. 'And why do they have to play in the rain? I don't even like football. I mean, it's okay, but I'm no good at it.'

'That's why we need you in this club,' Harper says. 'So you can get better.'

'Dad loved football,' Dexter says, so quietly it's as if he's speaking to himself. 'He'd want me to play, wouldn't he?'

'I think so,' Harper says, even though the truth is Jamie never pushed Dexter to do anything he didn't love.

And now, standing at the side of the football pitch, with drizzle threatening to turn into hard rain, Harper wonders if this was a mistake. There are other ways to get to Kate, that's becoming very clear.

Ellis walks over to her, his lips pursed and frown lines on his forehead. 'Hi,' he says. 'I'm sorry, but I did say there isn't a place for Dex. Once the kids start here they rarely leave unless parents move away. And it seems like every kid wants to play.'

'I know,' Harper says. 'We're just here to watch, aren't we, Dexter?'

Her son nods and looks away, once again focusing on the game.

'Sorry,' Ellis says. 'I'm just... it's not been a good week.'

'Tell me about it,' Harper says. 'Do you ever wish you could erase certain moments from your mind? That would certainly help.'

He smiles. 'Yep. If only.'

They both turn to watch the game. 'I'm sorry there isn't a space for Dex,' Ellis says. 'He's clearly passionate if he's willing to come down here just to watch. I can let you know if a space comes up.'

Harper nods and smiles. 'Thank you. Anyway, no rush. Dexter wants to support Thomas. The two of them have become really close.'

A strange expression crosses Ellis's face; this might be harder than she'd hoped.

'I really like Thomas,' Dexter says, turning to Ellis.

'Me too, buddy,' Ellis says.

Harper smiles. 'He's a special kid,' she says. 'I can tell that already. I'm so glad they're friends.'

'Mum,' Dexter says. 'Can me and Thomas play in the playground after this?'

Harper glances at Ellis. Perhaps this will work out after all. 'Yes, of course. If Thomas isn't busy.'

'Um, I guess it would be okay if the rain doesn't get worse,' Ellis says. 'For a little bit. Um, it's not my weekend with him so I need to get him back to his mum.'

'Oh, yes. Of course. Kate. Shall I message her and let her know? So that she's not worried?' Harper pulls out her phone.

Doubt creeps onto Ellis's face. 'Okay... maybe just for a short while,' he says. 'I need to get back to the game.'

'See you after,' Harper says, watching him head to the other side of the field. She types a message to Kate.

Hi Kate, just at football with Dexter. Bumped into Ellis. The boys would like to go to the playground for a bit after so Thomas will be home a bit later. Take care x

She rereads the message. It's warm and friendly, nothing that would raise any concern if Kate were to show it to anyone.

And then Harper deletes it and places the phone back in her pocket.

Harper is fully aware that Ellis must feel awkward being in the playground with her. The boys have disappeared to the basketball court on the other side, joining in a game with some older boys, and the only other people in here are a toddler with his grandparents.

For a few moments they sit in silence, watching the boys. 'Dex is good at basketball,' Ellis says.

'Football too,' Harper says, smiling

'You seemed annoyed about it before,' he says. 'On the phone that time. When I said there's no space for Dexter.'

'I was. But... it's just been difficult and... I suppose I took it personally. I just want Dexter to fit in. He's been through so much.'

Ellis nods. 'You both have. I get it.'

'What about you?' Harper asks. She doesn't want talk of Jamie to infect this conversation. She needs to choose her words with precision, and be on guard for any surprises. 'You said earlier you'd had a bad week?'

He looks away. 'Yeah.'

Clearly he's not keen to open up to her. Harper takes a gamble. 'Forgive me for saying this, but Kate mentioned that you'd split up with your partner. I'm so sorry.'

His eyes widen. 'Kate told you? Why—'

'Oh, sorry. Yeah.'

He stands and folds his arms, his cheeks flushing. 'Why would she talk about my personal business? It's nothing to do with her, or anyone else.'

Harper holds up her hand. 'You're right. I'm sorry. Please forget I said anything.'

'I think we both know that's not possible.'

'We don't have to talk about it. Look, I can tell Dexter we have to go.' Although she's not superstitious, Harper puts her hand in her pocket and crosses her fingers.

Ellis glances at the boys then shakes his head. 'No, let them play. Thomas told me all about Kate cutting short their playdate yesterday.' He shakes his head. 'To be honest, Kate's been acting strangely lately. I know you haven't known her long so you won't have noticed but, she's been saying some—'

'Actually, I have noticed.'

He stares at her. 'What d'you mean?'

Harper tells him Kate knew all about the playdate, then claimed she'd forgotten it was arranged. 'And I found a photo of my husband in her house. I don't know what she was doing with it. It was just a print out of a photo that was online. But... what do you make of that?'

Creases appear on Ellis's forehead. 'Very strange. I know something's going on with her. And if it's having any impact on my son then I need to find out what it is.'

. . .

In the evening, she sits with Dexter in the living room while he plays on his Xbox. Jamie's Xbox. The one Dexter seems to have somehow inherited without her having agreed to anything. Yet it's numbing his pain, so Harper's reluctant to take it from him. 'Ten more minutes,' she warns, knowing those minutes will grow into twenty, then thirty.

Dexter glances at her. 'Okay.'

In the end Harper cuts his time off after seven minutes; she wants to talk to him about Jamie, ask him about things she's been wondering about. It's probably still too soon for him to want to talk about his dad, but Harper needs to try.

'Can I watch TV now, then?' Dexter asks.

'No. Enough screen time. Can we just talk for a minute?'

He shrugs.

'It's about your dad.'

Dexter's body stiffens.

Harper moves across to him on the sofa and takes his hand. 'I know it's difficult to talk about and I'm so sorry to ask you this, but do you remember much about the last day we saw him?'

It floods her with guilt to see the way her son stares at her, and the pain he must be feeling to conjure memories of Jamie.

'I dunno,' Dexter says. 'I remember him being in the kitchen with you. And you were fighting.'

The breath is sucked from Harper's lungs. Dexter's never mentioned this; she'd thought he hadn't heard them. He was on the top floor of the house, playing in the spare room – even with their voices raised, their son shouldn't have been able to hear them.

'Do you know what we were fighting about?' Harper ventures.

He shrugs. 'Not really. I couldn't hear. Just shouts. Angry voices.'

Harper lets out a sharp breath. 'I'm sorry your dad and I were fighting. I feel bad about that every single day. Our last words to each other were angry, and that makes me really sad.'

'What were you arguing about?' Dexter says, glancing at the TV remote control, his fingers twitching.

'We were trying to sort things out,' Harper explains. 'We'd been having a few problems. Sometimes it's hard for adults and we disagree about things. But it was all being sorted out – I promise you.'

The doorbell rings and they turn to each other. It's past eight p.m. and Harper isn't expecting anyone. 'Stay here,' she says. 'You can watch TV.'

When she opens the door and sees Ellis standing there, her confusion quickly turns to concern. This won't be a friendly visit – there's no reason for him to be here. Is this because of Maddy? Her insistence that she recognised Harper from somewhere is a loose thread that might unravel at any moment. And Harper needs control of this. 'Hi,' she says. 'Is everything okay?'

'Sorry to just turn up like this. But I thought you might want to know that a space for Dexter has just come up in the team. A kid has dropped out. Parents said they were struggling with the time commitment.'

Harper frowns. 'That's a coincidence. We were only talking about it this morning.'

'I know. Bit of luck really.'

Harper's not sure she trusts him, but she'll give Ellis the benefit of the doubt for now. 'Do you want to come in? Dexter's just watching TV but we can go through everything in the kitchen.'

Ellis glances back at his car. 'If you're sure? I really don't want to intrude.'

'No, come in. To be honest, I'm glad of the company. Dexter and I were just talking about Jamie and it's all a bit much. I could do with a distraction. I was just about to open a bottle of red – like to join me?'

Ellis hesitates. 'I would, but not when I'm driving.'

'Sensible. But you don't mind if I have one, do you?'

'Not at all.'

In the kitchen, while Harper opens the bottle, Ellis takes in his surroundings. 'Nice place,' he says. 'Reminds me how much my place needs doing up.'

'No, it's not.' Harper says. 'It needs gutting. My husband Jamie and I never got around to it before he died. And now I just can't imagine ever feeling like I want to sort this house out. I'm sure you heard all about Jamie dying?'

'Yeah. Sorry. It's only been a short while, though, hasn't it? You need time.'

'Yeah, I know you're right,' Harper says. 'But knowing something doesn't make it easy.' She pauses. 'Don't you want to sit down?' Ellis's hovering is making her uncomfortable.

'I've been driving a lot today. Feel better standing.'

'Okay.' Harper frowns, and leans on the worktop. 'So, how is Kate?'

'She's... acting strangely. I feel like I don't know her any more.'

'That's worrying. She's the mother of your child. What exactly is going on with her?'

Ellis reaches into his pockets, his eyes darting around the room.

'Are you okay?' Harper asks. 'I know you've had a rough week, and I'm the last person you'll want to talk to about Kate. I mean, we're friends so it must feel strange. Shall we go through this football stuff?'

There's a long pause before Ellis speaks again. His mouth twists as if he's debating the words he wants to say.

'What is it?' Harper asks.

More silence. 'There... is no space in the team.'

Harper frowns. 'I don't get it. Then why are you here?'

Slowly, Ellis pulls out a small package from his pocket, then with a deep sigh, he tips it upside down to drop the contents on the table.

Harper stares at the tiny white objects. 'What are those?'

'They're cameras. And they're the real reason I'm here.'

TWENTY-TWO

SUNDAY 2 FEBRUARY

Kate hasn't heard from Ellis since last night, when he'd messaged to say he was on his way to Harper's, cameras in hand. The four messages Kate's sent since then have been ignored, and now she's starting to worry.

And now, while Thomas is still asleep, Kate calls Ellis again, surprised when he answers this time, his voice heavy with sleep.

'Finally! Why haven't you answered?'

Kate hears the rustle of sheets.

'Because I've been sleeping. It's not even six o'clock. Is Thomas okay?'

'Yes, he's fine. Did you, do it?'

Ellis sighs. 'So that's why you're calling? Yes, the cameras are installed.'

'Oh, good. Can I get the app on my phone?'

'I don't think so because it's on mine.'

'Have you watched her? Has she done anything?'

'Yes. She's currently making breakfast. Real criminal stuff, Kate.'

'Can you come over? Now?'

Another pause. 'Yeah... but there's really nothing to see right now.'

'It's not that. I need to talk to you. It's important.'

'You're doing it again, Kate. Acting weird. You need to tell me what's going on with you. Talk to me. Or someone at least. Are you still seeing that therapist? Because I'm not convinced he's doing a good job.'

'I have to go,' Kate says, ignoring his flurry of questions. 'See you soon.'

Ellis arrives within half an hour, and Kate's surprised to find him looking so unkempt.

'Before you say anything – I rushed straight here. And I left my phone at home by accident. Didn't have time to brush my hair or shave. I know this must be important for you to drag me here urgently. So what's going on? Is this about us, Kate?'

Kate registers the glimmer of hope in his eyes. 'Come in the living room. I don't want Thomas waking up.'

Ellis follows her, standing too close.

'This isn't about us,' Kate says, backing away. 'There is no *us* any more. I can't keep saying that.'

For a moment Ellis is silent, scrutinising her. He looks upset, until his expression changes into something colder. 'Then what is this?' he snaps. 'What is going on with you, Kate? First, you're interfering in my relationship and then discussing my personal business with people. Getting me to spy on people. This isn't you – what are you playing at?'

She backs away – it's not that she fears Ellis; he's never lifted a finger towards her – but the legacy of Graham White lives strongly in her mind and body.

'Hey,' he says, stepping back and holding up his hands. 'I didn't mean to get in your face. I just want to understand what's happening here.'

Kate straightens up; she won't cower to any man. 'There's nothing going on. And I could ask you the same question.'

'What's that supposed to mean?'

She's about to tell Ellis that she knows he's lying about not recognising Jamie Archer when she showed him Jamie's photo, but right now she needs him to stay with Thomas – there's somewhere Kate needs to be. They will have this conversation later. 'Nothing,' she says. 'Sorry. I'm just... there's some stuff I need to take care of.'

'So that's the real reason I'm here.' Ellis sighs.

'I need you to stay here with Thomas,' Kate says. 'Just keep an eye on him. Watch him like a hawk. I won't be long.'

'Watch him like a hawk? What aren't you telling me, Kate? And don't tell me nothing's going on.'

Kate switches off – the exasperation in his voice is too much for her. She scrawls a note to Thomas and slips it under his cereal bowl. 'I won't be long,' she says, pulling on her coat and rushing outside before Ellis can question her further.

Reaching the car, her eyes fix on the piece of paper under the windscreen wiper. Her throat constricts when she unfolds it and reads the typed words.

R.I.P Jamie
R.I.P Graham
Who's next?

Kate knows Rowan's home address because she'd followed him one day, after their third or fourth session, when she knew he was the therapist she wanted, but she needed to be sure about him. To get a picture of the man he was outside of his practice, to be sure she could trust him.

Now, though, as she stands across the road from his house in Fulham, Kate feels like a stalker, and guilt clutches her chest, destabilising her. She shouldn't be here. Rowan would report her to the police if he saw her, particularly as he's made it clear that he can't be her therapist any longer. He wouldn't hesitate to tell the police what she told him about Jamie Archer. But Kate knows she didn't harm Jamie. She knows it as sure as she knows that Thomas is her son.

She won't let Harper Nolan reduce her to this. Kate takes a deep breath and crosses the road. Rowan's is the only car in the driveway, so there's every chance his wife is out. But as Kate gets closer to the house, a light comes on in one of the downstairs windows, and a woman appears, closing the shutters.

Kate turns around and walks back across the road. She can't knock now. Instead, she picks up her phone and calls the mobile number Rowan gave her over a year ago in case she was having a panic attack and needed help getting through it. But Kate has learned to deal with those attacks herself, and has never had to call him for help. Until now.

He picks up on the fourth ring. 'Hello?'

'Hi, it's Kate. Kate Mason.'

'Where are you? Is everything okay? I'm sorry I haven't sent you the name of a new therapist yet. I promise you I'm working on it – it's just got to be the right fit.'

'I know. I understand. But can we talk? Please? Everything's got worse. There's stuff happening and I don't know where it will lead.'

Rowan sighs. 'Kate, I really don't think this is—'

'I promise you I'll go to the police straight after. Just meet me. In an hour. At Labakery on Kensington High Street. I'll explain everything.'

There's a long pause before he answers. 'Okay. I'll see you there at ten.'

Kate heads straight to the coffee shop to wait. She orders a chai tea and wraps her hands around the large mug to warm them. Snow has been forecast, and grey clouds hang ominously in the sky. When her phone pings, she rushes to read the message, assuming it might be Rowan telling her he's running late. But it's an email from FHeld@beneaththesurface.com.

Hi, Kate.

This is Faye Held, podcast host of *Beneath the Surface*. You contacted me a couple of years ago to complain about my podcast episode.

I'm working on a new episode and I could really do with your help. It's about the murder of Jamie Archer. I believe you know his wife – Harper Nolan.

I'd love to speak to you about her as a matter of urgency.

Best,

Faye Held

Numb with shock, Kate re-reads the email, carefully scanning for underlying meanings. This woman's podcast brought back all the memories Kate had so carefully buried, sending her spiralling, seeking out help from Rowan Hess. And Kate won't forget that Faye Held had suggested there might be more to his death than self-defence. Kate should reply immediately and tell her to go to hell, before deleting the email and blocking Faye Held.

But she wants to know what this woman has to say about Harper. It could be the lead Kate is looking for.

With her stomach churning, Kate ignores her tea and checks the time. Quarter to ten. She needs Rowan to get there fast, as inappropriate as it is for her to drag her therapist into this. Ex-therapist. She's not sure what help she's expecting from him; all she knows is that she needs to see him, and it's fast becoming clear that there's no one else she can trust.

She begins drafting an email to tell Faye Held to stop contacting her, but changes her mind. Maybe Faye Held can help her. She deletes what she's written and sends off a different response: *I can meet today.*

By ten past ten, Rowan still hasn't appeared. Kate looks up every time the door opens and lets in a gust of icy air. But it's never Rowan. And then a text comes. Rowan telling her that he can't come. He's sorry, but it's for the best. He'll send her the name of a therapist as soon as possible.

Kate drops her phone and it crashes to the floor, and all eyes in the coffee shop turn and stare.

She reaches down to retrieve it, smoothing her finger over the spiderweb of cracks on the screen, blurring the photo of her and Thomas that she loves so much.

It was Faye Held's choice to meet in Hyde Park. A strange request, considering the weather. And now, as Kate sits shivering on a bench, heavy doubts set in. Saying even one word to this woman, whose only goal will be to get as many listeners as possible, is dangerous. But clearly she knows something, and Kate needs to know what that is.

Faye is right on time, strolling towards the bench with a confidence Kate has never possessed, and Kate knows immediately that it won't be easy to lie to this woman. She's wearing a long, belted coat and flat knee-length boots, with a bobble hat over neat braids. Faye smiles when she reaches the bench, holding out her hand. 'Thanks for coming. This will be so helpful for me.'

Kate takes her hand. 'Tell me why I should help you after you dragged my name into your podcast?'

Faye's eyes widen. 'It was nothing personal. You do know

that, right? Just doing my job.' She appraises Kate. 'There were a lot of people who vowed that Graham White was a decent man. That he would never have attacked a young girl.'

But Kate knows the truth. 'That's what people have said about murderers before. Things like they were kind and thoughtful neighbours.'

Faye raises her eyebrows. 'True. But normally you'd expect some kind of unusual behaviour. Even if it's only picked up in hindsight. With Graham White there was nothing. Zero. Zilch. Nada.'

'That doesn't mean anything. I was there. I know what he did. And even if I agree to talk, I'm not sure how you think I can help you.'

'Let's sit.' Faye says, gesturing to the bench. I'll get straight to the point. Like I said in my email, I'm covering the Jamie Archer case on my podcast. First time I've covered something that's current. And I'm looking into his wife. They say always start with the person closest to the victim, so that's what I've done.' She smiles.

'I barely know Harper,' Kate says. 'I'm not sure what help I can be.'

'Oh, any acquaintance of Harper's will be able to shed light on her. By all accounts she's a bit of an enigma. And I've discovered some... disturbing things while I've been doing my research.'

'Like what?'

Faye pulls out her phone, tapping on it with bright orange fingernails. 'Firstly, I can't find any record that she and Jamie were actually married. Yet she's calling herself his wife.'

Kate sucks in her breath. 'But wouldn't the police have checked that?'

'Have you read any of the articles about Jamie Archer. None of them mentions he was married.'

'But they have a son. And I've seen their wedding pictures in their house.'

'Well, I can't explain the photos but this isn't the nineteen twenties,' Faye says. 'You can have a kid without being married. Now, I think I've said enough. Your turn.' She folds her arms and waits.

Kate clutches her bag to her chest. She doesn't trust this woman, and Faye already knows too much about her. And what Faye doesn't know, Kate's sure the woman will make it her job to find out. 'I told you I don't know Harper that well. But since I met her a couple of weeks ago, she's been doing some weird stuff. Pushing our sons into a friendship. Messaging me all the time. She sent me dead lilies and left a threatening note on my car. And she put a photo of her husband in my son's school bag. She insisted it wasn't her, but I know it was.'

Faye raises her eyebrows. 'Is that right? And why do you think she'd do something like that?'

Kate shrugs. 'To get to me.'

'Why would she want to get to you?'

'I have no idea,' Kate says. 'Because she's disturbed.'

Faye considers this. 'Okay. So I've gone over several scenarios. Jamie left her, or cheated on her, and she killed him in a jealous rage. Or... there's some other reason she had for needing Jamie dead.'

Kate stares at her, unsure how to respond. She's had her own suspicions about Harper, but hearing someone else say it is still surprising.

'Oh, I can tell you're shocked,' Faye says. 'But it's my job to go over all this stuff. It's not for the faint-hearted, is it? The trouble is – she has an alibi. She was at home with her son. And there's a Ring doorbell in the house opposite them that would have shown if she'd left for any reason. She couldn't have gone out the back as she'd have had to climb over several garden fences to get out of her road.' Faye crosses her legs. 'Still, doesn't mean she didn't find a way to get out and slaughter Jamie. People do manage to evade cameras.'

Kate takes in Faye's words – is it possible that Faye might actually be on her side after all? 'She could have got someone else to do it,' Kate says. 'Then she wouldn't have had to leave her house at all. You said she might have had another reason for wanting Jamie dead. Like what?'

'That's what I'm hoping to find out,' Faye says. 'Was he abusive? Threatening her in some way?'

'I wouldn't know about that. She's barely said anything about their relationship. But then, why would she to me? We've only just met.'

Faye studies her. 'And you never knew Jamie?'

'No.' Kate forces herself to maintain eye contact with Faye.

'That's a shame,' Faye says, sliding her phone back in her pocket. 'And also interesting.'

'Why interesting?'

'Because if you didn't know him, how come I have a photo of the two of you together. And let's just say you don't look like strangers in it.'

TWENTY-THREE

2015

Jamie looks pitiful, standing across from her, too agitated to sit down. Two weeks after she'd seen him in the restaurant with the older woman, Jamie had turned up at her place, begging for her forgiveness. Harper had momentarily given in and let him stay the night. A big mistake. In the harsh morning light, she'd come to her senses and told him to leave. That was five months ago, and now, Jamie stares at the large mound of her belly, unable to avert his eyes.

'Why didn't you tell me?' he asks.

Harper's never seen him so shocked, and she's enjoying this novel experience. 'Because I can't trust you. Look what happened last time – I didn't want you to know about this baby. I want to keep him or her safe.'

Jamie's face is distraught as he stands staring at her, his hands in his pockets, his shoulders hunched. 'I'm sorry, Harper. But you can't blame me for what happened to Molly. It would have happened even if I'd been there. That's what the doctors said. She just wasn't meant to be.'

Harper itches to punch his face. 'I felt her move. The evening you didn't come home. She was fine. And then I couldn't find you... and I was so worried and got so stressed. And then she died. It's your fault. You lied to me about being with Sam. You're not even friends any more.'

Jamie lowers his head and stares at the soft mink-coloured carpet they'd just had fitted before she lost their baby. 'I'm so sorry, Harp. I would never do that to you again.' He still doesn't look at her. Things got a bit... out of control. My whole life has got out of control.'

Harper knows this. It's clear for everyone to see. 'Who was that woman you were with in the restaurant? The last time I saw you.'

'I already told you when I stayed over that night. She was a friend. Who was that man *you* were with?'

'Stop!' she screams. 'I told you that's none of your business. And you're lying. Who was she?' Harper rubs her stomach, relishing the sense of life growing in her body, the limitless possibilities for her unborn child.

'Okay! Just calm down. I don't want you getting worked up.' Jamie sits on the arm of the sofa, knowing full well she hates it when he does that. 'I've made mistakes, Harper. But it's not what you think,' he begins. 'With that woman. She's just helping me out with something. I wasn't *seeing* her.'

Harper shakes her head. 'It's exactly what I think. You told me I'd messed everything up when I confronted you outside her house. What were you talking about?'

'We had a nice flat, didn't we?' Jamie says, ignoring her. 'A decent life.'

'I don't care about that. I'm happy here in this place.'

For a moment, Jamie stares at the ceiling. 'Where do you think it came from? The money. And you got to keep all your salary. Did what you liked with it.'

Jamie doesn't know, but what Harper was doing with it was saving it, spending as little as possible; perhaps she'd somehow sensed that sooner or later it would all be snatched away from her. Did she subconsciously realise that Jamie would let her down?

'I don't care about money.' She rubs her stomach, relieved when she feels a small flutter.

Jamie notices her gesture and moves towards her. 'Is the baby moving?'

'Don't come near me,' she says.

He holds up his hands and takes a step back. In his pocket, his phone rings.

'Aren't you going to get that?' she asks.

'It's not important.'

'More lies.'

The phone keeps ringing, blaring into the silence until finally it stops and they're left with their painful silence.

'I'm not a good person,' he says.

Harper takes a deep breath. She's been waiting for so long to hear some honesty from Jamie. She has no idea what she'll do once she hears the truth from him, but this is a start.

'What have you done, Jamie? Who was that woman?'

He sinks to the floor, pulling his knees up to his chest. 'I've been lying to you. To everyone. About who I am. The business has failed, and I... I'm in a lot of debt. I... I had to get a job. In that new high-end gym in Covent Garden. Remember I told you I did that personal trainer course before I went to uni? Well, I lied on my CV to get that job. Told them I'd been working as a PT for years. They snapped me up.'

Harper stares at him. Jamie started developing properties two years ago, and she's never seen him worry about money. That's how he's earned his money. They've gone on holidays, eaten out whenever they've felt like it. Not many people their age are so fortunate. 'What the hell, Jamie? But you've had money. Surely more than you'd get for working at a gym. We go out for dinner all the time.'

'That's what I'm trying to tell you. The business failed. I... I couldn't make it work. And it's left me crippled with debt. But I didn't want to burden you with this. I wanted you to keep thinking things were okay. So I had to find a way to keep funding this life we have.'

'What are you telling me, Jamie?'

'That woman you saw me with in the restaurant. She was one of my clients at the gym. She's wealthy. So much money she doesn't know what to do with it. But women like that... they get lonely. Sick of their partners or husbands. When I train them, they start telling me stuff. All their problems. And of course I listen. I didn't intend for any of it, but the opportunity was right there. I could see how much I make them feel like they're the only woman in the world. I tell them whatever it is they want to hear.'

Harper can't register his words – they don't make sense. This can't be Jamie talking. She'd prepared herself to hear about an affair, probably more than one, but she struggles to comprehend what exactly Jamie is telling her. She knows, though, that this is something worse. 'Them?' she asks, as what he's telling her starts to register. 'There are more?'

He nods. 'You'd be surprised how willing women are to throw money my way. Invest in my fictional company for the promise of more money. They believe me when I tell them I want to start up my own personal training business. But they don't really care about money, they don't need it. It's my company they want – to feel as if someone still wants them. I'm there for them. I give them my time, and emotional support. I show them I'm invested in them. They're clearly not getting any of that from their husbands.'

Stunned, Harper shakes her head.

'They believe me when I tell them I'm having difficulties with investors. And they want to help me out when someone's threatening me or doesn't pay me on time. It's like... they just can't see what I'm really doing. Or they do, but just don't want to believe it, because it shatters the life they're desperate for. And money means nothing to these women.' He shakes his head. 'I almost want them to confront me and demand their money back. I've tried to push them to, many times, but they never do. I've silently begged them to tell me I'm a fraud and that they're calling the police. It would be a relief.'

The blank expression is back on Jamie's face, making Harper want to smash her fist into it. There are two different people inside Jamie, like Jekyll and Hyde, and what he's just told her is proof of that.

'How many women?' Harper asks, her whole body numb.

'Only three.'

'So you sleep with them?' Harper asks, part of her not wanting to hear the answer yet the rest of her desperate to know, so that there can be no going back.

'Most of the time I don't have to. I make excuses not to. It's not about sex, Harper,' Jamie says, as if this should be obvious.

'It's about you conning them out of money.'

Jamie hangs his head.

And now she wants to know everything. 'How long have you been doing it?' she repeats, slowly this time. Anger sweeps over her and for a moment she forgets the little life growing inside her, until she feels those reassuring flutters again. Signs of life.

Jamie averts his eyes. 'Around a year. Since the property company failed, I've done this for us, can't you—'

'Don't you dare!'

'I can stop doing it,' he assures her. 'Leave the gym and start afresh. There's a job being advertised at the FCA for an economist. That's what I'm qualified to do, Harp. I'd have a good chance of getting it.'

She hates it when Jamie shortens her name. 'I don't believe you. And if you've had debt problems, you'll never get a job with them.'

'Then I'll get something else. Please give me a chance.' Jamie gestures to her stomach. 'Let me be a father to our child. I'll never lie to you, or keep you in the dark again. Cards on the table, always. I swear, Harp.' His phone rings again, and he pulls it from his pocket and throws it across the floor.

'Please,' he begs.

Harper closes her eyes, and focuses on the jolts and kicks in her stomach. This baby is full of life, strong and healthy. *So was Molly, until she wasn't.* Harper opens her eyes again and looks at Jamie. She's loved him so deeply, but now all that's left is simmering anger that she needs to use. For the baby's sake more than anything.

She moves over to Jamie and sits beside him, taking his hand and placing it on her stomach. She senses the change in his body language as he begins to relax. He thinks he's got her now.

And that's exactly what she wants him to believe.

The first thing Harper does when she wakes up is check her phone. It's now more important than ever that she finishes all this – before Kate ends it herself. Harper hadn't expected her to be so defiant, to not crumble and fall. It shouldn't surprise her, though – Jamie would never have picked someone who wouldn't defend herself. She dreads to think what would have happened if Ellis hadn't come clean about the cameras.

There's no message from Faye Held, but there's a text from an unknown number. Harper opens it, adrenalin coursing through her as she reads the message.

> *Hi, this is Mona Shaw. I don't like raking up the past, but Faye convinced me to message you. I live in St Albans now so you'll have to come to me if you want to talk.*

Harper wastes no time replying, telling Mona she can meet her today at eleven. Mona replies: *Fine. Meet outside Forest Town Church at 11.*

Harper climbs out of bed and goes to check on Dexter. He's still asleep and she doesn't want to wake him to drag him to St

Albans. Besides, how would she explain what she's doing? So far she's managed to keep Dexter out of this mess that Jamie left behind. She puts a message out to the school WhatsApp group, asking if anyone can recommend a babysitter, and within minutes a flurry of recommendations floods in. Harper picks one at random – Phoebe Helsopp, recommended by a parent she's never spoken to.

She sends Phoebe a message, asking if she's available right now, and is surprised when Phoebe replies immediately and agrees, on the condition that she's paid double for the short notice.

It takes Harper over an hour to get to St Albans – a place she's never been before. Her satnav directs her to Forest Town Church and she finds a parking space across the road. It's three minutes to eleven when she gets out of the car and makes her way to the church.

It's silent in the church grounds, and the cold chill pinches her skin, despite the long, padded coat she's wearing and her fleece-lined boots. She hovers outside, checking her phone every few seconds in case Mona Shaw has changed her mind.

Finally, at five past eleven, a woman who Harper assumes is Mona steps out of the church, heading towards Harper. She's tall, with curly dark hair tied in a side ponytail. There's a harshness about the angular lines of her face and she doesn't smile at Harper, even when Harper greets her and holds out her hand. 'Thanks for meeting me.'

Mona looks at Harper's hand with distaste, but lightly takes it. 'Nearly changed my mind,' she says. 'I've buried that whole incident. Tried to forget it happened. Do you mind if we walk? I can't sit still when I'm talking about all this.' She points to the back of the church. 'There's a nature reserve we can walk to if we head that way.'

'Of course,' Harper says. She glances at the church. 'Do you mind me asking why you wanted to meet here?'

'Oh, it's nothing weird. I help out here on Sunday mornings with the kids' sessions. I like to do my bit for the community. Let's walk.'

'Do you have kids, then?' Harper asks, walking fast to keep up with Mona.

'Not yet. Haven't met the right person. How about you?'

'A son. Dexter. He's ten, and—'

'Can we cut the small talk, please?' Mona says, stopping to face Harper. 'I'm really not cut out for it.'

Harper raises her eyebrows. Something tells her she's not going to like this woman. 'Okay.'

Mona resumes walking. 'You're here because you want to know about Kate. What I want to know is why you're asking about her?'

'Didn't Faye Held tell you anything?' Harper asks.

'Not much. She just said that you know Kate and you're concerned about her behaviour.'

'Kate slept with my husband. And now he's dead.'

Mona stops walking again. 'Oh. That's... I'm so sorry.'

'She was the last person to see him,' Harper continues. 'But she's not admitting to anyone – including me – that she even knew him. Nobody knows except for me. And now Faye Held.'

'And how exactly do you know she slept with him?'

Harper lets out a deep breath. 'I know how this sounds, but I had a camera in the flat. Jamie and I had a property we rented out and we were between tenants. I... let's just say I had suspicions that he was using it to take women back there.' Harper takes out her phone and scrolls to the picture of Jamie and Kate. 'Here's the proof.'

Mona stares at the photo. 'Kate's changed a lot. I wouldn't have recognised her. Her hair's completely different. Darker than I remember.'

'I think it's common for people to alter their appearance if they're trying to start over and forget the past. Run from something.' Harper puts her phone back in her pocket.

'Makes sense I suppose. But sleeping with someone doesn't make you a murderer, does it?' Mona says.

They continue walking. 'But if you've killed someone before...'

'Graham White. Hearing that name... it makes me... well, in a way, it was my fault. Kate shouldn't have been walking home that day. She should have been hanging out with us by the canal. Then it would never have happened.

'You can't think like that,' Harper says. She doesn't know all the details, but she needs to keep Mona talking. 'You are *not* responsible for what happened to Graham White. And I'm not responsible for what happened to Jamie.'

Mona pauses, dabs her eyes. 'But I'm the one who set off the whole chain of events. Kate and I had had an argument, and I keep thinking what if we hadn't? Even now I think like that. It's stayed with me all these years. Then maybe he never would have crossed paths with Kate. She points to a bench on the other side of the trees. 'Let's sit over there. I think I'm ready to share this story.'

'Kate and I fell out that day. Badly,' Mona says, once they've reached the bench. 'It was over this boy – Kian. It seems so trivial now, but back then it was colossal. We were only fifteen.'

'Friends and boys are everything when you're that age,' Harper says, remembering the huge crush she'd had at that age on Craig Summers. She never did have the courage to speak to him, and the two of them only ever eyed each other from a distance. Kids' stuff. But huge at the time.

'We both liked Kian,' Mona says. 'But we never talked about it, and I felt bad because even though I'd liked him first, Kate was always talking about him so I could never explain how I felt. But she knew. Once when she was at my house, she found an old diary I'd written in. It had everything in there – all my feelings about Kian. About my whole life. I caught her reading it but she never said anything. Just shut it and slipped it back under my bed. Kate was strange like that. A closed book. She refused to talk about what I'd just seen her doing. And what can you do if someone refuses to speak?'

That fits with everything Harper has witnessed from Kate. 'So what happened on the day Graham White was killed?'

'We were all hanging out by the canal. We'd broken up from school early as it was the last day of the summer term. Anyway, I was kind of seeing one of Kian's friends – Robbie. Kian always seemed to have a girlfriend so I'd given up waiting for him. Anyway, Kate needed the toilet and there weren't any nearby so she went into town. She was gone for ages. And in that time, I'd broken up with Robbie and admitted to him I had feelings for Kian. He was a real arse about it – shouting out to everyone that I wanted Kian. Calling me a slut. Humiliating me in front of the other boys. It was horrible. But then, Kian came to my defence and told Robbie to back off. They had a fight, then Kian and I were left alone. We were just talking and I admitted it was true that I liked him. That's when he kissed me and… it probably went too far, and I didn't think Kate would see us. I thought she'd decided to go home. She'd been gone for so long.' She stares at Harper. 'Please don't judge me – I'd liked him for so long. You know that feeling when someone is under your skin and you just can't shake them?'

Harper understands. Jamie was under her skin the second she met him. And he still is. But her deep-seated love for Jamie turned into something else. And even now he's dead, Jamie underlies all her actions. 'I get it,' she says.

Mona folds her arms across her chest. 'I don't like talking about this. I've blocked it out all these years.'

Harper nods. 'I understand. But I need justice for my

husband. Please, Mona. Help me make sure Kate Mason pays for what she did.'

Mona hangs her head. 'Kian and I were... you know... *together*. In the woods. And suddenly Kate was there screaming and shouting. She ran over to me and grabbed me by my hair, dragging me away from Kian. She told me Kian was her boyfriend and I'd betrayed her. But they weren't together, I swear. She was just infatuated with him. She was grabbing me, throwing punches, and I was terrified. She'd always had a bit of a temper but I'd never seen her that bad before. Kian dragged her off me and told her to calm down, but it was like she didn't even hear him. She ran off, and I remember how her face looked – so red with rage. She screamed that I'd pay for this as she was running off.'

'Did you tell the police all of this?'

'No. They never asked, and I just wanted to forget it happened. Robbie was already spreading it around that I was some kind of whore and I'd slept with Kian. I had to keep my distance from all of them when we went back to school. I just shut myself off and then my mum moved us to St Albans.'

'I know this is hard, but it's been a long time... You could go to the police now if it helps me to prove Kate killed Jamie.'

'Just because Kate and I had a fight and she basically attacked me – it doesn't prove anything about what happened with Graham White.' Mona shakes her head. 'I've already told Faye that I won't speak about this publicly to anyone, and that includes the police. I've got my job and the church to think about. I can't get dragged into that awful mess.'

But there is another way. 'What about Kian?' Harper says. 'He could testify to Kate's behaviour that day.'

Mona's defiant expression falls. 'That might be a bit difficult.'

'Why?'

'Kian died a few years after it all happened. He got really

drunk at a party and ended up walking in front of a car. Funny, though – Kian never seemed the type who'd drink excessively. It always seemed like he was just drinking for the sake of it. To look cool or something.'

Yet no one is who they seem – Harper knows this more than most.

'Were you in contact with him after Kate's attack?'

Mona shakes her head. 'I told you – I had to avoid them all. He approached me at school, though, on the first day we went back, to try and explain himself. He apologised to me for what happened in the woods. Said he'd had a lot to drink and he was sorry for how he behaved. But he had nothing to apologise for. I knew what I was doing.' She sighs. 'Kian and I never spoke again.'

'When did you hear about Kate's attack?' Harper asks.

'From people at school. Everyone was talking about it. Imagine if we'd had social media then. But it was just word of mouth. At first, I felt awful for Kate. First she'd lost Kian, even though he was never hers to lose, and then she got attacked. I even went to her house to try and see her but her mum told me she didn't want to see anyone. But then I saw a picture of Graham White and I recognised him straight away. I'd seen her talking to him in the park once and assumed he was just one of her mum's friends. I don't even remember if I asked her. I didn't even tell Faye Held this – you're the first person I've admitted it to. Because now, I know I should have mentioned it. But I was fifteen. I didn't know what to do. And Kate was my friend.'

'But the police investigated,' Harper says. 'They would have found out if Kate had known Graham White.'

'I don't know if she *knew* him. Properly. I just know that they'd bumped into each other in the park because they were talking. Who knows what that means? Anyway, they weren't looking into all that. They believed her story about being thrown into the van. There was no CCTV that picked anything up. And what reason would they have to doubt it? She was a child, and he was a grown man. Case closed.'

Harper struggles to piece this all together. Even though Mona Shaw is growing on her, she wonders if things might have played out differently if Mona hadn't kept this to herself all these years. If she'd just told someone – anyone – then there might be a chance Kate would never have met Jamie.

'That day was the day my life spiralled out of control,' Mona says. I'd be living a completely different life if it wasn't for what Kate did. I had every right to be with Kian that day – and she knew it. It was me he liked.'

Harper doesn't care about any of that. She only wants to know what Kate has done. To Jamie and to Graham White. 'I need to know the truth, Mona. Do you think Kate killed Graham White on purpose? Nothing you say will go any further than this.' Harper taps her head. 'I promise. I just need to know.'

There's a heavy silence, and Harper listens to the roar of traffic coming from the other side of the trees, silently praying for the outcome she needs. When she can bear the waiting no more, she turns to Mona. 'Well? Can you help me?'

'I really think she did it on purpose,' Mona says. 'And if she can do it once, what's to stop her doing it again? Justice needs to be served.'

TWENTY-FIVE
2006

Kate has barely left the house this summer. She was allowed to leave school and study for her GCSEs in college, with a small group of children who can't deal with the school environment. To start with they'd terrified her, but slowly she began to get to know them, and that's when it hit her that fundamentally everyone is the same under all the complex layers we think make us who we are.

And now she's finished her A levels and got a place at Brighton University, and the thought of leaving South Norwood is the only thing that keeps her sane. Her mum's been working on getting them out of there – but the house has only just sold, and even then they've had to take thousands off the asking price. But her mum has never once complained, or made Kate feel guilty for this disruption to their lives.

Sometimes, even though it's been three years since Graham White, Kate catches her mum staring at her. And she never wants to ask what her mum is thinking.

Kate looks around the house and barely recognises it – packing boxes stacked against every wall in the house, blank white walls with darker shadows where photos once hung.

Kate's hoping that the ghosts of her past will stay here in this house, while she puts miles between them. But there's one thing she needs to do to help that happen.

'I'm going out for a bit,' she says.

Her mum glances up from her book, with that anxious look on her face again. But Kate's eighteen now – she's an adult and her mum needs to let her go.

'Oh. Where?' her mum asks. 'I thought we could play Scrabble again.'

Her mum hates Scrabble, and they've been playing all summer. Kate humours her because she knows her mum can't cope when Kate leaves the house. Not since Graham White. How different things would have been if that day had never happened. Kate often ponders what kind of person she would be now. But still, the anger that's been there since she was a child is always within her, lying low, waiting to erupt.

'Just for a walk. Maybe to the high street. Might look around the shops.'

Her mum frowns. She knows Kate hates shopping and would rather spend her time drawing. 'That's a lovely idea. I'll come with—'

'I'd rather go alone. If you don't mind.'

A shadow passes across her mum's face, and Kate can't bear to see the sadness on it. She leans down to give her a hug. 'I won't be long, Mum.'

Kate's known where Jennifer Seagrove lives since it happened. Even though this is London, people still talk. They take pleasure in pointing out where horrific things have happened. And Jennifer was talked about a lot that year.

She often comes here, sitting on the wall across the road, pretending she's waiting for someone instead of watching Jennifer from afar. Kate is intrigued that Jennifer still wants to live here – shouldn't she want to be far from the ghost of Graham White, with whom she shared this house?

Once Kate and her mum move, Kate won't be able to come here any more, so she studies the house, committing it to memory, even though she has no idea where the urge to do this comes from.

Kate watches a couple further down the street, who appear to be arguing, so she doesn't notice a woman approach her, until she's right in front of her.

Jennifer Seagrove.

Close up, she doesn't look like the Jennifer who was plastered across the local papers. Her shoulder-length hair is blonde and short – not the long dark hair she had three years ago.

'I know who you are,' Jennifer says. 'I've seen you out here several times. What are you doing here?'

'I... I don't know...'

Jennifer frowns, and her face softens. 'I think you'd better come in for a chat, then.'

Stepping inside, Kate wills her heart to stop hammering. She's not prepared for this meeting, and no words come to her.

'Come in the kitchen,' Jennifer says. 'I'll get you a drink. Do you drink tea? Or coffee?'

Kate doesn't want either, but she's compelled to accept Jennifer's offer. Now that she's here, she needs to put things right somehow, in whatever small way she can. 'Tea please.'

Kate steps inside, following Jennifer through the narrow hallway. She pictures Graham White in here – taking his shoes off by the door, hanging his coat. Greeting Jennifer after a long day at work.

Jennifer makes tea and hands it to Kate, leading her to the living room, where the sweet scent of flowers fragrances the room, coming from the huge vase of white lilies on the side table.

'They're beautiful, aren't they?' Jennifer says. 'I bought them for myself. I do it every year on Graham's birthday.'

Kate stares at her. 'Oh. I thought... I thought you'd left him.'

'That doesn't mean I didn't care about him. And I don't want to remember the day he died, just his birthday.' She shakes her head.

'Are you going to tell me why you've been watching my house?' Jennifer says, gesturing for her to sit.

'I'm moving away tomorrow. With my mum. To Brighton. I... I wanted to come one last time.' Kate wonders if her voice betrays how nervous she feels coming face to face with this woman. She sits on an armchair, locking her fingers together.

'Why?' Jennifer asks, sitting on the sofa, perching on the end as if she doesn't want to let herself get comfortable.

'I'm not sure.'

Jennifer closes her eyes and sighs. 'It's not healthy, is it? You must know that, Kate.'

Kate chews her lip, clutching her stomach to stop the stabbing pain that's just started. She feels like a child again, instead of the young woman she now is.

'It wasn't true what they said about him,' Jennifer says. 'None of it was true. People are vile. He wouldn't have tried to kill you. I don't believe that for one second.'

'How can you be so sure of that?' Kate says, finding her voice because she knows different.

'I know because I was with him for long enough. He would never... and if that's what you believe then you can get out of my house.'

Now she's here, though, Kate doesn't want to leave just yet. Not until she's spoken her mind. 'He... he wasn't a good man.'

Jennifer stares at her. 'Graham didn't deserve to die.

'It was... it was self-defence.' Kate's hand shakes and she places her mug on the coffee table.

Jennifer's eyes bore into her. 'Is that the lie you've told yourself all these years? Does it make you feel better about taking his life? What a neat little story.'

Kate shudders at the harshness of these words. 'No... that's not—'

'I don't care!' Jennifer says, raising her voice. 'I left Graham. The day before you killed him. He was nothing to do with me when you... when you did that.' She stares at Kate. 'You don't look well. Your face is all... pale. I'd better get you some water.' She rushes off to the kitchen, leaving Kate alone, sitting on a chair that Graham White must have sat on countless times.

When she returns, Jennifer's manner is softer. 'Here you go. Please don't go collapsing on me now or anything. I really don't want to have to take you to A & E.'

Despite the situation, Kate smiles at Jennifer's kindness. And Kate has to keep in mind that Jennifer hasn't done anything to her. She is as much a victim as Kate is. 'Thank you.'

'I don't blame you, you know,' Jennifer says, sitting back down. 'I never have. You were a child. But I will never understand why it happened,' Jennifer continues. 'What you were doing in his van.'

Kate looks away. She could repeat that Graham White attacked her and forced her into the van, but Jennifer will clearly never believe her. 'What was he like?' Kate asks, looking at Jennifer through a hazy window of tears.

'Do you really want to know? It's not going to change your mind about him, is it? Like I said, none of this is healthy.'

'I'm eighteen now,' Kate says. 'I need to try to heal. I need to know this stuff.'

'Fair enough,' Jennifer says. 'Graham was... he had this way of making you feel special. Like you were the only person in his world. Whenever I was with him, his whole attention was on me. Nothing else mattered. He made me feel like a queen. It was intoxicating, really.' He had his faults. A bit of a short temper. Easily irritated. But nothing I was ever concerned about.' She lets out a deep breath. 'People said that because I'd just left him, he was angry and lashing out at someone. Anyone. They tried to make out he must have been angry with all women. But that couldn't be further from the truth.' She pauses. 'When I left him he was crushed, no doubt about it. But he handled it with dignity. He didn't get angry with me. If anything, he got more... I don't know. Determined? He was going to get on with his life.'

'Why did you leave him?' Kate asks, her fingernails digging into the palms of her hands.

Jennifer frowns. 'Now why would you ask me that question?'

'What do you mean?'

'I mean – why would you ask me why I left him when you already know.'

'I... don't know what you're talking about.'

'Really? You're playing that game, are you? Just what is it you're really doing here, Kate?'

Kate shakes her head. 'I'm not playing any games. I really don't know.'

The room falls silent as Jennifer stares at her. 'Are you wondering why I didn't go to the police?' she says.

'I don't—'

'Come on, you seem like an intelligent girl. There was no way I could have them knowing the truth about Graham. Because how would that have made me look? I would have been tarnished by what he'd done.'

'What do you mean? I don't understand.'

'It was better this way,' Jennifer continues. 'Better that everyone thought he attacked you. But I know the truth, Kate. I know all about you two. It was going on for months, wasn't it? You were fifteen and he was thirty-nine! Did you seriously think no one would ever find out about your relationship?'

TWENTY-SIX

SUNDAY 2 FEBRUARY

Kate stares at Faye Held, hoping she's only imagined Faye's words.

I have a photo of the two of you together

'What... what photo?'

'Glad you've asked,' Faye says, tapping on her phone. 'This.' She hands it to Kate, who slowly takes the phone.

And there it is. A photo of Kate with Jamie in his bedroom, taken from a camera that must have been high up in the corner of the bedroom. The satin sheets she remembers from that night wrapped around their naked bodies. An intense rush of heat surges through Kate's body.

'That's you, isn't it?' Faye says, easing her phone out of Kate's hand.

Kate nods. There's no point in lying now. She needs to tell the truth to this woman and convince her that she's innocent.

'Where did you get this?' Kate asks. 'Was it Harper?'

'I never give away my sources. Confidentiality means everything to me. Sorry.' She gives Kate an apologetic smile. 'Care to explain the photo?'

'I was at Jamie's flat for a few hours, but I left his house around two or three in the morning. And he was fine. We talked before I left.'

Faye studies Kate's face, and her absence of words is excruciating. 'D'you know what? I'm actually inclined to believe you, even though you've clearly just lied to me by telling me you didn't know him. But I still think there are things you're not telling me.'

Relief surges through Kate's body. 'I keep wondering if there's a connection with Graham White. It just seems too much of a coincidence that I'm linked to two dead bodies.' Especially when that note on her windscreen mentioned both men.

'That thought crossed my mind too,' Faye says. 'So I looked into it, but I can't find any hint of a link between the two men. I'll continue digging, though.' She pauses. 'But there's something about Harper Nolan I can't trust. I can't put my finger on it – call it instinct – but I'll find out what it is. And in the meantime, I find it hard to believe you would have killed this man – Jamie. I've researched you. You live a quiet life with your son and you work as a vet, caring for animals. Now I know that doesn't mean anything, but the vibe you give off doesn't scream murderer to me. You met Jamie Archer that night – there's no record anywhere of you having known him before. So I ask myself – why would you suddenly kill him after sleeping with him? What would your motive be? And there's always motive. Harper, on the other hand, had plenty – a wronged wife. Or girlfriend. So let's say they were still together. She finds out you've slept with Jamie, waits until you leave then confronts him. It gets messy. That's a much more likely scenario. I'm keeping an open mind, though. Not saying I trust *you* yet. But, when it comes down to it, we all have to pick a side, don't we? Run with it until we're proved wrong.'

'You won't be proved wrong,' Kate says. 'And thank you for your trust.'

.   .   .

As she pulls up to her house, Kate cuts the engine and stays in the car. Her conversation with Faye has unsettled her; she wants to believe that the podcaster is on her side, but if Kate can't even trust the people closest to her, then how can she trust this stranger? Especially one with a professional agenda.

Kate still hasn't heard from the one person who might have some answers, so she tries calling again, but as always it goes straight to voicemail. Hanging up, Kate throws her phone on the passenger seat and starts the car. Ellis can stay with Thomas for a bit longer – there's something Kate needs to do.

She knocks on Harper's door and waits. It's time to put an end to this campaign of Harper's. And whatever happens will be caught on the cameras Ellis hid. Seconds pass and nothing happens. Harper's car isn't anywhere on the road, but there are lights on in the living room. 'Where are you?' she whispers.

She's about to turn away, when the door eases open and Dex is standing there, a confused frown on his face.

'I thought you were Mum,' he says.

'Hi Dex. Do you know where she is?'

He shrugs. 'No. She just had to go out. A few hours ago.'

Kate peers into the house. 'And who's with you?'

'No one.'

Kate frowns. 'No one? But you can't be on your own.'

Dex shrugs. 'I wasn't. The babysitter was here. But then she said she had to go. It was only a few minutes ago.'

'In that case, I think I should come in and stay with you. Just until your mum gets home.'

He shrugs again. 'Okay. Can Thomas come?'

'He's with his dad, but maybe another time.' Kate steps into the house, fully aware that this could be a trap of some kind.

She wants to question Dex more, but he's a child and no matter what, she won't involve him in this. It's between her and Harper.

'Does your mum know that the babysitter left?'

'No. Phoebe just rushed off and said it was a family emergency. I told her I'm ten and I'll be fine until Mum gets back.'

'What were you up to?' Kate asks, unzipping her coat.

'Just watching TV.'

'Well, how about you carry on and I'll just get myself some water. That okay?'

'Yeah,' Dex says. 'I really wish Thomas could come, though.'

'I know,' Kate says.

While Dexter goes back to his TV programme, Kate roots through the kitchen cupboards until she finds a glass – even though she has no intention of drinking anything. Then she searches through the drawers. She's sure she won't find anything, but she'll never again get this opportunity to be alone in Harper's house.

'What the hell are you doing?'

Kate spins around to find Harper standing in the doorway, her arms folded across her chest.

'Dex was alone. I came in to stay with him until you got back. The babysitter walked out and just left him here.'

Harper rushes to the living room, calling for Dex, and from the kitchen Kate listens.

'Dexter? Did Phoebe just leave?'

'She said she had an emergency and I told her I'd be okay. I said you'd be back soon.'

'Weren't you scared?'

'Mum, I'm ten! Nearly in Year 6.'

'Come here.' There's panic in Harper's voice that Kate's never heard before – she almost sounds like a different person. 'Promise me you'll get someone to call me if anything like this happens again. Not that I'm leaving you again. I'm never leaving you again.'

'Mum, I'm fine,' Dexter insists.

Harper walks back into the kitchen, shutting the door. 'Looking for these?' she says, reaching into her pocket. She crosses to Kate and slips something into her hand. Two miniature cameras.

Kate stares at them. How is this possible? She grabs them from Harper and shoves them in her pocket. 'I... I wanted to make sure Thomas is safe when he comes here. I'll do what I have to, to protect my son. But you need to stop all of this, Harper. Before someone gets hurt.'

'Like Jamie, you mean? I'll take my chances. You know, Kate, there are consequences of our actions, and sooner or later we all have to face them.'

'Is that why Jamie's dead? Was it a consequence of his actions?'

'Why don't you tell me, Kate?'

'Jamie's death was nothing to do with me.'

'But you slept with him.'

Harper knows, there's no point denying it. 'So it was you who gave that photo to that podcaster. I had nothing to do with Jamie's murder. And you weren't even married. You've been lying to everyone.'

'You're talking about a little piece of paper that doesn't mean anything,' Harper says. 'Jamie and I were bound by something much more important than a pointless marriage certificate. We have our son.'

'Jamie was telling me the truth, wasn't he? When he said you were separated. What about that wedding photo in your living room?'

'Easy to fake online. Can't believe anything you see these days.'

Kate is rooted to the spot, unable to find any words in

response to Harper's admission, which confirms what Kate already suspected.

Harper smiles. 'You really fell for every word, didn't you? I can assure you that Jamie and I were very much together. What else did he say to get you into his bed?'

'I'll find a way to prove that you killed him,' Kate hisses. 'Don't fuck with me.'

'You do know I'll never let that happen?' Harper moves closer to Kate, forcing her to shrink back. 'Don't you ever get sick of all the lies you tell?'

Kate pulls herself straighter. 'Don't *you*? You need help, Harper.'

'Just doing what it takes to protect my son.'

'And so am I,' Kate snarls. 'You'll never win this, Harper. I've got truth on my side, that's all that matters.'

Dex barges into the room. 'Need some water,' he says.

'Bye, Kate,' Harper says. 'Thanks for stopping by. So thoughtful of you to check up on us.'

'Can Thomas come over, Mum?' Dex begs.

Harper raises her chin and glances at Kate. 'Yes, of course. Any time. I'm sure Kate will ask him when she gets home. We're free tomorrow after school.' She doesn't give Kate a chance to respond. 'I'll see you out.'

At the front door, Harper shakes her head. 'Pull a stunt like this again and I'll make sure Thomas knows just what kind of mother he's got. Does he know about your past? Maybe it's about time he did.'

Driving home, Kate sees Aleena and Theo walking their dog. Screeching to a halt as they turn into their road, she jumps out of the car and rushes over to them. 'Can we talk?'

Aleena glances at her son then instructs him to go to the

house. 'Dad's there,' she says. As soon as he's out of earshot, Aleena turns on her. 'What are you doing here?'

'I was just driving past and saw you. I hate us not speaking. I'm so sorry, Aleena. Please can we put things right?'

Aleena sighs and stares at Kate. 'I'm scared of you, Kate.'

Of all the things she could say, Kate hasn't expected this. 'Please don't say that. I'm still the same person and this doesn't have to change our friendship.'

'I've done a lot of thinking about it,' Aleena says. 'And maybe I've never noticed before, but you've always had... anger issues. But there was no reason for me pay it much attention before because... I thought I knew exactly who you were. But the way you were with Ellis sometimes. Losing it with him when he'd hardly done anything. I just dismissed it. Especially as you were never like that with Thomas. But then when I heard about Graham White, it all made sense.'

'Don't say that. I told you – I was being attacked. What would you do if it was you?'

'It *was* me, Kate. Remember? And I didn't end up killing him.'

'That's not fair.'

Aleena stares at her. 'I know it's not. But I don't believe it was as black and white as that. There's more to this – I know it. So what is it?'

'It was self-defence,' she says quietly.

'I want to believe that, but how can I? You've been lying for too long. Please, just leave me alone.' Aleena turns away but then changes her mind and spins around to face Kate. 'You need to watch out. You're in a lot of trouble, and I don't think you can run from it this time.'

TWENTY-SEVEN

SUNDAY 2 FEBRUARY

Harper knows she shouldn't call him. They have a pact, made months ago; each of them bound to keep its promise – but this is an emergency.

She closes her bedroom door and dials his number, holding her breath while she waits for him to answer. Two seconds. Three. Four.

'Hello.'

'We need to talk.'

There's a pause so long she assumes he must have ended the call, until he finally speaks. 'What's happened?'

'Not on the phone. Can you come over? When Dexter's asleep?'

There's a heavy sigh; he must be weighing up the consequences of this decision. He's cautious like that, and they both know this is risky.

'I don't know,' he says. 'I don't think it's a good idea. We said—'

'I know what we said and I don't care. You need to come tonight. Dexter goes to bed around nine so should definitely be asleep by ten. Come then.'

Another heavy sigh. 'I'll see.'

The beeps on her phone warn her he's gone. But he'll come; she knows he will.

Downstairs, she finds Dexter in the living room, playing on his Xbox. 'Enough screen time,' she says, when the truth is he's probably only just gone on it – he's spent most of the evening doing his homework in the kitchen.

'Just ten more minutes,' he pleads.

'Five. And then shower.'

Dexter nods and resumes his game.

There are three hours to fill, and Harper can't bear idly waiting. She's nervous – a feeling she's tried so hard to push from her body whenever it surfaces. Normally she can do it, but right now it's overpowering her. She grabs the vacuum cleaner from the cupboard under the stairs and sets to work on carpets that are already spotless.

When she gets to Dexter's room, she's surprised to find it messy. He's normally particular about things; Jamie's death is affecting him in unpredictable ways. She needs to provide him with answers if he has any hope of healing.

She picks clothes and books off the floor, taking her time to make sure everything is neat. There's a scrunched-up tissue down the side of his bedside table, and when Harper picks it up something drops to the floor. It takes her a moment to realise what she's looking at. She bends down to pick it up, and her breath is snatched away from her. Jamie's ring. The one she got him even when they decided they wouldn't marry. It made her feel better, somehow. And he'd done the same for her, even though she never wore it. The one she's holding now is just a plain gold band with a bevelled edge, yet she knows it's Jamie's. But she examines the inside, just to be sure, and there it is – the italicised message that Jamie thought would be funny to have engraved in both their rings. *It's just a piece of paper*.

This doesn't make sense. Why would Dexter have Jamie's

ring? Jamie never took it off, at least not in the house. Harper has no idea what he did with it when he wasn't here. All part of his act. Perhaps he did leave it here that night; it's plausible given that he was going to that bar in Putney to meet Kate. Dexter must have found it and kept hold of it. But why wouldn't he mention it? Harper studies the engraving again, picturing Jamie's laugh as he'd made his suggestion for their rings. *We don't have to be the same as everyone else. Love doesn't conform to rules – it can't be caged.*

Then Harper sees the speck of dark red blood opposite the engraving.

Numb with shock, her mind whirs with all the possibilities of what this means, and she rushes downstairs, clutching the ring so tightly it digs into her skin.

'Dexter!' She bursts into the living room. 'What are you doing with this? I found it in your room!' She tries to keep her voice measured, but panic drowns her words. She holds up the ring.

Dexter stares at it and then at Harper, his eyes wide. 'I... I found it.'

'Where?'

A suffocating silence surrounds them. 'Answer me!'

'At... at Thomas's house.' Dexter only stutters when he's nervous.

Harper takes a deep breath to calm down, and sitting next to Dexter, she takes his hand. 'I need to know everything,' she says. 'Whatever it is, you can tell me and we'll work it out together.'

Dexter nods, but takes his time to speak. 'It was when we had a playdate there. Thomas went to the toilet and I was just... just looking around. I found it. In a drawer in the kitchen.' He stops, his lips quivering like they do when he's about to clam up.

Harper puts her arm around him. 'You're not in any trouble, Dexter. 'I just need to know exactly what happened.'

'I thought it must be Thomas's mum's, but then I read the writing and it's the same as yours. So I knew it was Dad's. I thought Thomas must have taken it from our house and I didn't want to get him in trouble so I just took it back. I was scared I'd get into trouble. For going through their stuff.'

'It's okay. Everything's okay. You're definitely not in any trouble and I won't say anything that will get Thomas in trouble. He might not have realised what it was.'

'Who did that to Dad?' Dexter says, burying his head in her arms, wailing, finally letting out all the emotions he's been bottling up.

'I don't know. But whoever did it will be found out, Dexter. I promise you.'

He takes his time to calm down, but gradually his sobbing subsides and his breathing returns to normal. And once she's sure he's okay, Harper smiles.

It's ten past ten and there's still no sign of him. He won't come – he's washing his hands of this now, walking away because he thinks it's nothing to do with him. But now she has evidence to show him that he's wrong. This is *everything* to do with him. She hopes his tardiness is just a precautionary measure. Harper checks on Dexter again, to make sure he's still asleep.

Finally, at ten seventeen, there's a knock on the door. Listening to make sure there's no sound coming from Dexter's room, Harper rushes to check through the peep hole before she opens the door.

'Thanks for coming,' she says.

'What choice did I have?'

She holds the door open and peers outside. 'Come in, then.'

Ellis steps inside, and Harper closes the door behind him.

TWENTY-EIGHT

TWO MONTHS AGO

Harper's been following him for a few days now, cataloguing his every move, getting a feel for him. It's staggering what you can learn about someone just by following them, learning their routines. All of this was necessary before she could even think about approaching him.

Harper has learned that he works for PricewaterhouseCoopers in Embankment as a senior manager in network information security. She has little idea what it involves, something to do with cyber security, but she does know that he works from home two days a week, and when he comes into the office, he leaves work at around the same time every day. He's usually on his own, and heads straight for the Tube where he takes the District line to Wimbledon. It's easy to follow someone when their movements rarely vary.

And this evening she'll approach him, when he gets off at Wimbledon. There's a coffee shop by the station and she somehow needs to convince him to go there with her. That will be the tricky part – once he's in there, the minute she opens her mouth she'll have his full attention.

But Harper is a stranger – will she even be able to get him alone?

She starts to feel sick as the Tube stops at Southfields, and there are only two more stations to go. But Harper is fully prepared for this moment.

Outside Wimbledon station, she approaches him from behind, and, taking a deep breath, taps him on the shoulder.

Ellis spins around, frowning. He's a private person, she's worked out. 'Yes?' he says, his voice laced with annoyance. He probably just wants to get home.

'Hi, I know you don't know me, but I really need to talk to you about your wife.'

Everything changes now, and he stares at her. 'Kate? Is she okay?'

'Yes, yes – it's nothing like that. Please – can we just talk quickly? There's a coffee shop just over there.' Harper points across the road.

He flicks his wrist and glances at his Apple Watch. 'I suppose so. But Kate and I are separated. I'm moving out soon and we're getting a divorce. Unless this is about our son, then—'

'It's not about Thomas. But this is very important.'

He raises his eyebrows; Harper has got his interest now.

'Let me buy you a coffee,' she says. 'Or would you prefer a drink? There's a bar just a bit further down the road.'

Ellis nods. 'Okay. Let's have a drink.'

Once they're inside the bar, nerves get the better of her. It was one thing getting him here, quite another to convince Ellis to believe what she's about to say.

She offers to get the drinks, but he insists on getting them and heads to the bar without giving her a choice. At least it gives her a few more moments to prepare.

'There's no easy way to say this,' she says, when he comes back with a beer for himself and tonic water for Harper. 'And I know this situation is a bit... bizarre because I'm a stranger to you. But... I recently found out that my husband is having an affair.'

'Oh. I'm sorry,' Ellis says.

'And the woman he's been having an affair with is your wife.' She watches him, registering the shock on his face.

Ellis composes himself and puts down his glass. 'I don't think so. That doesn't sound like something Kate would do. Honestly. Let's just say she doesn't agree with people having affairs.' He drinks some beer, wiping froth from his mouth with a napkin. 'I know that from personal experience.'

Harper knows all about Ellis's affair with the woman he worked with. A one-night silly mistake that came back to haunt him. Hardly comparable to what she's sure Jamie and Kate Mason have been doing. It was weeks ago she first found that picture of Kate on Jamie's phone. 'Forgive me, but isn't that why Kate left you? Because *you* had an affair?'

'How do you know that?'

'Does it matter? Am I right? Kate ended your marriage because you made a mistake. Once. No second chances.'

'It doesn't matter,' Ellis says. 'I betrayed her. And the whole time we'd built our marriage on trust. I don't blame her for leaving me. She's always been completely honest with me about... everything. And I threw it back in her face with my deception.'

'Are you listening to what I'm saying, though?' Harper says. 'Why did your marriage end?'

Ellis hangs his head. 'Because I slept with another woman. But it was just once.'

'So Kate left you because you had an affair, but she's been having one too!'

Ellis lifts his head. 'What?'

'It's true. I found a photo of her on my husband's phone. A few weeks ago. And the date on it was six months ago. That's before you had your affair, right? And that means that Kate was cheating way before you did.'

In silence, Ellis studies her, scrutinising every inch of her. The atmosphere has changed now, just as she'd expected. 'Why are you telling me this?' he says eventually.

'Because I need proof. I need to get Jamie out of my life and this will help me.'

'Just confront him. Tell him you're leaving him.'

Ellis is right – if Jamie were a normal person, then she could do that. But he isn't, and she will never be rid of him unless she confronts him with irrefutable proof. Conning all those women out of money is one thing, but whatever he's doing with Kate is something else, and she needs to know what it is.

'We have a son,' she says. 'It's not straightforward just to walk away without proof.' She pulls out her phone. 'This is Jamie. Can you think of any other reason your husband might know Kate?'

Ellis studies the picture. 'I've never seen him. And I've never heard Kate mention anyone called Jamie.' He sighs. 'We have a son too. Divorce messes kids up.'

'Then please will you help me?' Harper urges. 'So I can make sure I'm doing the right thing. For *my* son's sake.'

Ellis considers her request. 'Not sure what you think I can do? Kate and I are separated now. I'm moving out as soon as my new place is ready.'

'But you're still there now. Can you see if you can find any evidence of them being together? Anything at all. Look through her things. There might be something there.'

When he doesn't answer, Harper pushes. 'Don't you want to know if you've been lied to? She ended your marriage because of your affair. But what if that's not the case? She's been lying to you, Ellis. Pretending she's innocent in all of this, and that it's *your* fault. And I need to know why. I need to know what she and Jamie are doing.'

Ellis's cheeks drain of colour. 'Okay. I'll try and help. Give me your number.'

TWENTY-NINE

SUNDAY 2 FEBRUARY

'I shouldn't be here,' Ellis says, shuffling from one foot to the other. He hovers in the hallway, his eyes darting around the house.

'It's fine,' Harper assures him. 'Dexter's asleep.'

Ellis still doesn't move further into the house. 'What's this about? We said we wouldn't have contact unless it's to do with our sons.'

'That's rich. You didn't exactly keep your distance when you turned up here with those cameras. I think you were intending to plant them for Kate, and you only changed your mind at the last minute. And don't forget you're the one who came over to me at football earlier in the day.'

'All part of the act.' Ellis closes his eyes and exhales. 'I don't want any part of this any more, Harper. It's over, it has to be.'

'Just come in the kitchen. I don't want Dexter waking up and hearing us.'

Reluctantly, Ellis follows.

'You make it sound like we're having a relationship,' Harper says, closing the door.

'No, this is worse than an affair. An affair people might understand. But this deception—'

'Is necessary. Your wife's a murderer, Ellis.'

'Soon to be ex-wife.'

Harper rolls her eyes. 'That's irrelevant. But if it makes you feel better, I'll rephrase – the mother of your child is a murderer.'

'All you've got is that photo of them together. That doesn't mean she was the one who killed him. How do I know it wasn't *you*?' Ellis shoves his hands in his pockets and stares at her.

'Don't you think the police have looked into me? Harper asks. 'And that photo was taken on the night he was killed. Which means Kate was the last person to see him.' Harper walks to the door and listens out for Dexter. 'There's got to be something in Kate's house,' she says.

Ellis ignores her. 'That photo was taken from a camera that *you* were watching from. Highly illegal.'

'Yes, but I had to do that. I had to know what Jamie was doing. Because Kate didn't fit his normal mould. I just wish the camera hadn't stopped working. Otherwise it might have shown Kate coming back in the bedroom. She could have had Jamie's blood all over her.'

Ellis shakes his head. 'This is crazy. What more do you want from me? I told you that was the end of it. I'm not doing this any more.'

Harper needs to get through to Ellis, and so far it's not working. She steps closer to him. 'Remember Maddy? Surely you haven't forgotten her already? Love really is fickle, isn't it?'

'What's Maddy got to do with this? Leave her out of it.'

'It wasn't Kate who warned her off you.'

Ellis's eyes narrow to slits as he digests this new information. 'So Kate was right. It was you. What did you do? Why bring Maddy into it? She had nothing to do with it.'

'I needed to prove to you how easy it is to mess with someone's life. Jamie was having an affair with your wife – that gives you every reason to want him dead. What would the police think about that?' Harper forces a smile. She's not enjoying this – Ellis hasn't done anything to her – but she's doing what needs to be done.

'I was with my son that night,' Ellis says. 'What do you want from me, Harper?'

'It's time you got Thomas away from Kate,' Harper says, her voice softer now.

'On what grounds? Kate's a good mum. She'd never hurt our son.'

'How do you think Thomas would feel if he knew you and Kate had been lying to him his whole life? Keeping it a secret that his mother killed someone. Make that *two* people.'

Ellis moves towards her. 'He's not old enough to understand. It would destroy him. We made a decision together to spare him from it. At least until he's an adult.'

'Then it would probably destroy him if he found out now. Wouldn't it?'

'Are you threatening me?' he snaps.

'Thomas must have seen that Kate has a temper, even if it's never directed at him. He's a smart boy – he'd quickly piece it all together.'

'What the hell do you want from me, Harper?'

What she wants is to mess up Kate's life, like Kate has done to her by taking Dexter's father away from him. 'Tell Kate you want full custody of Thomas. You don't think she's fit to be a mum and if she doesn't let you have him, then you'll be going to the police to tell them she was with Jamie Archer the night he was murdered.' She could tell him about Jamie's wedding ring, how Dexter found it in Kate's house, but she can't prove that's where it came from, and she doesn't want to drag her son into this.

Harper catches the fear in Ellis's eyes as he turns away from her, walking over to the patio doors. Then, with a jolt he spins around to face her. 'No. Go to hell.'

Harper doesn't sleep after Ellis storms out, and by the time dawn approaches, she's sure of what she needs to do. It took a horrific act of violence to start this, and that's what it will take to end it.

Dexter walks into the kitchen, rubbing his eyes.

'Morning,' she says, forcing her voice to be breezy. 'Did you sleep okay?'

Dexter ignores her, and marches to the cupboard, pulling out a box of Cheerios.

'What's the matter? Are you okay? Did you have a bad dream again?' Since Jamie's death, Dexter's often been forced awake by nightmares.

'No, just stop!'

Shocked at the sharp tone he's never used towards her before, Harper grabs the milk from the fridge and places it next to his bowl. She reaches for his arm but he pulls away.

'Leave me alone!'

'What's going on, Dexter? You're really worrying me. Please talk to me.'

He shakes his head, but Harper persists and eventually he gives in. 'I saw Thomas's dad here last night. I was coming downstairs for water and heard voices. Then he came out and ran out of the house. Why was he here in the middle of the night? Is this about Dad?'

Harper takes his hand and leads him to the table to sit down. She places his bowl in front of him. 'No, sweetheart. This is nothing for you to worry about – I promise you.'

'It's happening again, isn't it?'

'What?'

'It's just like you and Dad. Whispering all the time. Stopping talking when I walk in. Lying to me. You think I don't know but I do.'

'Dexter, that's not what your dad and I were doing. I'm so sorry you felt that way. We had some difficulties – I know that might be hard to understand, but sometimes relationships can be challenging. I love you, Dexter. And so did Dad. Everything we've done is for you.' As Harper says this, she wonders how much of it is true on Jamie's part. What he did was for himself more than their son.

'You're lying!' Dexter shouts, swiping his bowl aside. It smashes to the floor, landing in a pool of milk and cereal. Dexter rushes upstairs and Harper begins picking up the broken pieces, the sharp edge of a shard piercing her skin and leaving a bright red bubble of blood on her finger.

They walk to school in silence, and bump into Aleena and Theo on the way.

'Are you okay?' Aleena asks. 'You don't look so good.'

'I didn't sleep last night,' Harper explains, glancing at Dexter.

Aleena places her hand on Harper's shoulder. 'I'm sorry. Let me know if there's anything I can do. I can't say I understand what it's like to lose a husband but I'll listen if you need to talk.'

'Thanks,' Harper says, her voice cracking. She's touched by Aleena's kindness, but this has nothing to do with grieving for Jamie.

'Can Thomas and Dex come over after school?' Theo asks.

'Not today,' Aleena says. 'You've got Rugby. And Thomas is staying at his dad's tonight. I just ran into Ellis.'

'Oh, how is Ellis?' Harper asks. 'I got to know him a bit at football last week. He wasn't doing so well after his break-up with Maddy.'

'Well, I'm not sure why I'm defending Kate but Ellis deserves this after having an affair. What goes around comes around,' Aleena says.

'True. But things are rarely black and white.'

'I suppose so,' Aleena says. 'Maybe I'm just so used to hearing Kate's side of it that I never stopped to question the truth of what happened. Before that, I always thought Ellis was a good man.'

'How well do we ever really know anyone?' Harper says, as they reach the gates. 'Well, at least I won't bump into Kate at pick-up.'

Aleena frowns.

'You said Ellis was having Thomas tonight.'

'Yeah,' Aleena says, but her attention is caught by a mum waving at her from the gates.

The boys walk in together and Harper watches them for a moment before turning back to Aleena. 'Well, might see you later. Have a good day.'

Aleena smiles. 'Yeah, you too.'

Harper rushes home. Talking with Aleena has helped cement a plan in her head, and there's a lot she needs to get organised before tonight if she's going to pull it off.

THIRTY

MONDAY 3 FEBRUARY

There's silence on the other end of the phone, and Kate wonders if they've been disconnected. 'Ellis?'

'Yes, I'm here.' But his tone of voice suggests he'd rather not be. A guilty conscience?

'Harper found the cameras. Where did you hide them?' Kate won't tell Ellis she thinks he might have given the cameras to Harper. Now that Kate knows Ellis knew Jamie, any trust she had left for him has withered away.

'I did what you told me. Look, I'm about to leave for work.'

'Can you pick Thomas up from school today and have him at yours? For the night?'

There's a brief pause before he answers. 'Yeah. No point me asking why you need me to have him?'

Kate thanks him and tells Ellis she needs to go.

David is the next person she needs to call. Once again Kate is asking him to cover for her, but she'll make it up to him when this is all over. And to Ellis.

As soon as the call ends, Kate dials Faye Held's number, glancing at the clock to see how long she has before she'll need to wake Thomas for school. And Ellis won't be long.

'Hi. What's happening?' Faye's voice is chirpy, as if she's already been up for hours.

'Can we meet? Today?'

'Not even a little hint? I'm a busy woman, you know.'

'Please, Faye. Harper's dragging my son into this... and that terrifies me more than anything. I need to prove that she's the one who killed Jamie. If we go over everything together, maybe you can help me see something I've missed?'

'Not sure what you think I can do. And that's a big leap to make about Harper being a killer.'

'Yesterday you said you trusted me, so—'

'That's not exactly what I said, Kate. I said we all have to pick a side. It doesn't mean I trust you. I just said I don't trust Harper.'

'Please, can we meet today? There's got to be a way we can prove Harper's responsible for Jamie's death, and if we get our heads together then—'

'Hey, I'm a true-crime podcaster not a detective.'

'Yes, but you're a very creative one. Please, Faye.'

Faye exhales loudly. 'Okay. But you'll have to come to my place. I have a home studio and I'm a bit chock-a-block today. Say around lunchtime – one o'clock? I'll send you my address.'

'Thanks,' Kate says, 'I'll see you then.' She hangs up before Faye can change her mind.

Kate gets to Stoke Newington before twelve and finds a coffee shop, slipping inside to escape the biting cold while she waits.

After forcing down a barely lukewarm coffee that's far too bitter, Kate wraps her scarf around her neck and makes her way to Brighton Road.

She sees the glaring lights of the ambulance as soon as she turns onto Faye's road; two police cars are parked haphazardly, and a swarm of onlookers are huddled on the pavement.

Kate walks faster, checking door numbers as she goes. Outside number fifty-two – Faye's house – a police officer stands guard by the door, while two paramedics carry out a woman on a stretcher. It's Faye, her long braids dangling over either side of the stretcher.

Rushing over to them, Kate tries to get closer, but she's ushered away by the police officer. 'You can't go in there,' he says.

Kate stares at him, then looks back at Faye. Her face is unrecognisable under the deep red blood and purple bruises. Kate claps her hand to her mouth.

'Do you know her?' the officer asks, his voice warmer now.

Kate's about to tell him she does, but she can't be any part of this. 'No... sorry, I thought it was a friend of mine but it's the wrong house. How awful. Will she be okay?'

'I'll need you to move back, please,' he says, ignoring her question.

'Will she be okay?' Kate repeats, feeling as though she in a trance.

'It doesn't look good. Now stand back, please.'

Kate slowly moves back, folding herself into the crowd of onlookers that's expanding by the second. And then when no one is paying her any attention, she slips away and rushes back towards the station.

The first thing she does when she gets home is check her phone again. There's no news about Faye on any social media so she calls Homerton hospital, the closest one to Faye's house, only to be told that they can't give out any information about patients over the phone.

Frustrated, Kate ends the call and scrolls through Faye's Instagram. It's too much of a coincidence to believe that this has nothing to do with Kate. She'd only just spoken to Faye and arranged to meet her, and then she's attacked. *Because she was helping me.* But with no news of it anywhere online, Kate can only speculate.

Putting her phone in her pocket, Kate grabs her coat and leaves the house.

By six p.m. she's outside Rowan's practice in South Kensington, hovering on the pavement, waiting. A young man leaves, pulling up the hood of his coat to shield himself from the cold, and then a few moments later, Frieda steps out.

Kate waits until she's disappeared around the corner, then crosses the road and heads inside. She can't worry about what Rowan will think of her turning up like this – there's too much at stake.

She calls his name as she steps inside, just to warn him of her presence.

His door opens and Rowan stands there, frowning, his arms folded in front of him. 'Kate. Um... this really isn't—'

'I know what you're going to say – but there's no one else I can turn to. Please will you just listen to me for a minute? And then I'll leave you alone – I promise. I'll go to that person you're referring me to. It's just... you're the only one who knows everything.'

Kate can tell from the way his eyes narrow that Rowan's not convinced she'll go to another therapist this easily. He doesn't want her in his clinic, but she will stand her ground.

Rowan glances past her. 'Come in, then,' he says. 'But I don't have too long. I'm going to the theatre tonight.' He leaves the door open and gestures for her to sit. 'This is highly inappropriate, Kate. I know you must realise that. You're putting me in a very difficult position. All the things I know – I really have to be informing the police.'

She nods. 'But aren't you always telling me things are never black and white? You're the only person I can speak to about what's happening. And isn't it okay now that technically you're not my therapist any more?'

'Sadly, it doesn't work like that. Ethically. You were my patient for two years. I've referred you to someone else but that hasn't quite gone through yet.'

Kate ignores him. As soon as she talks, Rowan will understand. And he will help her. 'I think Jamie's wife tried to kill someone today.'

Rowan's eyes widen and he stares at her. 'Why do you think this? Who?'

Kate explains about her meeting with Faye Held yesterday, and how the two of them were due to meet this afternoon. How Faye was going to help her gather evidence that Harper was responsible for Jamie's murder.

Rowan is attentive as he listens, his expression unreadable. 'Kate, I must insist that you tell the police this. Immediately. Have you even gone to see them yet? You promised, Kate. You know that's the right thing to do. Even more so if what you're saying has any plausibility.'

'It does,' Kate says. But now she needs to lie to Rowan – it's the only way she'll get him onside. 'I *have* been to the police.' It's all she can do not to look away from him.

Rowan's shoulders relax. 'Okay. Good. I know that won't have been easy. What did they say?'

'They're looking into everything.'

'Did you tell them everything, Kate? That you were with Jamie Archer that night?'

She nods, shame flooding through her body.

'Okay. But I'm a bit confused – you said you need my help.'

Kate stares up at the ceiling. 'I don't know how this happened. How my life turned in this direction. All I care about is Thomas. Keeping him safe. Protecting him. He doesn't deserve to be dragged into this.'

'You *are* protecting him, Kate. It's always been clear to me how much you love him. And even with your... challenges with anger, you've always been calm and rational with him.'

'I would never even raise my voice to him,' Kate says. 'Even when he's trying my patience. So you understand my need to protect him, no matter what?'

'Yes,' Rowan says, frowning. 'But what is it you need me to help with?'

'It's very difficult. When I think... I think Ellis might be tied up in this. I don't think for a second he'd hurt Thomas, but—'

'Kate... this is hard to believe—'

'I know. But... he was seen with Jamie in the summer. They were in a bar together. Socialising. But when I showed Ellis a photo of Jamie, he claimed he'd never seen him before. And I've been thinking about finding that photo of Jamie in Thomas's school bag. Ellis picked him up that day and was alone in the house until I got home. He could easily have slipped it in there ready for when I got back. He knew Thomas would never bother checking in his bag after school. He just waits for us to check it. What if I've got it wrong and it wasn't Harper at all?'

'I suppose that's possible,' Rowan says. 'But it doesn't really prove anything. Circumstantial. Maybe Ellis is telling the truth. And the person who saw them is mistaken? You have to look at it from all angles, Kate.'

'I know. And I am. But... I'm scared, Rowan. It feels like something awful's going to happen. Well, it has already – to Faye, the podcaster. And she was only involved on the periphery. I'm right in the middle of it all.'

'Again, I need to ask you, what do you need from me?'

'I need you to take me back as a patient. I didn't realise how much I'd come to depend on our Friday sessions. You helped me rebuild my life, and now it's crumbling and I need to get it back.'

'Kate. You just said you'd be happy to move on to a new

therapist. And you *can* get your life back. You did it before and that was without me – you've done all the hard work yourself.'

'Please reconsider, Rowan.'

'Kate, I'm sorry, but I can't. It's not possible.'

'Please. You need to reconsider, Rowan.' Kate says, feeling her cheeks flame. She'd been so certain that Rowan would change his mind.

They both turn around at the sound of a gentle cough to see Rowan's wife standing in the doorway, smiling.

'I'm sorry,' she says. 'I thought you'd finished with your patients for the day.'

'I have,' Rowan says, standing 'Kate is an ex-patient who just came in to update me on how she's doing. Kate, this is my wife, Daniella.' He turns back to his wife. 'I thought we were meeting at the theatre?'

'Thought I'd surprise you. Tear you away from your paperwork.' Rowan's wife wanders towards him and kisses him. 'But I can wait in reception if you need to finish your chat.'

Kate stands, pulling on her coat. 'No, it's fine. I was just leaving.'

Daniella Hess smiles. 'Oh, please don't let me interrupt if you haven't finished.'

'Oh, we're finished,' Rowan says, before Kate can respond.

Kate heads to the door. 'I'll see you at my usual appointment time on Friday,' she says, walking out and closing the door.

Thomas is quiet this evening as they eat the pizza Kate hastily threw in the oven. She knows the cause of his silence – he was confused and disappointed when she'd changed the plan for this evening without warning and turned up at Ellis's to collect him

'I know you're confused about me picking you up from Dad's when you were meant to be staying with him,' she says.

'But... my plans changed and I didn't need his help after all. And I think it's better if you stay here on school nights. We're a lot closer to school.'

The truth is, after her visit with Rowan being cut short, she couldn't bear the thought of being away from Thomas, of him being with Ellis any more than necessary, so she'd rushed straight round there to take Thomas home.

'It's weird, Mum,' Thomas says. 'You've never done this stuff before. And now you're picking me up early from play-dates and from Dad's.' He pulls red pepper off his pizza. 'Are you angry with Dad again?'

'No, sweetheart. I'm not.'

Thomas scrunches his face; Kate knows he doesn't believe her.

'Will you just trust me?' she says. 'I want the best for you. Always.'

He nods, picking up a slice of pizza. And for the rest of the evening, he barely says another word.

Sometime in the night, Kate wakes with a start. Instinctively she knows something is wrong. Her body feels way too hot. Then everything comes into focus: the crackling sounds, the smoke drifting in beneath the door.

'Thomas!' she screams.

THIRTY-ONE

Kate jumps out of bed, shoves her phone in her pyjama pocket and races to the bedroom door. The hallway is clogged with smoke, but shielding her face, she makes her way through it to Thomas's room, screaming his name.

'What's happening?' he asks, drowsy from sleep. And then he realises and jumps up.

'Hurry, Thomas! Come with me!'

He's screaming at her, trying to resist her hold, but she's still stronger than him and manages to drag him back to her room. He tries to rush to the door, screaming, but she can't make out any words; the roar of the fire is too loud. He's trying to get out of the room. Panicking. And then she realises that Lula must have been in his room, where their cat always sleeps curled up on Thomas's bed.

'Thomas, I'm so sorry – we can't go back to your room – we need to get out of here right now!' They have only moments before the upstairs is consumed in flames.

He stares at her, horror in his huge eyes, frozen. 'Come on,' she says, pulling her duvet from the bed. 'Do you think you can grab hold of this and use it to climb down onto the kitchen roof? I'll hold it so you don't fall. You have to trust me, okay?'

Thomas gives a barely detectable nod, but still doesn't move.

'Quick,' Kate says, pushing him towards the window in the en suite. She closes the bathroom door.

Kate helps Thomas climb out, then she follows him through the window, dragging the duvet behind her. She dangles it down from the kitchen roof, leaning over so it's as close to the ground as she can get it. 'You need to hold onto this,' Kate explains.

Her son stares blankly.

'Thomas – listen! We need to hurry. Grab onto this and climb down.'

Finally he moves towards the edge of the roof, but Kate can tell he's in shock. She helps him over the side and watches as he climbs down, clinging to the duvet.

'Don't let go!' she shouts. 'You're nearly there.' But she can see the fear and horror on Thomas's face.

Once he's safely at the bottom, Kate throws the duvet onto the ground then climbs over the edge, hanging down as far as she can before making the jump to the ground. Her body hits the pavement with a shocking thud; the duvet does little to lessen the impact.

Thomas rushes over to her but doesn't say anything, he just stares up at the house, consumed with flickering orange flames.

'Lula might have gone outside,' Kate assures him. 'She sometimes likes to go out all night, doesn't she?' Kate has to believe this – she can't bear the thought that Lula is still in there. She calls Lula's name and scans the garden but there's no sign of her. Then, as Kate stares up at the house, contemplating whether she could try and look for her, Lula crawls out from the bush at the back of the garden.

Kate rushes over to her and picks her up, handing her to

Thomas, who still doesn't speak. 'We need to go round the front,' Kate says, pulling out her phone and calling 999.

Liv Cross, the neighbour across the road rushes over to them and wraps them in blankets. 'The fire brigade is on the way. I woke up to get some water and saw the fire so called straight away.'

Through spluttered coughs, Kate manages to thank her. Then she turns to Thomas, pulling him towards her. 'Are you okay?'

He nods. 'But... but Dex...'

'Dex? What do you mean?'

Thomas stares at her. 'He... he ran away. And came here. I let him in. You were in the bath. He said he didn't want to go home so I said he could stay over. But I didn't see him in my room just now. He... must have gone to the bathroom.' Tears stream down his face.

Kate's stares at her son, then back at the house. 'He was there tonight? In our house?'

Thomas nods.

'Oh, Jesus!' Kate feels in her pyjama pockets for her phone. She calls Harper, watching as flames engulf the house.

'Why are you calling?'

'Harper – is Dex with you?'

'What? Of course he is. What the hell is this?'

'Go and check on him. Thomas said he ran away and was sleeping in Thomas's room. But the house is on fire and he couldn't see Dex anywhere. I managed to escape with Thomas, but he's saying Dex is in there!'

Harper gasps and Kate hears running footsteps. 'He's not in bed!' Harper screams. 'He's in your house! Get my son out of there!'

Kate pushes the phone into Thomas's hand. 'Stay on the call with Harper.' And then she rushes to Liv. 'Can you wet this blanket for me? It needs to be soaking. Please hurry!'

'What? Why?'

'I think Thomas's friend is in there!'

Liv rushes into her house, returning with the sodden blanket. Kate drapes it over her head, then races towards the house.

'Mum!' Thomas screams. 'No!'

Kate rushes around to the back of the house, and that's when she sees a figure on the kitchen roof. It's Dexter, screaming for help. 'Don't move! I'm coming.'

Kate checks all the windows and the door, but the downstairs is a furnace of orange flames. There's no way she'll be able to get in there. She scans the garden, her eyes fixing on the shed. Rushing towards it, she's relieved to find it open. She hauls out the ladder and drags it over to the house. She positions it against the wall and climbs up to Dex.

'I'll hold the ladder while you get down,' she says. 'Go!'

He makes his way down the ladder, as sirens sound in the distance, and Kate follows, knowing that she'll never forget the look of fear in Dex's eyes just now.

Back in the street, an ambulance has arrived, as well as the fire engine, and Harper's car pulls up, stopping right in the middle of the road. She jumps out, running towards Kate and the boys.

'Dexter!' she screams, hugging him tightly.

'I'm sorry, Mum. I'm so sorry for running away.'

'It doesn't matter. All that matters is you're safe. And Thomas.' Harper kisses the top of his head. 'Stay here a minute, I just need to talk to Kate.

'Thank you,' Harper says. 'No words are enough. Thomas told me you... you went back to save my son.'

Kate nods, and turns to the paramedic standing near them. 'Are the boys okay?'

'We'll need to get them checked at the hospital, but hopefully neither of them inhaled enough smoked to do any major damage. We'll just give then a quick check here, though, first.'

'Okay, thanks.'

Harper pulls her aside as the paramedics check the boys over.

'You could have died,' Harper says. 'But you still went to save my son.'

'There was no way I was going to let Dex die in there.'

'You didn't even know for sure he was in there.'

'I had to see. I acted on instinct.'

'I don't know what to say. I...'

'Did you do that to my house?' Kate asks.

'No!' Harper protests. 'I had nothing to do with this. I would never do anything like that.'

Kate shakes her head. 'And I'm supposed to believe that after everything you've done? Tell me the truth, Harper. And all that other stuff.'

'I would never put your son in danger.'

'He wasn't supposed to be there,' Kate says, her voice almost a whisper.

'What?'

'Thomas was meant to be staying with Ellis tonight. I changed my mind at the last minute and went to get him. I was supposed to be alone in the house. Did you know?'

'How... how would I know that?'

They're interrupted by the paramedic who's finished checking the boys. 'We need to get you all to the hospital now.'

Kate's relieved to be pulled away from Harper – however she feels about the woman now, she will sort through it once she knows for sure that Thomas is okay.

She's had no choice but to call Ellis. All of her belongings went up in flames, and all she has on her is her phone and pyjamas. But at least Thomas is okay; tonight could have ended differently. And now Ellis stands beside her in the hospital, hugging them both, clinging on to them as if he's already lost them. 'What happened?' he asks, speaking into her hair. 'How did the fire start?'

Kate pulls away. 'I don't know. But it wasn't an accident. No way.'

Ellis stares at her, horror scrawled on his face. 'But... then who would do something like this?'

'I don't know. But everything's gone. All our things. Clothes. There's nothing left.'

He pulls her closer. 'Those things don't matter. You and Thomas are okay – that's what's important.'

For now. Someone tried to kill me, and what if they succeed next time?

'We'll sort out new things,' Ellis says. 'Don't think about that now. And you're both coming to stay with me of course. For as long as you need.'

Kate's already realised this is her only option. 'It won't be for long,' she says. 'Just until I can sort somewhere for us to rent until the insurance money comes through.'

'You don't need to rent somewhere,' Ellis insists. 'You and Thomas will stay with me as long as you need. And Lula, of course. You've got a home with me, Kate. Always.'

Kate's too fraught to say any more. 'Can we just go now?' she says. 'We need to get Lula from Liv's house.' Kate shudders at the thought of going back to their road, seeing the remains of the house she'd loved so much. All those years of memories also burned to the ground. She turns to Thomas, who's barely said a word since they got to the hospital. 'Are you okay?'

He nods, and stares at the shiny white floor.

In the corridor, Harper is waiting, holding two gigantic carrier bags. 'These are for you,' she says, handing them to Kate. We're about the same size and you'll need some clothes.' She looks down at the slippers Kate's wearing, offered to her by Liv.

'There are shoes in there too. And some of Dexter's school uniform for Thomas.'

Kate stares at the bags, her body unable to move, to take anything from this woman.

'Thanks,' Ellis says, reaching for them.

Harper nods and turns away, heading back to where Dexter is waiting for her. Kate resists the urge to go after her, to question her again about the fire.

'Come on,' Ellis says, watching Harper walk away. 'Let's get out of here.'

With sinking dread in the pit of her stomach, Kate takes Thomas's arm and they head outside.

They get in the car and when she turns to watch Ellis climb in, she sees that he's smiling.

THIRTY-TWO
2015

The moment Dexter is born, Harper knows she's done the right thing. In the chair next to her hospital bed, Jamie is holding him, giving Harper time to recuperate – her labour was long, and she was moments away from having to have an emergency C-section. But Harper doesn't care how traumatic the birth was – her son is here, breathing and healthy.

And she has let Jamie back in because she's playing the long game now. What goes around comes around, and sooner or later he will learn that.

Jamie is smiling at Dexter, his eyes shining brighter than she's ever seen before. Being a father suits him – this is what it takes for him to feel love. 'I can't believe he's here,' Jamie says, his eyes fixed on the baby. 'Everything's going to be all right now,' he says. 'This little guy will keep us on track.'

Harper wants to scream. *It wasn't me who went off track.*

A phone rings and she glances around the room, unable to work out where the sound is coming from.

'I think that's yours,' Jamie says. 'And it's in your locker under there.' He points to the bedside table. He's splashed out for a private room for her, and although she was tempted,

Harper never asked him where the money came from. 'I'll get it,' he offers.

'No,' she says, swinging her legs off the edge of the bed and reaching into the locker. She grabs the phone just as it stops ringing, and her stomach lurches when she sees who the missed call is from. Pierre. The man she hasn't seen since the night she saw Jamie with a woman in that restaurant.

'Who was it?' Jamie asks.

'Nothing important,' Harper says.

Jamie nods, smiling down at Dexter, while Harper climbs back into the bed and tries to compose herself. She hasn't seen Pierre since the night they had that meal. She hasn't wanted to, and seeing his name now makes her shudder. The past never stays hidden; she should have learned that from everything Jamie has done.

Later, when they're at home, with Dexter napping in his Moses basket, Pierre messages her. She deletes it without reading his words, but now thoughts of him are imprinted in her mind, making her feel sick.

The baby begins to grizzle, slowly stirring, and before she can reach to pick him up, Jamie is by her side, lifting him out. 'Are you hungry little Dex?'

'It's Dexter,' Harper snaps. 'Not Dex.'

'I like Dex.'

She opens her mouth to yell at Jamie, to tell him it's not up to him, but she thinks better of it. Her silence is what will pay Jamie back for everything he did to her. To their little girl. 'Let me have him,' she says, unfastening her maternity bra. Her breasts are heavy and sore and she needs to get this milk out.

Jamie helps her get Dexter into position then watches while he feeds. 'Do you think he looks like me?' he says, stroking Dexter's soft smooth head.

'Babies don't always look like their parents.'

'But normally there's something, isn't there?'

'Maybe he'll have your charm,' she says.

He ignores her jibe. 'I just don't see any resemblance.'

Harper smiles. Of course Jamie doesn't. And when she looks at their son, all she can see is Pierre.

THIRTY-THREE

TUESDAY 4 FEBRUARY

'You're not going to school today,' Harper insists.

Dexter pauses with his spoon in the air then places it back in his cereal bowl, shooting milk onto the table. 'I'm fine, Mum. I don't want to stay at home.'

She reaches for his hand. 'Listen, you're not in any trouble for running away. I know you were upset with me. I just feel awful that I didn't even notice you'd gone.' Harper will never forgive herself for thinking Dexter was in bed. She'd said goodnight to him and then didn't go in his room again. She'd thought she was doing the right thing by giving him some space to cool down. If only she'd checked.

'How did the fire happen?' he asks.

This is the question that's kept Harper up all night. 'I don't know,' she says. The police had found a large rock by the back door, which someone had used to smash the window, so clearly Kate didn't do it herself. And for all her faults, Harper can't question the love Kate has for Thomas.

And the other thing Harper knows is that if it wasn't Kate, then someone tried to kill her and Thomas. They wouldn't have known Dexter was there, so this can't be about Harper.

'Do you think Thomas will be at school today?' Dexter asks.

'I don't think so. He'll need time. Just like you do.'

'The doctor said I'm fine.'

'Physically, yes. But things like that leave scars we can't see, Dexter.'

'What does that mean?'

'It means not everything that hurts us can be seen,' Harper says, standing and taking her unfinished toast to the food bin. 'Look, if you really feel like you'll be okay, then fine. But if you change your mind at any point during the day, just tell the teacher and I'll be straight there to pick you up. Now, finish your breakfast – I just need to make a quick call.'

Upstairs in the bedroom, she waits for Ellis to answer, counting the seconds until he picks up. 'What the hell happened?' she says, the moment he answers.

'Why are you calling? I can't talk to you.'

'My son could have been killed last night. Yours too. And Kate.'

'So it wasn't you?' Ellis says.

'Of course it wasn't me! Why the hell would I do that?'

'Because you hate my wife. And you want to destroy her life.'

'Ex-wife.'

'We're not actually divorced yet. You've been tormenting her for weeks, haven't you? Trying to turn her life upside down. Trying to get me to take Thomas from her.'

'Don't act all innocent. I know this fire was something to do with you.'

Ellis snorts. 'I'm going to pretend I didn't hear that, because what you're saying is dangerous. You need to learn when to keep your mouth shut.'

'Why would someone want her dead? Aren't you asking yourself that?'

Ellis takes his time to answer. 'Someone other than you, you mean? And Kate's not dead. Thomas is fine. Now they're safely here with me, where I can keep an eye on them and make sure nothing like that ever happens again. Don't call me again.'

He cuts her off, leaving Harper staring at her phone, shocked at the icy tone in Ellis's voice, and the smug satisfaction. Now he's finally got what he wanted all along.

Harper sits in her car opposite Ellis's house, waiting for him to leave for work. It had been easy to find out where he lived from asking Thomas a few harmless questions when he was at her house with Dexter.

It's crossed Harper's mind that Ellis might have taken the day off, to stay with Kate and Thomas, and the thought of that chills her. Now that Kate and Thomas are in his house, what lengths will he go to in order to keep them there? Ellis knew about Kate's affair with Jamie, and he never said a word. That would make him hate Jamie. It's enough to send him over the edge. To lash out at the man he held responsible. The police would be interested to hear more about this, but telling them will only put Harper on their radar.

At ten past eight, the front door opens and Ellis steps outside, followed by Thomas, dressed in the school uniform Harper gave him and trainers he must have had at Ellis's house. Like Dexter, he must have insisted on going in to school.

As soon as they drive off, Harper gets out and rushes to the front door, glancing back at the road in case they come back for any reason. She knocks and waits.

'What are you doing here?' Kate says when she opens the door. She's wearing a large towelling dressing gown, which must belong to Ellis.

'I had to come. I've... I've been wrong about you.' She glances back at the road. 'Has Ellis gone to work? Can I come in? Please, Kate.'

Kate frowns, and Harper understands her reluctance. 'Please. I just want to talk. We need to put an end to all of this. Things are already bad enough, and I think they'll only get worse.'

'Why are you doing this?' Kate says, folding her arms. 'You can't stand me. You think I killed your husband. And I'm certain it was *you*. So tell me – how the hell is us talking things over ever going to work?'

'I know things are crazy,' Harper admits. 'And a lot of that's my fault. But I did *not* start that fire. You have to believe me. And I know it wouldn't have been you – not with Thomas in the house. So just think about this – if it wasn't either of us, then someone else is trying to hurt you.'

Harper lets that sink in. If this doesn't work, then she'll never be able to get through to Kate. Seconds tick by and Harper turns back to check the road again, convinced that any second now Ellis will reappear.

Finally, Kate stands aside and lets her in. 'Five minutes,' she says. 'That's all I'm giving you. And don't think for one second that I trust you.'

When Kate doesn't invite her further into the house, Harper suggests they go and sit down. 'I know you want me out of here fast so let's lay all our cards on the table.'

Silently Kate walks into the living room and sits on the sofa, her arms still folded, while Harper sits opposite her, taking a deep breath. She never thought she'd be opening up to this woman. 'If I'm honest with you, will you do the same for me?' she asks.

Kate slowly nods. 'But how do we know we can trust each other? After everything that's happened.'

'Because we're both mums, and we could have both lost our sons in that fire. Tell me about your affair with Jamie, Kate. How did it start?'

'There was no affair! It was one night – that's all. And I thought he was separated.'

Harper wants to believe this, but given all that's happened, she's still not sure she can trust Kate. She needs the truth. Now. 'Think of the boys,' she says. 'Nothing is more important than them – not me, or you. Nothing. This is far from over and we're both in the dark. If we tell each other everything, maybe we can get to the truth. Before someone gets hurt. If anything had happened to either boy—'

'Stop! Don't you think I know that?' Kate yells. 'And I would never have forgiven myself... because however I look at it, it all comes back to me. And now Faye, the podcaster, is in hospital. She might not make it and—'

'*What?*'

'I was going to meet her at her house. She... she was helping me. And when I got there an ambulance and police car were already there. She'd been attacked. It was horrific. She looked... barely alive.'

'Oh my God.' Harper tries to process what this means. 'I only saw her on Thursday. Why would someone attack her?'

'I thought it was you,' Kate says, heavy suspicion in her eyes as she scrutinises Harper. 'But you seem shocked by it.'

'What have the police said?'

'I checked just on social media and according to what everyone's saying, apparently there's no new information. No suspect. Nothing.'

'This doesn't make sense. And if she was helping you, why did she put me in touch with Mona Shaw?'

Kate's face is ashen. 'What?'

'I'm sorry. But after what happened when you were fifteen, I had to know if there was any connection to Jamie.'

'I wasn't lying about any of that!' Kate shouts. 'Graham White attacked me. It was self-defence.' She stands up and walks to the window then turns back to Harper.

'I don't know what happened to you back then or what you did,' Harper says. 'I only care about what happened with Jamie. I need you to tell me all of it. How long was it going on for?'

Kate takes her time to answer. 'It was just one night. That was it. I'd never met him before that night.'

'You're lying to me, Kate. I found a photo of you on Jamie's phone, months ago. And I followed him to your work the week before he was killed.'

Kate's face folds. 'I swear to you – I'd never set eyes on him before that night. But I think he was following me for some reason. Targeting me. But he never approached me until that night in the bar.' Her eyes drop to the floor. 'My partner at the surgery told me he'd been in asking for a female vet. The week before. It was weird. It didn't make sense. I'm the only female vet there – it's a small surgery, just me and my partner, David.'

Harper already knows this; she's done plenty of research on Kate Mason. Perhaps it's foolish to believe Kate, but for some reason she does. 'Okay. Let's say I believe you. Tell me how he actually approached you.'

She listens as Kate recounts the details of how she met Jamie, what she thought at the time was a chance meeting, and her words seem laced with honestly.

'He told me he was separated,' Kate says. 'And I think because it was the day Ellis had moved out, I felt some kind of bond with Jamie. Like we were both a bit adrift. I had no idea about you still being... together – otherwise I would have stayed away from him. You weren't even—'

'Jamie had affairs before you,' Harper blurts out. 'Lots of them.' She hasn't planned for it all to come out like this, but now she's said it, she feels the heavy burden lifting from her body. 'But they weren't exactly affairs.'

'What do you mean?'

'We'd been together for years when I found out Jamie was cheating. Only, when I confronted him, I found out it was something completely different.' Harper pauses to gather her thoughts – these are words she's never uttered before. 'He met these rich women in the gym where he got a job as a personal trainer. He'd start some kind of relationship up with them but all he was doing was taking their money. Jamie had got into a lot of debt, and lost the business. I never even knew. He had people demanding money from him. And these clients at the gym just threw money at him. He knew how to charm them, and I guess in return he gave them his company. But however you look at it, he was conning these women out of their money.'

Kate's mouth hangs open as she clearly struggles to comprehend what Harper is telling her.

'Jamie was very careful about the women he targeted,' Harper continues. 'He'd study them for months, making sure he knew every detail of their lives so he knew how to appeal to them. Whatever they looked for in a man, that's what he'd become. He'd develop a relationship with them and somehow convince them to invest in his fictitious company. When really, the money was paying off his extreme debts.'

'But what did he want with *me*? I don't have much disposable income. I do all right with the practice, and we don't want for anything, but I'd never have enough to give away to anyone.'

'That's what I've been struggling to understand,' Harper says. 'You don't fit the mould of the kind of woman Jamie would have targeted. Of course you're attractive, anyone can see that, but it was never about looks for Jamie. And the other three were all clients at the gym. Older. Forties. Fifties. And extremely wealthy.'

'Why me, then?'

Harper shakes her head. 'I wish I could answer that. I thought it must have been different for him this time. I thought maybe he'd fallen in love with you. That your affair was nothing to do with money.'

'There was *no* affair!'

'But I thought there was.'

'Why?'

'Because of that photo I found of you on his phone. It terri-fied me more than anything. Not because I'm weak and couldn't let go of him, but because Jamie and I had unfinished business. I wanted to hurt him how he'd hurt me.'

Kate gasps.

'Not as in kill him. No, I wanted to pay him back for what he did. Not just because of the other women, but because he... it was his fault our baby girl died.' Feeling the suffocating sadness as if it had only just happened, Harper tells Kate about Molly.

Kate comes over and puts her arm around Harper. 'I'm so sorry. I can't imagine how heartbreaking that must have been.'

Harper takes a moment to compose herself. It feels strange to be comforted by a woman who until now has been her enemy. 'That's why I didn't want him to fall in love with someone else. Because then he would easily have walked away and I would never have got justice for our girl. If he moved on with his life, then Molly would be out of his mind, and he'd be free. I couldn't let that happen. That's why I stayed with him. I wanted to punish him. Every day. I'd talk about Molly all the time, drive him crazy with it. And then eventually I was going to leave him and take Dexter far away. Until I realised that I couldn't do that to my son.'

Kate stands again, walking across to the window once more. 'You weren't married, were you?'

Harper takes her time to answer. She's never been honest about this before; it was just between her and Jamie. 'No, but we were very much together,' Harper says. 'Jamie always said marriage was just a piece of paper and I agreed with him. So we never actually got married. But we felt like we were, and that's what we told people.'

Kate sighs 'I knew that. And Faye confirmed it.'

'It doesn't take a private detective to work it out,' Harper says. *It's just a piece of paper.* 'But like I said, we were as good as married. We even had rings.' Harper reaches into her bag and notices Kate flinch. 'This was Jamie's. And Dexter found it in your kitchen.' She hands the ring to Kate, who stares at it but doesn't take it. 'It's got an inscription. Look. That's what Jamie and I used to say to each other. It's just a piece of paper.' Harper feels the sting of tears in the corners of her eyes. 'How did it get in your house? It had blood on it!'

'I've never seen that before,' Kate says. 'I swear. I don't know how it got in my kitchen. But Jamie definitely wasn't wearing a wedding ring that night. Otherwise I would never have slept with him. And the blood could have come from anywhere.'

Hearing her say those words forces Harper to picture Jamie and Kate, and it's all she can do to push the image away. 'Then we have a problem. It doesn't make sense. Why would Jamie's ring be in your house?'

Kate shakes her head.

'And that photo of you on his phone I found months ago. That's what convinced me you were having an affair. Jamie never kept photos of those women on his phone. Only yours.'

'I can't explain that,' Kate says. 'But why didn't the police find it?'

'Because Jamie's phone was never found. Whoever killed him must have taken it. The police said it hasn't been switched on again.'

'Who else has been in your house since Jamie died?' Kate asks.

'No one. Ellis. That's it.' Harper considers this. It always comes back to Ellis, but she needs to be sure Kate is being honest. 'What aren't you telling me, Kate?'

Kate buries her head in her hands, taking her time to answer. 'Jamie and I arranged to see each other the next afternoon, so I went back. The door was unlocked so I assumed he'd left it open for me. I went in and... saw him on the floor. He was already dead.' She looks up, her eyes pleading with Harper. 'I panicked and ran. I know that was wrong – I should have called 999, but after Graham White I was terrified. It all came crashing back to me so I had to get out of there. I even dropped my keys.'

'Where?'

'In the apartment.'

'I never found any keys and the police didn't mention any.'

The two women fall silent, and Kate is the first one to broach what they're both thinking. 'Then that means someone has the keys to my house.'

'Does Ellis have a key?'

'Not any more – he gave it back the day he moved out. Why?'

'Because the more I think about this, the more I think Ellis must have something to do with it.'

'Ellis wouldn't have done all that stuff. The dead flowers. The running tap. That note left on my car. He wouldn't...' Kate doesn't finish that thought.

'None of that was me,' Harper insists. 'All I did was call Maddy and pretend to be you. And the school that time to say I was picking up Thomas. I'm sorry. I swear I didn't do anything else.'

Harper is expecting some resistance to this claim, but Kate doesn't flinch. 'You already think that, don't you? Because you know Ellis doesn't want to let you go. Kate, there's something I need to warn you about.' She takes a deep breath. 'Ellis knew you were having an affair with Jamie. Or at least he thought you were, like I did. And I'm the one who told him. A couple of months ago.'

'What? How? You didn't even know me, and I didn't know Jamie until that night—'

'But I'd found that photo of you on Jamie's phone, and I

managed to find out who you were. It's not that hard to do. I tracked down Ellis after work one evening and told him you were having an affair with my husband.' Harper gives Kate a moment to process what she's just said. 'He never confronted you, did he?'

'No.'

'Don't you think that's weird. Especially when you found out about *his* affair. He never mentioned what he thought you'd done with Jamie. Why is that? Why are you staying in his house, Kate? Ellis is clearly tied up in this. It's the only thing that makes any sense, if it wasn't you who killed Jamie.'

'I'm staying here because I need to be close to him. It's the only way I'll find out what he's doing. Because I've been thinking this too. He had access to Thomas's bag that day I found the photo of Jamie. And if you say it wasn't you—'

'It wasn't.'

'Then—'

Harper's phone beeps in her pocket, and she fishes it out and stares at the screen, her face draining of colour.

'What is it?' Kate says. 'What's going on?'

'It's Faye's sister. I set up an Instagram account so I could contact her. Told her I'm a good friend of Faye's and asked how she's doing. She just told me that Faye's dead.'

Kate feels as if she can't breathe. She hasn't allowed herself to believe that Faye would die. Granted, the state she was in splayed on that stretcher didn't look hopeful, but hearing this outcome floors Kate. 'No,' she says. 'No...'

Harper stands up and walks over to her. 'We have to work together to stop whoever's doing this. It *has* to be the same person who killed Jamie. The person who's been targeting you for some reason.'

'I thought that was you,' Kate mumbles.

'Only the phone calls. To mess with your life because I thought you'd killed Jamie. But now it's clear there's someone else with an agenda.'

'And you think that's Ellis.'

'There's no other conclusion I can reach,' Harper says. 'If it wasn't you.'

Kate realises that they'll never be able to trust each other, but she clings on to the hope that because Harper is a mother, just like her, they have a common bond that might pull them together. The fire has already changed things between them.

'You need to get out of here,' Harper continues, gesturing

around the room. 'I don't trust him.' She draws in breath. 'You and Thomas could stay with me. There's enough space.'

'No.' The words instinctively shoot from Kate's mouth. 'I have to be here. If I'm here then Ellis won't hurt me – like you said, it's what he wants. Plus, I'm still convinced this is something to do with Graham White – it has to be.' Even though Kate hasn't found any connection, and neither could Faye before she died.

'Jamie had no connection to that man,' Harper says. 'I've been through his things and there's nothing.'

'That we know of. But Faye was looking into it – maybe she found something?'

'We'll never know now.' Harper sighs. 'I liked her. She didn't deserve to be caught up in any of this. Whatever it is.' She looks at Kate, her eyes narrowing. 'Your friend Mona tells a different story about what happened with Graham White.'

'I'm not explaining or defending myself again,' Kate says. 'I had to do it back then and I won't now. Believe me or don't. Either is fine with me.'

'Just keep your son safe,' Harper says. 'And yourself. I've done this already, but I'm going to check out those three women Jamie was involved with at that gym. I don't think I'll find anything. He'd cut ties with them all months ago – I could tell from the messages begging him to contact them or asking about their investments. I'm surprised none of them went to the police. I figured it's because they were ashamed and embarrassed. Anyway, Jamie had told me before Dex was born that he'd stop what he was doing but I'm not convinced he did until we moved to Wimbledon. I think he really did stop then, around the time I found that photo of you. That's why I was convinced about your affair. Because he'd finally stopped conning those women, and you were different. Everything pointed to you meaning something different to him.' Harper lets that thought hang in the air.

'I'm going to pay Mona a visit. It's a long time overdue.'

'Why?' Harper asks. 'I know you think this is tied to your past, but there's nothing to prove that.'

'Maybe not. But Mona and I have unfinished business. Do you have her address?'

'She wouldn't give it to me. We had to meet in public. I've got her number, though.'

Kate will have to find another way. 'No, she won't speak to me on the phone.' She walks to the living room door, hoping Harper acknowledges the signal to leave.

Evelyn Shaw stares at Kate as if she's an apparition. Mona's mother always had a stern face, but now it's lined with the deep trenches of age she looks even fiercer. 'What are *you* doing here?'

'I need to see Mona.'

'No. You've done enough to my daughter. You're the reason kids were spreading lies about her at school. Making sure she had to change schools. And you just walked away from it all.'

'I didn't do anything to Mona. I never said a word about her.'

'Well, all those rumours started about her because of you. What you did to that man.' She spits her words, looking at Kate with disgust and loathing. 'I'm not giving you her address.'

'Please, Mrs Shaw. Things have been happening to me and... I think it's to do with Graham White.'

'The man you killed.'

Kate forces a deep breath. 'Please. I just need to talk to Mona. Someone set fire to my house last night while my son and I were sleeping. We could both be dead. He's ten years old!'

Evelyn's face softens as she takes in this information. 'Well... that's awful. But what's that got to do with Mona? I hope you're not trying to suggest—'

'No! Course not. I just need to talk to her about what happened. I think it's related to this. It has to be.'

With a heavy sigh, Evelyn takes her phone from her pocket and taps her passcode into it. She places it on the hall table and steps back. 'Well, it's not my fault if you find my phone and scroll through it, is it?' And then she leaves Kate alone and disappears into the living room.

'Hello, Mona.'

Mona spins around, her eyes popping as she registers that it's Kate standing behind her. Kate has turned up at Mona's house at precisely the moment Mona was putting her key in the door.

'What the...? Go away, Kate. I've got nothing to say to you.' Mona scrambles with her key, but it jams in the lock, giving Kate time to grab the keys from her.

'I've been trying to call you. I'm sure you got all my messages. We need to talk. It's a long time overdue.'

Mona tries to grab her keys back, but Kate is too fast. 'How did you find me?'

'It doesn't matter. And believe me, I wouldn't be here unless I had no choice. Now, let me in. I'm at breaking point, Mona, and who knows what I'll be capable of.' She dangles Mona's keys, and after a moment, Mona grabs them and opens the door.

The second Kate's inside Mona's flat, she gets an instant picture of what Mona's life must be like now. Far different from how Kate expected Mona would be living when, as school kids, they'd planned their adult lives down to the minutest detail. Mona had wanted a bright, modern place in the heart of London, in the middle of everything. But this flat is dingy and dark, cluttered with things that seem to belong to an elderly resident rather than a thirty-seven-year-old. None of the furniture matches and it all looks as though it's other people's cast-offs.

'Don't judge me,' Mona says, watching Kate take in her surroundings. 'It's rented. This isn't how things will always be.'

'I don't care how you're living,' Kate says.

Mona removes magazines and clothes from the sofa. 'Sit down, then.'

'No, I'm fine standing.' Kate folds her arms. 'Did you know Faye Held is dead? I know you knew her – she spoke to you for the podcast episode she was doing about Graham White a couple of years ago. Remember?'

There's a flicker of something on Mona's face, but she quickly composes herself. 'How did she... what happened to her?'

'You don't seem surprised. Are you lying again, Mona? You're good at that, aren't you?'

'Get to the point, Kate, and then get out of my flat.'

'Shall I tell you what's been happening in my life over the last few weeks?' Kate says. 'I've had a woman stalking me because her husband was targeting me for some reason, my house has been set on fire with me and my son in it, my closest friend has cut me out of her life because I didn't tell her about my past, and I can't trust a single person in my life.'

Mona doesn't respond.

'And do you know when I think it might have all started? When Faye Held did that podcast episode on Graham White. And you spoke to her, spewing lies about me.'

Again there's no response.

'Do you know anything about Jamie Archer?'

'I'd never heard that name until that woman contacted me and told me all about it.'

'Do you know what, Mona? Some small part of me can even understand why you spoke to Faye. We can end up telling so many lies that we actually start to believe the narrative we've sold ourselves. We rewrite it, and don't even realise it's been altered.'

'Why are you here? What do you want?'

'It's time to tell the truth, Mona. For both of us.'

Mona looks as if she's about to throw up as she sits clutching her stomach. 'I don't know what you mean,' she says.

'Yes, you do. This all started because of you. You owe me the truth, and I'm not leaving until I get it.'

There's a long pause. And when Mona speaks, Kate wishes she'd never asked.

'I... I loved him,' Mona begins.

THIRTY-FIVE

2003

It's the day after her fifteenth birthday when she first meets him. He's sitting on a bench in the park near school, staring at the lake, and he looks a little bit like Leonardo DiCaprio. She can't pull her eyes away from him. But there's a sadness about the way his gaze fixes on the ripples, and something compels her to walk over to him and sit beside him.

He moves up to make room for her, even though there's plenty of space, but he doesn't look at her. She could be anyone: an elderly man sitting down to catch his breath, or a mum watching her children play basketball on the court by the lake. She wants him to *see* her, although she can't explain why.

'Are you okay?' she asks. 'You don't look okay.' She feels her cheeks flush. What a ridiculous thing to say to a grown man she's never met. He'll probably tell her to eff off, and who could blame him? He's a proper adult, why would he talk to a schoolgirl?

But he doesn't tell her to eff off. Instead, he turns to her and smiles, which makes him even more attractive. 'Is it that obvi-ous?' he says, with a small chuckle. 'I thought I was doing a decent job of hiding it. Of looking like I'm just out here for the fresh air. To take in the views of that beautiful lake.'

Now it's her turn to smile. 'Need to try harder next time.'

'Well, you're bold,' he says, raising his eyebrows, looking her up and down. 'For someone so young.'

She rolls her eyes. 'I'm fifteen. Not that young.'

Again he raises his eyebrows. 'Is that right? If only you knew just how young it really is.'

'How old are you, then?' Her heart pumps faster. She silently prays that he's not too much older. Twenty is fine. Maybe even twenty-five.

'Old enough to be your dad,' he says. 'I'm thirty-nine last time I checked.' Although when you get to my age, you kind of stop keeping count. Gets too depressing otherwise.'

Disappointed, she does a quick calculation. 'You're right. You *are* old enough to be my dad.' But still she wonders how someone so attractive can ever feel depressed.

He laughs. 'Told you. What's your name?'

She tells him and asks him his.

'Graham,' he says.

'So why are you sad, Graham? Wife left you?' She's already noticed the absence of a wedding ring on his finger.

'Are you always this sassy?' he asks, smiling. 'That will get you far in life, I'm sure.'

'Guilty as charged,' she says, feeling flattered that she's making him smile when he'd looked so down before.

He stands up, and holds out his hand. 'Nice to meet you, Miss Sass.' And then he's gone, leaving a yearning ache in her stomach.

She sees him five more times in the park, on the same bench where they first met. She's never worked out what he was sad about, but since then he's always seemed happy when he's talking to her. Maybe she's as good for him as he is for her.

Each time they meet, they talk – for nearly an hour most times, before he says he has to get home. She doesn't want to ask him if there's a girlfriend waiting for him at home – that would ruin everything. Instead, she keeps him in their bubble, one that no one outside it would ever understand.

It's a Friday evening when she next sees him in the park, this time playing football with his friends. She told her mum she's studying at Collette's house. She doesn't even get on with Collette, but her mum wouldn't know that – she never listens, too wrapped up in work and her own busy life.

Graham spots her on the bench – their bench – and winks at her before turning back to his game. A jolt of excitement passes through her, something she's never felt, even though she's messed around with boys before.

For forty minutes she sits watching the game, and as it ends and Graham's friends disperse, she's once again alone with him. He takes his time gathering his things and then glancing around, brings them over to the bench and sits down, bending down to untie his football boots. 'Like football, do you?' he says, grinning. 'Noticed you were watching us.'

Not 'us' – you. 'I like things about it,' she says, fluttering her eyelashes.

He raises his eyebrows just like he did when she first met him, and she feels as if she'll explode. How can a man this age do this to her? She doesn't understand it, but she wants to feel more of it, to see how good he could make her feel.

'Where have all your friends gone?' she asks, to keep him talking.

'They're not really my friends. We just play football every week. I don't usually socialise with them.' He packs his football boots in his bag and stands. 'Well, enjoy your evening.'

'Wait,' she says. 'Are you going already?'

'Yeah, it's late and I need to eat. Sorry, Miss Sass.'

'We could eat together somewhere?' she says, unsure where this bold proposition has come from. 'You could buy me a drink.'

He laughs, a loud splutter that makes her feel small and pathetic, and then his expression changes. 'I think you should go home now.' His tone is soft and kind, but this makes her feel even more pathetic. She's tried to seduce an older man and he's turned her down.

She stares at him, defiant, longing for him. 'Don't go.'

He sighs. 'This is dangerous,' he says. 'I shouldn't even be talking to you. I'm an adult and you're... you're not.'

'I practically am,' she says.

'Listen – you need to do me a favour.'

'Anything,' she says.

'Go home. And never, ever talk to men like this again. You're young – there's plenty of time for all of... all of this. Don't be in such a rush.'

And then he's gone, not even looking back at Mona to see the damage he's inflicted on her.

Mona is off school for the rest of the week. Her mother has a job interview on Monday so she's too wrapped up in preparing for it to doubt Mona's story about feeling sick. And when she leaves Mona alone in the house and heads off to work, Mona puts her plan into action.

Every day she heads to the park, knowing that sooner or later she's bound to see Graham again. But it's not until Thursday lunchtime that she spots him, sitting on their bench, this time eating a sandwich. She assumes he must live or work around here, so she waits and watches, from behind the gigantic oak tree she used to climb when she was younger. He never looks around, and she's quite certain that he's forgotten all about her. Yet he is imprinted on her mind, on her whole body, and she can't shake him.

Maybe he's realised he's made a mistake by dismissing her? That's why he's sitting on their bench, hoping she'll come along. Mona wants to believe this, but doubt niggles away; he'd crushed her so cruelly and then walked away.

Graham gets up from the bench, and she follows him, not even bothering to keep a safe distance. He turns down several roads and then he heads up the driveway of a house on Pearson Street. Mona holds her breath and her pulse races. Is this his home?

Then everything changes when he knocks on the door and a blonde-haired woman answers, pulling him towards her and kissing him on the mouth.

Mona wants to throw up. So this is why he wouldn't do anything with her. She'd never entertained the possibility that he might have someone. She watches them – sees how tenderly he touches her cheek, kisses her forehead, wraps his arms around her.

When the door shuts, Mona turns away, seething with rage. He'd led her on, made her think that he was interested in her. And then this.

Graham White has fucked with the wrong girl.

Over the next few days, Mona feels herself changing. Robbie keeps trying to talk to her, and normally she wouldn't entertain the idea, but somehow, being with him feels like she's getting Graham out of her system. She's aware it's a temporary solution, though – she's not attracted to Robbie, whereas it's clear that Graham adores that blonde woman he spends so much time with. Five days out of seven last week. Mona's keeping a diary. Times, places. Every detail of his life. And he always leaves her in his house when he goes to work – he must really trust her.

PE started ten minutes ago, but Mona's still in the girls' changing room, on her own. If she could, she'd make herself invisible so that nobody would ever find her. Who would even care? She can't bear the thought of going out there to play tennis, so she'll wait here until the teacher comes looking for her.

Five minutes later, when the changing room door opens, it's not Miss Bright but Kate who strides in. 'There you are! I've been looking everywhere for you. Miss Abbott said you need to hurry up or she's marking you absent.'

Mona shrugs. 'Let her. I don't care. Who gives a shit about tennis?'

'Mona, what's going on? I thought you didn't mind tennis?' She pauses. 'You've been acting really... I dunno. Strange. Just talk to me. I'm your friend. Tell me what's wrong.'

Then it all pours from her mouth, words Mona never imagined she'd ever be saying.

'I... I was attacked. By a man in the park. A few weeks ago.'

THIRTY-SIX
2003

For a second, Kate thinks Mona is messing around. Not a good thing to joke about, but still, Mona is the sort of person who has no filter. She says what she thinks and nothing is off limits. But Kate sees through her vulnerability, and it's part of why she feels connected to Mona. She sees the pain in her friend that no one else knows is there. 'What... what do you mean?'

'I met him in the park about a week ago. He was playing football with his friends and then they all left. He... he came over to me and started trying to talk to me. You know... all flirty. I told him he was old enough to be my dad and he just... he just laughed. Then the next thing I knew, he grabbed me and dragged me into the wooded part, behind the bushes.' A stream of tears flows down Mona's cheeks. 'I screamed but there was no one around.'

Horrified, Kate grabs her friend and hugs her tightly. Mona's been acting differently – withdrawn and distant – and this explains why. For a while they sit silently in the changing rooms until Mona's ready to speak again. 'When he'd finished, he just got up and walked off, as if nothing had happened. He even smiled, and said he'd see me around. As if... as if I'd wanted him to do that to me! He knew how old I am. He's a... I can't even say it.'

'We need to go to the police,' Kate says. She's got to be strong for her friend, help her through this. 'I'll come with you.'

'No! Then I'd have to tell Mum and you know what she's like. She'd focus on how I was out at night when I shouldn't have been. And everyone at school thinks I'm a slut already – they'll say I wanted him to do it.' She stares at Kate with large, frightened eyes. 'But I swear I didn't! He's in his thirties!' Mona wails again, her chest heaving with her heavy sobbing.

Kate holds her tighter. 'He can't get away with this, Mona! You can't let him.'

Mona's crying subsides. 'I know. That's all I can think about. I don't want him to get away with it. But there's another way.'

'What do you mean?' Kate asks.

'We can make him pay without me going to the police.'

'How?'

Mona takes a deep breath. 'Okay, I know this will sound crazy... but I need to take things into my own hands.'

Kate's used to Mona's scheming and plotting, and it rarely turns out well. Her friend is impulsive at the best of times, but this is starting to feel frightening 'That doesn't sound like a good idea. And what exactly do you mean?'

'He's a paedophile, Kate. And I need to put a stop to him before he does it to someone else. What he did to me has changed me for the rest of my life. I can't let him get away with that.'

'That's why we need to go to the police. It's the only thing to do, Mona.'

'They won't be able to do anything.' Mona is strangely calm now; she's already made up her mind. 'It's his word against mine, and any DNA he left behind on me will be long gone. It was weeks ago and I've had a million showers since then. And washed everything I was wearing – I couldn't stand the thought of him all over my clothes.'

'You should have told me!' Kate protests. 'I would have helped you. That's what friends are for. I thought you trusted me, Mona!'

Mona reaches for Kate's hand. 'Course I do. Best friends forever, right? Nothing can come between us. And that's exactly why I'm telling you all this now. It's just between us, nobody else can know what he did to me. Ever.'

Kate leans back against the changing room wall. 'So what's your plan exactly?'

'We're going to terrorise him. Let him know that he can't get away with abusing girls. Ruin his life. I know where he lives. He has a girlfriend too. I'm sure she'd be sickened to know what he did.'

'What if he calls the police?'

'He won't know it's me doing anything. And even if he does, he doesn't know where I live. I was just an anonymous girl in a park – an easy target.'

Kate exhales. She doesn't like the sound of this, but she needs to support her friend. That's all that matters.

For weeks the girls torment Graham White. They post used tampons through his door, and dog excrement they find in the park. They follow him around, pulling their hoods over their faces so he can't see them. They sit on the low wall opposite his house, sprinting off when he opens the door to question them about what they're doing.

And after her initial reservations, Kate throws herself into their mission, for the sake of her friend. It brings her to tears when she pictures what that man did to Mona. They are vigilantes seeking justice for the sake of all young girls; this is what Kate tells herself.

Then one day, Mona ups the ante. 'We're going to break into his house,' she whispers, as they're making their way to double science. 'Tonight. Do you think you can sneak out?'

'Mum will never let me out late on a school night.'

'Please, Kate,' Mona begs. I can't sleep at night when I think about what he did to me. How... he violated me.' Her eyes brim with tears.

'Okay, I'll do it,' Kate says, silently praying that Mona will have second thoughts.

The second they're in Graham White's house, Kate's hands begin to shake. Shards of glass from the window they've smashed shimmer on the floor; they've crossed a line there's no way back from. What if he comes home and catches them? There's no telling what he'd do to them. 'I don't think this is a good idea,' Kate whispers.

'We're here now,' Mona says, staring around the place, sucking up every detail of it. Kate finds it odd that she's doing this – she should feel sickened to be in the home of the man who attacked her. Still clutching the hammer she used to smash the back door window, Mona makes her way through the kitchen to a small living room.

And then without warning, she swings the hammer, smashing it into the television, spraying a waterfall of glass across the room.

Momentarily Kate is stunned; she'd half expected Mona to change her mind and rethink this terrifying plan. But when it becomes clear that Mona is only just getting started, and when she pictures how terrified Mona must have felt when that man was tugging at her clothes, Kate joins in, swiping ornaments from the mantelpiece, upending the coffee table, throwing sofa cushions to the floor.

'We don't take anything, though,' Mona warns. 'I want him to know for sure that this wasn't a burglary.'

After the break-in, Kate holds her breath every time her mum answers the phone. Her fingerprints will be all over Graham White's house, and he surely must have called the police.

The only respite from this worry is that at least now Mona can begin to heal, to feel that even the smallest sense of justice has been served. Nothing other than a prison sentence will be enough, but the satisfaction she saw on Mona's face that night is enough for Kate to believe that this is the end of it.

But Kate is wrong. Only days later, Mona is back to the shell of the person she was, once again becoming snappy and withdrawn.

'It's not enough,' Mona says, when they're walking home from school. 'I thought it might be, but it isn't. I still feel... hollow and empty. That man... he can replace the items in his home. Redecorate. Go back to his life. But I can't.'

Kate stops walking and faces Mona. 'What are you saying?'

'I'm going to send a letter to his girlfriend. And ruin his business. Did I tell you he's a mechanic and has his own garage?'

Kate wonders how Mona knows this but decides it's best not to ask.

'I'll tell all his clients he likes little girls,' Mona says.

'Please let that be the end of it. Promise me? If you're not going to the police, I mean.'

'Yeah, yeah,' Mona says, but she's only half listening. 'He'll be playing football this evening,' she says. 'And I'm going to be sitting right there on the bench where he first approached me. Let's see what he thinks of that.'

'No! You can't. He'll—'

'But this time I'll be ready for him,' Mona says, smiling. 'And I'll be fine because you're coming with me.'

'And what do you think I can do to defend you?' Kate says, holding up a scrawny arm. 'He's a fully grown man.'

'It's not going to come to that,' Mona says. 'I won't let it. I just want to freak him out and let him think I'm about to expose him to all his football buddies. You'll see. Everything will work out.'

There's no sign of him when they get to the park. The football game has started, and Kate crosses her fingers by her side, hoping Graham White won't show up.

None of the other men pay them any attention, and once the match has ended and they've dispersed, Kate turns to Mona. 'Let's go. I don't want my mum to realise I'm not in my room.'

'I wonder where he is,' Mona says.

'You've got to stop this. It's not healthy. If you don't want to go to the police, you have to let it go.'

Mona doesn't say anything for a moment, but stares straight ahead. 'Okay,' she says. 'I won't do anything. I'll let it go.'

Kate smiles, and takes Mona's arm. 'Come on, I'll walk you home.'

'Men are shits, aren't they?' Mona says. 'Look at my dad. Walking out on my mum when she was pregnant with me. All those affairs he had.'

'We can't think like that,' Kate says. 'They're not all like that. We just have to learn to spot the ones who *are*.'

Kate sees Mona to her house, then continues on to her own road, walking faster now she's on her own. The roads are eerily quiet tonight, and it spooks her, forcing her to turn around every few seconds to check she's not being followed.

There's never anyone behind her, but Kate can't shake the feeling she's being watched.

By the last day of term, Mona seems to have perked up, and glimpses of the girl she was shine through. She hasn't mentioned Graham White for days now, but somehow that worries Kate even more. When Mona goes silent, it means there are too many scrambled things going on in her head.

Somehow Mona convinces Kate to go to the canal after school – it's a half-day and the long summer holiday stretches before them.

Robbie is all over Mona, but Kate bites her tongue, refrains from lecturing Mona that she's not being fair to him if she doesn't like him. After what Mona's been through, perhaps this is what she needs to help her heal.

Kate sits on the grass with Kian. She likes him, and it seems like he's flirting with her, but she doesn't know for sure until he kisses her. As much as she likes it, she's finding it hard to focus on what's happening between them when her bladder is about to burst. She should have gone at school – the nearest toilets are on the high street and that's a fifteen-minute walk from here. She tells Kian she'll be right back, and heads off.

Everything changes when she gets back and finds Mona with Kian in the woods. All the years of friendship dismantled with one senseless act.

She turns and runs away from them, ignoring Kian's shouts.

And when she reaches the canal, a hand spins her around. Mona. Pleading with her to listen. But her words are muffled and Kate can barely take in any of it.

'I... I'm so messed up. I know that. It's because of what

Graham did to me. I... I'm not myself, Kate. Please, you have to forgive me.'

Kate shakes her head and continues walking. But somehow Mona has penetrated the surface of her anger, found a way to release it like air from a balloon. Still, Kate carries on walking, ignoring Mona, who is right beside her, pleading with her to stop.

They reach Kate's house, and Mona grabs her arm. 'Listen to me! I'm not in my right mind, Kate. I'm sorry. I'll say it a thousand times – please, Kate. I'm not—'

'Not what?' Kate spins around. 'Someone who's already been with half the boys in our year?' Kate's words are like knives hurtling towards her friend.

Mona's jaw drops, and slowly tears meander down her cheeks. 'I know that's what everyone else thinks of me... but I never thought you felt the same. I thought you understood me.' She swipes at her eyes. 'Graham White has messed me up. I... I can't even think straight. First my dad abandons us and now this...'

Slowly, Kate's anger dissipates. She's been there through the worst of it with Mona; she can't abandon her friend now, even after what Mona's just done. It was a cry for help. And it's all Graham White's fault. Mona needs help and support, not for Kate to turn away from her and reject her like almost everyone else in her life has done.

Before Kate has a chance to express this to her friend, an arm grabs her around her chest, and a clammy hand smothers her mouth. She's dragged backwards and all she can hear is Mona screaming before a heavy fist smashes into her face.

When Kate opens her eyes, she's in the back of what seems to be a van. Her arms and legs are tied, and beside her Mona is groaning, curled up like a foetus.

'Are you okay? What's happening?' Kate pulls herself up, coughing from the dust that floats up as she moves.

'My stomach,' Mona says. He kicked me and I think it's done some damage.'

'Try not to panic,' Kate says, shuffling over and putting her arm around Mona. We're together. We'll get out of this.'

'Who was he?' Kate says. 'Did you get a good look at him?'

Mona frowns. 'Didn't you notice?'

'What?'

'It was *him*! Graham White. He's the one who's done this to us and now I don't know what he's going to do.'

Panic swells in Kate's body. 'I told you we should never have broken into his house. He's going to kill us! He wants to keep you silent in case you tell the police what he did to you. And now I'm involved too. He knows you've told me!'

'We need to just stay calm. And think of a plan.' Mona pauses. 'There are two of us and only one of him. As soon as he opens the door, I'll kick him really hard between his legs and you run. I'm a bit faster than you so I'll be able to catch you up.'

'But we don't even know where he's taking us. Where are we supposed to run to?'

'I don't have all the answers, Kate. But I got us into this mess, so I'm going to get us out of it. Just... whatever happens, as soon as that door opens and I've done some damage – run!'

For what feels like hours, the van continues on, and soon Kate can tell they're off the main roads and heading down a dirt track. She throws up, her vomit pooling across the floor of the van. Beside her, Mona squeezes her hand.

Eventually, the van comes to a stop and the girls turn to each other. 'Get ready,' Mona says. 'This is it. We only get one chance to get this right.'

Kate crawls over to the door, her heart thumping in her chest. And when the door creaks open, like a wild animal Mona lunges towards Graham White, thrusting her knee right between his legs. He doubles over and Kate jumps out of the van, running into the darkness.

She waits to hear Mona's footsteps behind her, but there is only silence. He must have hurt Mona, otherwise she'd be right behind Kate.

Stopping to turn around, Kate squints into the darkness. Nothing but silence. And then she turns around and runs back the way she's just come, stopping short when she sees Mona up ahead, staring at something.

Graham White's lifeless body.

'What do you mean by that? Who did you love?'

Kate needs to hear it from Mona's mouth. The truth. After all these years.

'Graham,' Mona says, sinking onto the floor and drawing her knees up to her chin, childlike and vulnerable.

That's when Kate understands everything, the murkiness clearing away and leaving a bright light for her to follow. 'He didn't rape you, did he?'

Seconds tick by and all the while Kate fears the answer she's about to hear. It changes everything. On the floor, Mona shakes her head.

'And you let me take the blame for his death.' Anger rages inside Kate and she forces deep breaths to keep it at bay. But still her pulse races. 'The only reason I covered for you back then was because I thought he'd raped you! And then when I wanted to tell the truth, you forced me to keep quiet. For years people think I killed a man. And now, after everything you put me through, it was all based on a lie!' Kate stares at the woman who as teenagers she would have done anything for. 'Why did we break into his house, then? What did you want revenge for? Did he dump you? Is that it?'

Mona's voice is barely audible. 'No, that's not it.'

'What? I can't hear you.' It's getting harder for Kate to keep her rage contained.

'I offered myself to him on a plate, and he turned me down. Basically told me I was little girl and made me feel this small.' She gestures with her fingers.

Kate struggles to understand what she's saying. 'So Graham White didn't touch you at all? He never went anywhere near you?'

The shake of Mona's head leaves Kate seething. How easily she destroyed an innocent man's life. 'But why did he kidnap us?'

'I'm sorry,' Mona whimpers. 'It just got out of hand.' She falls silent.

'Talk, damn it! Why did you tell me he raped you?'

'Because I... I was obsessed with him.' Briefly Mona looks up before hanging her head again. 'We did meet in that park. And I saw him there a few times. We'd chat. He was really kind to me. Friendly. No one had ever been like that to me before.'

'*I* was!' Kate screams.

'I mean no boys. Ever. They just used me and threw me away.'

'Because you *let* them!'

'I don't need a lecture from you!'

Kate resists the urge to grab Mona and shake some sense into her. 'You owe me! My whole life changed because of you! I could have gone to prison! Everything I've ever done has been tainted by Graham White's death, by people thinking I killed him, when you're the one who did that to him!' Kate presses her palms against her temples. 'Did you kill him on purpose? You told me he'd tried to kill you and it was self-defence. Was that a lie, too?'

'It *was* self defence! I didn't want him dead – I loved him!' Mona shakes her head. 'I tried to make him like me, but he wasn't having any of it. He told me to stop and then he stopped going to the park except to play football with his mates. I was jealous and rejected and I couldn't handle it.' She looks up at Kate. 'I'm so sorry.'

Kate edges back. 'He abducted us because we broke into his house,' she says, her voice quiet now.

'I think he just wanted to stop me doing anything else. I... I sent his girlfriend a letter. The day before. It must have tipped him over the edge and he wanted to shut me up.'

'You told me you weren't going to do that. What did you say to her? More lies!'

Mona hangs her head. 'I told her I'd been seeing him, and that I was fifteen.'

'Why wouldn't he just go to the police?' Kate asks. 'And tell them what you'd done?'

Mona shrugs. 'He was probably terrified they wouldn't believe him. Accusations like that don't wash off easily. His life would have been ruined even if it never went to court. He had a business to protect. And once people get a whiff of a child abuser, they make their lives hell, don't they?'

'Jesus, Mona! That's so screwed up! You ruined his life, and then you killed him.'

'It was an accident!'

'Do you expect me to believe that when you've lied about everything else?' Kate's chest tightens. All these years she's taken the blame for her friend, protected her because she'd thought Mona was the victim of a paedophile. 'You forced me to cover for you,' Kate snaps. 'Remember? I was only fifteen – I wasn't thinking straight. You told me your life wouldn't be worth living if people thought you were responsible for someone's death and I let you talk me into it. You made me feel bad because you'd had such a troubled life and mine had been happy up to that point. I felt awful that you hadn't had a break in life.' Kate shakes her head. 'But what you did to me after all that was even worse.'

2006

Kate hasn't seen Mona since the night she killed Graham White, but every day regret has seeped into her body, spreading like cancer. She should never have gone along with Mona's suggestion for Kate to take the blame – she didn't want to, but she'd been too numb with shock to think rationally. And it was the flood of guilt Mona unleashed on her that cemented her decision.

Now, though, it's time to put things right. Kate can't do this to her mum any more – can't let her go on thinking her daughter is capable of taking someone's life, even in self-defence.

Her mum's at work this morning, meaning Kate doesn't have to lie about where she's going. She's already warned Kate to stay away from Mona after what she did with Kian; her mum knows nothing of Mona's involvement in what followed.

It's not even nine a.m., so Kate's sure Mona will be at home, still in bed. She was never good at waking up before lunchtime. And Mona's mum will have left for work hours ago.

Kate rings the doorbell, then stands back to look up at Mona's window, the blackout blind shutting out daylight.

Four times she has to buzz. Then six, seven, eight. Finally, Mona's face appears at the window, scowling. It's a shock seeing her again after three years. A painful eternity.

Mona pulls open the window. 'What the hell are you doing?'

'We need to talk. Now.'

'I'm sleeping. And there's nothing to say. We agreed not to contact each other.'

Wrong. It was Mona who dictated that's what should

happen. Kate naively went along with it, no questions asked, no time to consider what she was agreeing to.

'Let me in, Mona – or I'm going straight to the police.'

Mona's eyes widen but it takes her a few seconds to close the window. And another long minute before the front door opens and she stands there, her arms folded defensively. 'What are you waiting for, then? Are you coming in or not?'

The house smells musty, uncared for. Mona's mum is too busy to clean, and Kate doubts Mona would ever think of running the vacuum cleaner around the place.

'What do you want, Kate? Why are you here?' Mona doesn't invite her further in, but lingers in the hallway in her short pyjamas.

'I've changed my mind,' Kate says. 'We need to tell the truth about what happened.'

Mona's face drains of colour. 'No... what are you talking about? We can *never* do that, Kate.' She grabs Kate's arm and leads her to the living room, where the sofas are covered in so much stuff that there's no space to sit.

'We agreed,' Mona continued. 'You said you'd do it for me.'

'I... I wasn't thinking straight. And now I am.'

'It's been three years, Kate. You can't just turn around now and say you've changed your mind. We'll be... we'll both be arrested. For perverting the course of justice or something. Are you crazy?'

Kate perches on the arm of the sofa. 'I'm so far from crazy, Mona. I've never seen things more clearly. I want out of this lie. I came here to let you know that I'm going to the police. And I hope you'll see that it's the right thing to do and come with me.'

Mona stares at her, then shakes her head. 'I will never do that, Kate. I've got my life to think about. And I'm seeing someone now. I really like him.'

With those words, Kate sees just how disturbed Mona is. She killed a man, yet there she is getting on with her life, in a relationship with someone. While Kate hasn't been able to even look at a guy since it happened. Kate's body blazes with anger.

'I don't care!' she screams. 'I'm going to the police!' And she will – even though it will be hard dealing with them after last time. This time will be different – this time it's to clear her name.

Kate turns to leave but Mona grabs her wrists.

'You're not thinking straight. And I won't let you do this, Kate.'

Kate wrestles out of Mona's grasp and makes for the front door.

'I've got evidence that will prove you did it!' Mona shouts.

Slowly, Kate turns. 'What are you talking about?'

'I'll show you.' Mona runs upstairs, coming back with something in her hand. 'Look at this.' She hands Kate a photo.

Kate stares at it. It's Kate – in Graham White's flat, trashing the place. But still she asks Mona what it is.

'Exactly what it looks like. Evidence of you stalking Graham White.' Mona snatches the photo back. 'And if you even think about going to the police, I'll show this to them. And I'm sure I can find some other evidence if I put my mind to it.'

'I hate you,' Kate says, because right now that's all she can think of to say.

'If you ever go to the police, or tell a single person the truth, I will wreck your life, Kate. I don't care if it's two years or twenty years from now. If you ever have kids, I'll take them away from you. I've already killed, haven't I? Don't think I won't do it again if I have to.'

'You... you... wouldn't,' Kate stammers.

'Not worth the risk finding out, is it?'

Kate doesn't stay to hear any more; she runs from Mona's house. She never wants to set eyes on her again.

NOW

'I did what I had to do,' Mona says. 'Surely you understand that by now? If the truth came out then my life would have been over.'

'*You're* the one who's been doing stuff to me,' Kate says. 'Sending dead flowers. Getting inside my flat. Leaving notes on my car.'

Mona scrunches her face. 'I don't know what you're talking about.'

'Why would you do that when I've never said a word to anyone. I was too terrified because you're so unstable. And I have a son.'

'I haven't done anything to you,' Mona says. 'I've kept my distance and tried not to think about you. Until now.'

'And even back then, you planted that seed about me killing Graham on purpose! And I was too scared to challenge you.'

'*I* was scared too,' Mona says. 'I thought people would find out the truth. I... I just said stuff to make them think it was you, so that they'd never even consider for a second it could have been me.'

'No one even knows you were there,' Kate hisses. 'You didn't have to say anything at all.' Crushing silence descends on them as everything unravels. 'Did you attack Faye?' Kate demands.

'No!'

'Were you trying to silence her in case she discovered the truth? She was good at that, wasn't she? I'm sure if she kept digging, she would have found out the truth, or at least come close to it.'

'No. That's not possible. We're the only two who know.'

'Graham White's girlfriend knew. You just said you wrote her a letter telling her he'd been seeing you. So she knew.'

'But she never said anything to the police. I've thought

about that a lot – and I think it's because she didn't want people to think she'd been in a relationship with a paedophile. That's the only thing that makes sense.'

Kate recalls Jennifer's comment all those years ago about knowing Kate was with Graham. At the time Kate had no idea what she was talking about but now it's clear she was talking about Mona. She was probably disgusted that the man she loved could do that. 'How could you let Jennifer think her partner was capable of that? You've ruined so many lives, Mona!'

'Don't you think I know that?' Mona screams, shrinking back against the sofa.

'Who's Jamie Archer?' Kate says. 'Don't lie to me!'

'What? I don't know.'

'You're lying.' Kate scrolls through her phone and shows Mona a picture of Jamie.

'He's the man you were having an affair with. I met his wife – she told me everything. She's convinced it was you.' Mona's lips form a half-smile. 'Maybe we're not so different after all?'

Kate slams her fist down on the sofa, right by Mona's head. 'Don't you ever compare us. I'm nothing like you.' But as soon as she's said it, Kate realises this isn't true. She's been as much of a liar as Mona has.

Kate forces deep breaths. 'So you don't know him?'

'How would I know him? He's got nothing to do with me.'

'But he might have something to do with Graham White.'

'How? That was all years ago? This guy looks around our age – what could he have to do with it? I think you're just desperate, Kate. Maybe you need to look closer to home.'

'And what's that supposed to mean?'

'I mean that maybe you're the link to everything here. Not Graham White.'

. . .

It's late evening by the time Kate leaves St Albans and makes her way to Ellis's house, with sleet pattering against her windscreen.

Ellis has given her a door key, but she rings the bell, determined to show him that she's not settling in here, that this is a temporary arrangement.

What she's not expecting to see when the door opens is Harper, smiling at her and letting her in, as if it's her own house.

'What are you doing here?' Kate asks.

'Ellis had an emergency and had to go out. He tried calling you but you didn't answer. Apparently, Thomas begged him to let Dexter come over so he took me up on my offer of watching Thomas while he's... doing whatever he needs to do. He didn't like the idea of me being here, but I guess whatever he had to go and deal with was more important.'

Kate pulls out her phone, and sure enough there are three texts from Ellis and a voice message. 'I must have accidentally turned my phone to silent.' She can't think what kind of emergency Ellis would be having; none of it sounds right.

'This is our chance,' Harper continues, ushering Kate inside and closing the door. 'I can stay down here and keep an eye out in case he comes back, and you can have a root around. Start with his laptop. There's got to be something on there.'

Kate bristles, annoyed that Harper is dictating what she should do. She brushes past her and follows the sound of the boys' voices to the living room.

'Hey,' she says, forcing her voice to sound cheerful.

'Mum! Dad said Dex could come for dinner. His mum's making us pasta.'

'That's great. I've just got some things to do, okay?'

In the kitchen doorway, Kate watches while Harper busies herself with the boys' dinner. Still not convinced she can trust her, Kate reminds herself she needs to stay vigilant. Especially after what she's just learned about Mona. Graham White's death was so senseless now and Kate will never forgive herself for being fooled by her. Too many lies have been told, and she still doesn't know who killed Faye. Or who'll be next.

Upstairs, she slips into Ellis's bedroom and closes the door, surprised to find his laptop open on the bed. She rushes back downstairs and asks Harper if she's been up there.

'No. I literally just got here with Dexter. Ask him if you don't believe me. All I've had time to do is take off my coat and find the pasta.'

Kate heads back upstairs, and brings the screen to life, surprised to find he's still using the same password. She checks his email first, opening his Gmail and scrolling through. Nothing stands out. Just some spam and some from friends. His mum. A couple from Maddy. And then a name catches her attention that has no place in Ellis's inbox.

Jennifer Seagrove.

Sent two hours ago.

Sweat coats Kate's forehead as she clicks on it.

Hi Ellis,

I hope we can find a way to work this all out. Your wife is a liar and you need to put a stop to her. It's just getting worse. End this. Before it's too late.

Numb with shock, her hands shaking, Kate takes a photo of the email, then closes Ellis's laptop. She feels nothing as she makes her way downstairs to tell Harper what she's just found.

'What is it?' Harper says. 'What's happened?' Abandoning the saucepan of pasta, she rushes towards Kate.

'I found this email to Ellis.' Kate shows her the photo. 'It's from Jennifer Seagrove, Graham White's ex-partner.'

Harper takes the phone, frowning as she reads Jennifer's words. 'I don't get it. What is she talking about? Why would the two of them be in contact with each other?'

'You were right that Ellis is involved in this,' Kate says. 'I just don't know why or how.' *That message is clearly a threat to me.*

Harper reads it again then hands Kate's phone back. 'Did Ellis reply to the email?'

'No, but it was sent at four thirty-two, just a couple of hours ago. And she gave him her address.'

'Two hours ago was around the time Ellis called me and asked me to have Thomas,' Harper says. 'So this was the emergency he needed to go out for.'

Kate paces the kitchen. 'If he's gone to meet her,' she says, 'what does that mean?'

Harper rushes back to the pasta as it starts to boil over, and turns off the hob. 'What did Ellis say when you first told him about Graham White?'

'He was really understanding. I made sure I told him the moment I felt things were getting serious between us. He was really supportive – he stood by what I'd done and never questioned me.' Now Kate wishes he *had* questioned her more in the beginning, and somehow got the truth from her. 'But then a few months ago he started bringing it up. Asking things I didn't want to talk about. At the time I just thought he must have been struggling with it.'

'Well, clearly something changed and he was no longer happy about what you'd done,' Harper says.

'He stopped trusting me.'

Harper drains the pasta and serves it onto plates for the boys. 'None of that matters now; at least we know about it and that means we can take action. We can be a step ahead of Ellis – he has no idea we found the email. You stay here with the kids. I'll drive to Jennifer's house.'

Kate shakes her head. 'This isn't about you, Harper. I'm going,' she says. 'It's time for me to face Jennifer again.'

'It's not safe for you to go, Kate. How about I just go there and see if Ellis is there?' Harper insists. 'You stay here with the boys. I just think you should stay here where you're safe – and double-lock the doors. We have no idea what Jennifer meant in that email.'

Kate still can't allow herself to fully trust Harper, but she wants to believe in her, and until proven otherwise, what choice does she have?

'I'll call you when I get there,' Harper says. 'Just make sure you stay here.'

Once Harper's gone, Kate sits with the boys while they eat,

her legs anxiously jiggling under the table. They're both talking in between mouthfuls of pasta, but Kate doesn't hear a word they say.

As soon as they've finished eating, she scoops up their plates and cups and dumps them in the sink. 'Come on, boys, get your coats on,' she says.

Thomas frowns. 'Why? Where are we going?'

'It's a surprise. Come on.'

Outside Aleena's house, nerves attack Kate. There's no way to know how Aleena will react to her turning up like this, begging Aleena to take the boys for a couple of hours. Kate hadn't even known she'd be home until they pulled up and saw the lights on. There is no plan B.

'What's going on?' Aleena says, when she registers the three of them standing on her doorstep.

'Hi. I can't really explain right now, but it's an emergency. I'm looking after Dex for Harper but something urgent came up and I need to go somewhere. I'm sorry to ask this but I can't take the boys with me.'

Aleena looks from Kate to the boys, then ushers them inside. 'Theo will be thrilled to see you,' she calls to their retreating backs. She turns to Kate. 'What's going on? I thought you and Harper—'

'We've sorted through things. I'm sorry – Ellis isn't home and there was no one else I could ask. Harper had to go somewhere. She's... helping me with something.'

Aleena frowns. 'Is this about that man when you were fifteen?'

'Could be. I won't be long.' Kate rushes back to her car, raising her hand to Aleena as she drives off.

She drops the car off at Ellis's house then makes her way to the Tube station. At this time in the evening it will be faster

than driving. Her feet pound the concrete as she walks, determination fuelling her, masking her fear. She's sick of all the lies
– it's time for the truth to come out. Not just about Mona, but
everything else. Kate won't live in fear any more – no more
hiding in shadows, watching every word she says in case she
slips up.

She takes the shortcut to the station, walking through the
park, where in the darkness she can barely see a few metres in
front of her.

It comes from out of nowhere: the arm grabbing her,
yanking her towards the trees. The hand covering her mouth,
stifling her scream. *It's happening again. Graham White. But it
can't be – he's dead.* Kate tries to kick out, and her arms flail, but
whoever's got her is too strong and she can't wrestle out from
under him. She's sure it's a man – it *feels* like a man – although
no words have been spoken. They're behind a tree now, hidden
from view, and he spins her around. He's taller than Kate; his
face is covered in a black balaclava and his hair is hidden under
a beanie hat. Definitely a man.

He shoves her to the ground, kneeling on top of her, his
hands gripping her neck. And as his thumbs press down, Kate
realises she'll only have seconds to live. She musters every
ounce of her energy as she struggles against him, prepared to
fight to the end.

But it's getting harder now, and she's losing consciousness.
In the distance she hears shouts. Footsteps running, the sound
growing louder. The man choking her loosens his grip, pauses
for a second, then jumps up and runs off. Bodies gather around
her, asking her if she's okay, helping her up.

They're all young – teenagers she guesses. And they've just
saved Kate's life.

. . .

'It must have been Ellis,' Harper says, handing her a glass of water. It's been over an hour since the attack, and Kate doesn't want to be here, sitting still while there are things she needs to do. 'Ellis wouldn't hurt me,' she says, her words as fragile as cobwebs. Kate takes the water, but her throat is too sore to drink.

Harper is agitated, unable to sit, pacing Ellis's living room, peering through the blinds every few seconds. 'Don't take offence but you're not thinking straight. Ellis has already hurt two people. Jamie and Faye Held, so—'

'We don't know that,' Kate leans forward, rubbing her sore neck.

Harper shakes her head. 'Well, he wasn't at Jennifer Seagrove's house. No sign of him. Or her. Which means Ellis could have been anywhere. Including the place you were attacked.'

'It wasn't Ellis.' But even as Kate says this, doubts set in. The man who attacked her just now was around the same build as Ellis so it's possible.

'How are you so certain?' Harper asks, checking the window again. 'I know he's Thomas's dad, but don't be blinded by that. Look at Jamie...' She trails off. 'We need to get out of here before Ellis comes back. If those teenagers hadn't come along...'

'I'd be dead,' Kate says. 'You're right – I can't be sure, but if it is Ellis, then I'll face him – I'm not running from this. It's time for the truth to come out. 'I'll wait for him to come home and confront him.' Kate springs up and rushes to the kitchen, grabbing a knife from the drawer.' If it comes to it, she'll do whatever's necessary to protect herself.

Harper follows her. 'I get why you want that, but Ellis could easily overpower you.' She points to the knife. 'So that won't protect you. Come on, you need to come and stay with me. Aleena said she'll keep the boys overnight and get them to school in the morning, which gives us the night to figure this all out.'

Kate considers her options. 'Can Lula come too? I don't want to leave her here.'

Harper hesitates. 'Um, yeah. Course.'

'Okay, then I'll come. Let me just get some things together.' Kate goes upstairs to the spare room and packs some clothes into one of Ellis's sports bags. Glancing at the door, she carefully places the knife in the bag.

Everything feels different at Harper's house this time. The hostile atmosphere – that last time she was here permeated every room – no longer exists, and it surprises Kate how comfortable she feels, how safe being away from Ellis.

'I know you won't rest, but I think you should try,' Harper says, gesturing to the sofa. 'You're probably still in shock after being attacked. Again. Tonight must have brought all of that trauma to the surface.' She sits beside Kate.

Kate lowers her head and stares at her feet. 'I'm fine. Ready to do what I have to do. I don't need to rest.'

For a moment Harper silently appraises her. 'Okay, you can help me, then. I'm going to send an email to Jennifer Seagrove and see if I can get her to talk to me. And I'll carry on going through Jamie's emails.' She pauses. 'You just get some rest.'

Upstairs in the spare room, Kate gets into bed. She knows she won't be able to sleep, but Harper is right – she should at least try to rest. Lula is hiding under the bed, where she's been since they got there.

Even under the duvet, Kate shivers, and goosebumps coat her arms. She goes to the wardrobe, wondering if there's an extra blanket in there.

Jamie's clothing is still hanging from the rail. On the top shelf, she sees a folded fleece blanket on top of a cardboard box.

Kate reaches up and as she pulls on it, the box and blanket topple to the floor, papers spreading across the carpet. Glancing at the door, she kneels down to gather them up, studying each one as she places them back in the box.

It becomes clear that they all belong to Jamie, and most of them are credit card statements or loan agreements. His finances were a mess; Kate can almost understand why he resorted to conning those poor women out of money.

She pores over every document, drowning in guilt that she's invading a dead man's privacy like this. And then, halfway through the pile, Kate picks up an A4 sheet, folded in half. The letterhead catches her attention and time stands still, the room spinning as she stares at it and reads the words written under the letterhead. She glances at the door again, then folds the paper and puts it in her pocket.

Downstairs, she peers into the living room, where Harper sits with her laptop.

'I have to go somewhere,' Kate says.

Harper looks up from her laptop. 'What? Where? It's not safe, Kate!'

But Kate doesn't stay to explain herself.

THIRTY-NINE

TUESDAY 4 FEBRUARY

Kate scans the streets as she makes her way to the Tube station, retracing the steps she took earlier before being attacked. She's on her guard this time, adrenalin pumping through her veins. When she reaches Wimbledon station, she stops at the entrance, relieved that there are still plenty of people making their way in and out.

She dials Rowan's number and waits for him to answer.

'Kate,' he says, his voice still fused with kindness. 'This really isn't—'

'Something's happened,' she says. 'Lots of things. Awful things. I've found out stuff about Ellis and I really need to talk to you. Please. Just one last time. Then you'll never hear from me again.'

There's a long pause, and Kate crosses her fingers, willing him to say yes.

'I want to help you,' Rowan says. 'I really do – but my hands are tied, Kate. This goes against my professional code of conduct.'

She's expected this. 'I'm no longer your patient, so there's no reason you can't see me as a friend, is there?'

'That's still crossing a professional line. Barely a day has passed since I stopped being your therapist.'

'I was attacked,' Kate explains. 'Just now. And it could have been Ellis. I don't know for sure. I don't want to believe it but I have to face the possibility that it was him.'

There's a sharp intake of breath. 'Are you okay? What happened? How do you know it was Ellis?'

'Because now I know everything. And you're the only person I can talk to about it. Please, Rowan.' Kate hates begging, sounding needy, but she's doing what is necessary.

'I'm glad you're okay, Kate. I hope you've called the police?'

'Yes,' Kate lies.

'That's good. Look, I'm sorry all of this is happening to you but I'm going now.'

'No, please, Rowan.'

'I beg you, Kate – please don't call me again.' He lets out a deep breath 'Or I'm the one who'll have to call the police.'

Rowan ends the call, the silence he leaves behind deafening her.

Daniella Hess looks as glamorous as she did both times Kate's seen her at Rowan's practice. Her long black maxi dress skims her body, and her hair hangs in loose waves around her shoulders. She doesn't say anything, and there's no hint of recognition on her face as she waits for Kate to explain who she is.

'Sorry to disturb you. Is Rowan home?'

Daniella frowns. 'No. He's not. Can I ask what this is about?'

'I'm a patient of his. And I really need to speak to him. He said he tells all his patients that if they're struggling and need him in an emergency, he'll be there for them.'

Daniella sighs. 'Yes, that sounds like Rowan.' She studies Kate's face. 'Are you okay? Can I help you with something?'

Kate appreciates this offer, but she doesn't have time for Rowan's gatekeeper. 'Thanks, but I just need to speak to Rowan. He can always calm me down when I'm having a panic attack.'

Daniella checks her watch. 'Look, he shouldn't be too long so do you want to come in and wait for him?'

Kate hasn't expected this, and she's touched by Daniella's kindness. She contemplates refusing this offer – she can wait across the road and catch Rowan when he turns up – but she's safer inside Rowan's house, with his wife; outside there are too many shadows for someone to lurk in. 'Thank you,' Kate says, stepping inside.

Daniella makes her coffee and they sit at the kitchen table. It's a huge room with a leather corner sofa and large granite island in the middle. It suits Daniella, but somehow Kate can't picture Rowan here amid this luxury.

There's an awkward silence, until Daniella is the first to break it. 'I remember you,' she says. 'The other day when I went to meet Rowan at his practice.'

'I didn't think you recognised me,' Kate says. 'Why would you? Rowan has a lot of patients.'

Daniella nods. 'Have you been seeing him long?' she asks. 'Oh, actually, I'm not supposed to ask that. It's none of my business. You don't have to tell me anything.'

'I'm sure it's fine if I *want* to tell you, though,' Kate says. 'It's been just over two years.'

Daniella nods. 'A long time.'

'He's really helped me,' Kate says. 'Oh, that sounds like such a cliché, but it's true. I didn't know what a void I was living in until Rowan helped me see it. He helped me find myself.' Kate studies Daniella's face – it's kind, but there's fierceness underlying it. 'You're probably wondering why I went to him in the first place.'

'No, really, it's none of my business,' Daniella says, glancing at her watch.

'It looks like you're going out somewhere,' Kate says.

'I've got time.'

Kate takes a deep breath and tells Daniella all about Graham White, the whole truth; how for years she told everyone that *she* was responsible for killing him, because she'd thought she was protecting her friend. And Daniella seems to listen without judgement, sympathy etched on her face.

'My God – that's awful! Does Rowan know this?'

'Not the truth about Mona. I only found out today. I haven't had a chance to tell him yet.'

'Is that why you're here?' Daniella asks.

'I need to get everything off my chest,' Kate says. 'It feels good just to tell you, but I still feel as though there's a virus inside me I need to flush out.'

'Yes, I imagine it's cathartic finally speaking the truth after all these years, and—'

The front door opens and they hear footsteps in the hallway.

'That will be Rowan.' Daniella stands up. 'In the kitchen,' she calls. She turns back to Kate. 'Actually, I'd better go and warn him you're here.'

But it's too late – Rowan strides into the kitchen, his face falling when he registers that Kate is sitting at his kitchen table.

Daniella springs up and kisses his cheek. 'Kate was desperate to talk to you,' she explains. 'I'll leave you two alone to have a chat.' She leaves the kitchen, closing the door behind her.

Rowan waits a moment then rushes to the table. 'What the hell are you playing at?' he hisses. 'You can't be here. This has gone too far now. I'm calling the police.' He reaches into his pocket for his phone, but Kate springs up and grabs it, shoving it in the inside pocket of her coat.

'Kate, I'm going to need my phone back, okay? Just hand it back to me and we can talk. I promise.'

Kate stares at him for a moment, acknowledging the fear in his eyes; Rowan doesn't know what she's capable of. He doesn't trust her.

And he's right not to.

Kate pulls out the kitchen knife that's been in her pocket since she left Harper's house, and stares at the blade.

Rowan backs away, glancing at the closed kitchen door. But Daniella warmed to Kate, she can tell, so Kate's confident she's in another part of the house. 'Kate, what are you doing? Please, I'm truly sorry for what's happened to you, but this isn't the answer. Please give me the knife. Or just put it down on the table, and we can talk.

Kate moves closer towards him, relishing the fear in his eyes; it fuels her. 'Sit down, Rowan. And don't think for one second that I'm going anywhere.'

FORTY

ONE YEAR AGO

Today's session with Rowan was heavy going, and Kate feels as though he's delved deeper than ever. It's terrifying to think that she might say the wrong thing, and that the truth about Mona will come out, so she keeps any mention of Graham White vague. Mona's threat all those years ago still haunts Kate.

She's never been a big drinker, so hasn't paid much attention to the bar down the road from Rowan's practice, but this evening she's drawn to it. There's a book in her bag she's been meaning to read but never seems to have the chance. Kate steps inside, relieved to find it fairly empty, and heads to the bar.

Kate orders a gin and tonic from a female bartender with tattoos covering most of her skin, then finds a booth in the corner and takes out her book, losing herself in the words, pushing from her mind how strangely Ellis has been acting over the last few weeks. He's still there for Thomas, and for Kate if she needs any help around the house, but there's a vacant expression in his eyes when he looks at her, as if he's checked out of their marriage. It's as if there's a glass partition between them, allowing them to see each other but never quite reach each other.

'Hello.'

Kate looks up to see Rowan Hess smiling at her.

'Oh, hi.' Her cheeks flush. She's never seen Rowan outside of his office and she feels embarrassed. As if he's caught her doing something she shouldn't be. 'I don't normally come in here,' she explains. 'Just fancied a quick drink before I go home.'

Rowan holds up his hand. 'No need to explain anything to me. You have every right to go to any pub you wish. None of anyone's business.' He smiles.

'I don't normally drink alone,' Kate says.

'*I* do.' He laughs. 'Nothing wrong with that after a long day. And I know I pushed you today.'

Kate shrugs. 'Guess that's what I'm paying you for.'

He nods. 'Anyway, you're not drinking alone.' He gestures to her book.

'Oh... right.'

'We're never alone when we've got a good book, are we?'

'Well, I'm not far enough in to make that judgement yet, but I'll let you know.'

Rowan laughs. 'Well, I'm off to order a nice pint and read what's happening in the news. See you next week, Kate.'

He turns to head to the bar.

'Wait!' Kate calls.

Rowan stops and turns back, raising his eyebrows.

'Seems silly both of us sitting on our own. Would you like to join me?' Kate's boldness takes her by surprise, and she can only imagine what Rowan will think of it. There's no way he'll sit and have a drink with her.

There's a flicker of hesitation, and Kate prepares herself for his rejections, but then Rowan shrugs. 'Why not?' he says, taking off his coat and placing it over the back of the chair opposite Kate. 'Back in a moment.'

While he heads to the bar, flutters of excitement explode in

Kate's stomach. *Did Rowan Hess just agree to have a drink with me?* This can't be appropriate, but Kate doesn't care. She's done with being the good girl – always doing the right thing. Look where that's got her so far. If she wants to have a drink with her therapist, then she can. It doesn't have to mean anything. But if Kate's honest with herself, she does find Rowan attractive; he's not conventionally good-looking, but his aura is powerful and she finds that intoxicating. Even more so now that he's agreed to have a drink with her.

Even if Ellis has been acting strangely, Kate would never do anything. This is just a drink, and Rowan would never cross that line.

When he gets back to Kate's table, Rowan's eyes dart around the pub, while he only half focuses on what Kate is saying. She understands his anxiety – if anyone were to see them it would be easy for the innocent drink to be misconstrued.

'So how's life outside of being a therapist?' Kate asks, to set him at ease. She doesn't want this to feel like an extension of one of their therapy sessions, so she will turn the tables and get him talking about himself.

'My life's... complicated,' he says, downing too much beer in one gulp.

'How so?' Kate asks. She stares at her gin and tonic, her thirst for it has seeped away.

He clears his throat. 'You don't want to hear about my life,' he says.

Yes I do. In this moment, I want nothing more than to know the man beyond my therapist. She tells him this, and notices the slight flare in his cheeks.

'Well... my life's been complicated since... since *you* came into it.'

His words sit between them, as solid as stone.

'I don't understand,' Kate says. *Is this what I think it is?*

He shakes his head. 'I don't think I should say any more. I don't want to detonate *that* bomb.'

Kate stares at him, unable to comprehend Rowan's words. He's hardly had enough beer to be tipsy, so this isn't alcohol speaking for him. 'What exactly are you saying?' she asks.

'I've already said too much,' Rowan says, standing and grabbing his coat. 'I'm sorry, Kate.'

She stares after his retreating back, then grabs her bag and coat and rushes after him, catching up with him when he's crossed the road. 'Wait!'

He turns around, and she doesn't expect him to stop but he does, walking backwards so he's still edging away from her. He's scared.

'I feel the same,' she calls.

That stops him, and slowly he walks towards her.

'Maybe I didn't realise it until just now,' Kate continues, 'but it's there. It's been there for a while.'

'This often happens with patients and therapists,' Rowan explains. 'We have to acknowledge it and not act on it. I... I think it might be best if I refer you to someone else.'

'Yes, do that,' Kate says. 'But don't ignore *this*.' She moves towards him, as if she has no control of her body, and Rowan does the same.

'We're both married,' he says.

'I know.' She thinks of Ellis and how cold he's been towards her, how he's been asking a lot of questions about Graham White lately, even though he knows Kate doesn't want to talk about it. Is it possible Ellis can no longer accept what she did?

Rowan reaches for Kate. Pushing back a strand of hair that's fallen across her cheek, he leans down to kiss her on the mouth. Softly at first, then more urgently. Then he's pulling her into an alleyway between the parade of shops, and the two of them tear at each other's clothes, desperate to feel each other's flesh.

. . .

Their affair continues for months: snatched moments after their therapy sessions, whenever Frieda is out for lunch. Rowan's secretary never questions why he often tells her to take an extended lunch break. It's intoxicating; the pull of Rowan is so strong that Kate feels no guilt when she's with him. This is right where she's meant to be.

When those brief moments are no longer enough, they gravitate to hotels. There's a small one near Rowan's practice that never seems crowded. Rowan always insists on paying, and always does so in cash. All the hotel staff must know what they're doing – in and out within a couple of hours, never staying the night. It makes Kate giddy to think that she's doing something so illicit. Sometimes she and Rowan venture into the small lobby area and have coffee before they go their separate ways, and in those moments they pretend the world outside doesn't exist. And that this can never come back to haunt them.

Until the day Rowan tells her it's over.

They've just finished a therapy session, in which he's grilled her about Ellis and tried to make Kate see that she's being paranoid about her husband's behaviour. And then he says the words Kate's half expected, because deep down she's known this couldn't continue.

'I'm so sorry, Kate.' Rowan can barely look at her. 'I... I really do care about you. But I need to focus on my marriage, and get back on track with' – he flaps his arms – 'this place. I've been letting things slide, and I'm not proud of how I've carried on. I think we need to put an end to this now.' He stands up and crosses to the window, staring out at the street. 'I've never done anything like this before. And I never will again. I'm sorry. I took advantage of you and it's all my doing.'

Once the shock of his words passes, Kate takes a deep breath. 'All good things come to an end, don't they?' She smiles, to prove she's okay with this, and the truth is she *is* fine with it. Rowan was just a distraction, a way to escape her demons.

The relief on Rowan's face is tangible. 'I'm so glad to hear that.' He turns to her and glances at the clock, signalling their time is over.

'I'll see you next week, then,' Kate says, heading for the door. 'I'm booked in on my normal Friday.'

'What? No, hold on. You don't understand.' Rowan crosses to her.

She turns around and waits.

'Kate, when I said we need to end it – I meant our therapy sessions too. All of it. All of *us*.'

All the blood feels like it's draining from her face. Kate can easily accept their affair being over, but not this. Never this. She depends on Rowan. He knows all about her and there's no way Kate can start over with a new therapist. No way can she let that happen.

'No,' she says. 'Like I said, I'll see you next Friday.'

Rowan stares at her. 'Kate. Are you listening to me? I'm telling you I'm no longer your therapist. It's not possible. I'm going to—'

Kate walks towards him, standing close enough to smell his Calvin Klein aftershave. 'I'm going to pretend we've never had this conversation,' she whispers. 'Wouldn't it be awful if your wife were to find out what we've been doing? I'd really hate for that to happen. And I'd hate even more for your career to be over because someone reported you. What would you even do? This place is everything to you, isn't it?'

Rowan's eyes widen and sweat trickles down his forehead. 'No, Kate, please—'

'I'll see you next week,' she says, leaving his office without glancing back. She doesn't want to see the fear on his face.

FORTY-ONE

THE DAY OF JAMIE'S MURDER

Jamie knows in his gut that Harper doesn't love him. She puts on a good enough show, but he sees through her act. What he can't understand is why she's still with him after everything he's put her through. Of course it was his fault she lost their baby. He's tried to tell himself it would have happened even if he'd been at home and had managed to get Harper to the hospital sooner, but in the core of his being he knows he's responsible.

One more time. That's it. He's got to do it this one last time and then Jamie can get out of this black hole he's in. After tonight, he will be free.

He stands in front of the mirror in their bedroom, smoothing down his jeans. He doesn't notice Harper until he turns around and sees her standing in the doorway, watching him. 'How long have you been there?' he asks.

Her eyes narrow. 'Where are you going?'

'Out. With work people. Just for a couple of drinks.' *Don't push. Don't ask any more questions.*

'Where?'

He's used to Harper's questions by now – that's what happens when all trust is eroded. Again, his fault. 'Probably into town,' he says. 'Leicester Square. Somewhere like that.' *Nowhere near there.*

'You're doing it again!' Harper erupts. 'Lying. You said you weren't doing it any more!'

Jamie's too defeated to argue. What's the point? Harper always finds out anyway. He doesn't know how, but she has her ways. 'Just one more time,' he says. 'And that's it. This will pay off all my debts. I'll be free, Harper.'

A flash of anger crosses her face. 'I don't care! Find another way.'

'Harper, I don't have a choice.'

'There's always a choice. Choose me and Dexter. Isn't that what matters?'

Jamie hangs his head – Harper is right, this is the choice he should make, but he's trapped, buried alive with no way to get out until he sees this through tonight. 'I swear to you – this is it. Forever. Will you just trust me?'

Harper snorts. 'Trust you?' she screams. 'You're delusional, Jamie. You really are.' She folds her arms. Jamie hasn't noticed until now how thin she's got. 'I'm not putting up with it any more. It's over, Jamie.' She pulls off her ring and throws it at him. He tries to catch it but misses and it lands by his feet.

'Don't do this,' he says, picking it up. 'We can work all this out. After tonight. There's always a way to fix things.'

'I don't like the way you fix things,' Harper snarls. 'You don't give a damn about Dexter, do you? What would he think if he knew what you were doing?'

'He'll never know. And after tonight it's all in the past.'

'That doesn't make it right!'

'I know. I know.' Jamie flops down on the bed and buries his head in his hands. 'Don't you think I wish I'd made different choices?'

Harper closes her eyes. 'I don't care any more. You can stay in the Richmond flat tonight and then first thing in the morning

I'm putting this house on the market. Severing all ties. Dexter and I can move back to Southend. We'll both be happy there.' The hostility in her voice unsettles him.

'No! I won't let you take my son away from me.'

Harper shakes her head. 'Don't you get it, Jamie? Dexter isn't your son!'

Her words shatter in the air, turning Jamie's blood cold. 'What are you talking about? Of course he is. Just because I'm—'

'No, he isn't!' Harper screams. 'That night I followed you from that restaurant – I was on a date too, remember? His name's Pierre. I spent the night with him after I followed you to that woman's place. I was in a dark place and wasn't thinking straight.' Harper's voice is quieter now, flooded with shame.

But Jamie can't blame her for this act, not after what he's done. Lying about Dexter, though – that's unforgiveable. Rage overcomes him and his hands clench into fists. It's an involuntary action but he'd never hit Harper. Never hurt any woman.

Numb, he turns away from her and begins packing his clothes. He doesn't care if Harper's telling the truth and he's not Dexter's biological father – that boy is still his son and always will be. Nothing can take away the ten years that Jamie's been his dad. 'I'll leave,' he tells Harper. 'But I'm not giving up my son. I'd have to be dead before I let anyone take him away from me.'

Jamie tries to force Harper's words from his head as he walks along Putney High Street. He comforts himself with the thought that she's lying, and he vows to never think of it again. Dexter might not look exactly like him, but Jamie sees little of Harper in him too. That happens sometimes. Dexter is his son. End of story.

He makes his way to the bar with the silly name; he knows

that's where Kate Mason is headed tonight as he'd overheard her talking to her friend while they walked their kids to school. He was right behind Kate, as he has been for days now, getting a sense of her so that he knows how to strike when they're face to face. And what Jamie's learned about Kate Mason is that she seems like a decent woman. What she's done to deserve what's happening to her, he has no idea. He's just following instructions, and he tries not to dwell on the reasons.

In Tequila Mockingbird, he makes his way to the bar and stands next to a group of men, all of them dressed in suits. He assumes they've come straight from the office. Jamie's got his suit on too, minus the tie, so he easily looks like he's part of this group.

On a sofa in the corner, Kate and her friend are sitting with drinks, and Kate's rigid body language tells him she doesn't feel entirely comfortable here. Jamie can use this to his advantage.

In a stroke of luck, Kate approaches the crowded bar and stands right near him, and Jamie tells the guys he's near to make room for her. She'll appreciate that, and it gives him a way in. It might even make her think he's with this group, not a lone stalker like he is.

It's easier than Jamie thinks to strike up a conversation, and soon they're sitting alone, talking about their lives as if they're old friends. It makes Jamie sad. This isn't what he's used to doing – Kate isn't his normal target. And on top of that, she's nice. He likes her. Under different circumstances he might actually want to start something real with her. But he's got a job to do, and he needs to see this through, as much as he detests himself right now.

Again, luck is on his side and they end up sharing an Uber. Kate's idea. No coercion from him necessary. Which only makes him drown in guilt.

By the time the Uber pulls up outside Jamie's apartment building, Harper, and the bombshell she dropped, is far from his thoughts. Kate has helped him escape his life, even if only temporarily. He doesn't know what kind of trouble she's mixed up in; all he's been given is a brief to spike her drink with some concoction he knows nothing about, so that he can get her back to his place. But Jamie has no intention of slipping anything into her drink, and it's untouched in the inside zipped pocket of his coat. This isn't Jamie's world, and if he wasn't desperate for the large cash sum, he'd have no part of it. He doesn't know what the plan is for Kate, but he prays she won't get harmed. That was the assurance Jamie had demanded when he agreed to do this. But there's no honour among thieves.

Kate is laughing, and her smile lights up her face. All the tension she exhibited in the bar seems to have evaporated, and he's pleased to think that might be something to do with him.

His streak of luck continues when the Uber driver claims they've only made one booking, and the next Uber Kate can book is forty minutes away.

'Want to come in for coffee?' Jamie asks. 'At least you'll be dry while you wait.'

'I'm not going in your house – I don't even know you.'

'Actually, it's a flat. Does that make a difference?' Jamie laughs, to hide how nervous he feels now that this is really happening. He tells Kate about letting his wife keep the house, and mentions Dex, just to make her feel more secure.

It works, and Kate agrees to come inside for coffee, once he's shown her some ID.

'Here you go,' Jamie says, handing her his driving licence. 'Just ignore the mugshot.'

It hasn't been Jamie's intention to sleep with Kate, that was never what this arrangement was about. All he had to do was slip her the drug, then get her to his flat. Well, he's done that now – minus the drugging part – and now he's not sure what he's supposed to do.

But Jamie is enjoying Kate's company, more than he's done

with any other woman for years, including Harper. And now they're in bed together, ravishing each other's naked bodies.

Afterwards, while they're lying together and Kate talks about her son, Jamie wonders why he hasn't had a call or message asking if Kate is unconscious yet. Jamie looks at her and smiles. Twisting a strand of her hair around his finger, he allows himself to get lost in her. Fuck the money. He'll find a way to give it back the half he's already received. He wants no part of this.

'What are you doing tomorrow? Well, today actually,' he asks, when she's getting dressed to wait for her Uber. It's gone two a.m. and he'd asked her to stay, but Kate had insisted she needed to get home. *Probably better that way. She shouldn't be in this flat.*

Kate shrugs. 'No plans. Thomas will be with his dad.'

'Then come back and see me. I've got some things to do in the morning but you could come in the afternoon. Around two?'

She smiles and nods. 'Yeah, okay.'

He kisses her forehead, breathing in her scent. She smells like roses and he likes it. He likes Kate Mason.

The moment she's gone, panic overcomes him. He's taken a lot of money to get Kate to his flat – money that he's already used to pay off some of his debts – and now he's let her go. There will be repercussions, he's sure.

As Jamie clears their mugs away, there's a knock on the door. Kate must have forgotten something. Smiling, Jamie rushes to answer it.

And the minute he opens the door, he knows he shouldn't have.

She's lost count of how many times she's tried to call Kate. Harper should have stopped her leaving – she's got a terrible feeling that tonight won't end well.

A sudden pounding on the door startles her. She springs up from the sofa and makes her way to the front door, checking her doorbell camera on her phone. It's Ellis. And Harper knows why he's here.

'What do you want?' she shouts from behind the door.

'Let me in, Harper. I need to see Kate. Now. Where is she?'

'She's not here. Just go before I call the police.'

There's a moment of silence before Ellis responds. 'I think that's a good idea. Call the police. Because there's a lot I need to tell them.'

This has to be a ruse, and Harper's not falling for it. She puts the chain on the door and opens it a fraction. 'Why the hell would you want me to call the police, after what you've done?'

'What is it you think I've done, Harper? Just let me in before all the neighbours wake up.'

It's a split-second decision, and Harper has no idea what's

about to happen, but if Ellis knows where Kate is then Harper needs to find out. She pulls the chain back and slowly opens the door. 'I've got a video doorbell and it's filmed you coming here. If anything happens to me, then—'

Ellis steps inside. 'What do you think I'm planning to do, Harper? Why would I hurt you? Turns out you've actually done me a favour by trying to turn Kate's life upside down.'

She doesn't trust him, but time is running out. 'Where is Kate? What have you done?'

He frowns. 'I'm here looking for Kate – why would I be here if I'd done anything to her? I need to see her. Now.'

'If I knew where she was then I wouldn't be asking you, would I?' Harper snaps. 'It was you who attacked her, wasn't it?'

Ellis's face crumples. 'What are you talking about? Kate's been attacked?'

'This evening. She thinks it was you. I do too.'

Ellis's mouth hangs open as he digests Harper's words. 'But... what happened? Is she okay?' His voice is frantic.

'Thankfully a group of teenagers walked past and the man ran off before he could do serious harm. But he tried to strangle her. He wanted her dead.' She glares at Ellis, willing the truth to come out of his mouth.

'Jesus! Where is she now, then? We need to find her!'

'I told her to stay here but she said there was something urgent she needed to do. A bit like you did earlier. Now I don't know where she is.' She studies Ellis's face. His concern seems genuine, but then he must be adept at lying by now. 'It must have been you,' Harper says. 'Who else would want to hurt her? And you were with Jamie in a bar months ago – Maddy saw you! She'd come to meet you and saw you talking to Jamie.'

Ellis frowns. 'If you're talking about that time in the summer, that was a meeting with a potential client. He worked for the Financial Conduct Authority. But he never got back to me after that meeting. I never saw him again. I only saw him that once and I'm not great with remembering faces. He told me his name was Ewan.'

'That's his middle name,' Harper says.

'So that's why Kate kept showing me pictures of Jamie. I didn't recognise him – he looked different when we met up. He had facial hair.'

This all seems plausible, but Harper will never trust Ellis. 'I still don't believe you,' she says.

'Why the hell would I want to hurt my wife? I love her!'

Harper can tell Ellis is distraught, but still she corrects him. 'She's not your wife any more, Ellis. You need to accept that.'

Ellis shifts his feet. 'I know! But that doesn't mean I don't still love her. She's the mother of my son. We'll always be family. And that's why—' He stops short and stares at Harper. 'Why are you so concerned about Kate all of a sudden? You wanted to destroy her life! How do I know *you* didn't arrange for someone to attack her?'

'Because that fire changed everything,' Harper says. 'It's not likely that a woman who could rush back into a burning house to save a child could also be a cold-blooded killer.'

Ellis fixes his eyes on the floor. 'I know the truth, Harper. Finally, after all these years I *know.*'

'What are you talking about?'

'The truth about Kate. And I think you need to know it too. Everyone does.'

For a moment, Harper falters. Has she been wrong to trust Kate? Or is Ellis gaslighting her? 'What are you saying, Ellis?'

He takes a deep breath. 'I've just been with Jennifer Seagrove. She was Graham White's ex-girlfriend.'

'I know who she is. Go on.'

'I've been in contact with her. For months now. Because I know Kate's been lying about what happened back then.'

Harper swallows the lump in her throat and waits for Ellis to continue.

'I first reached out to Jennifer about a year ago. Something was bothering me about Kate's story and I wanted to find out the truth. I... I think I suspected that she might have... known Graham White.'

'What do you mean exactly?'

Ellis takes a deep breath. 'I mean – I wondered if he'd done something to her. You know – groomed her into having some kind of relationship with him. Child abuse. That's what I mean.'

Harper stares at him, numb with shock.

'So I managed to track down Jennifer and we struck up a kind of friendship. I suppose she found it okay talking to me as I had nothing to do with the past. I didn't know Kate then. I think maybe she saw me as another innocent victim in all the lies.'

'What lies?' Harper holds her breath; she doesn't want to hear that Kate killed Graham White deliberately. She's been so sure that she could trust Kate after all.

'Jennifer admitted she had a letter that was sent to her the day before Graham died,' Ellis continues. 'It was from a schoolgirl, claiming she was in a relationship with Graham. It had so many details that Jennifer couldn't ignore it. Times and places they'd meet, that sort of thing. And all of it tied in with when Jennifer wasn't with Graham. But it's been years and Jennifer couldn't find the letter to show me.'

Harper considers this. 'Jennifer could be lying about it, then. Where's the proof?'

'What would be the point?'

Harper's not sure – all she knows is that everybody lies.

'And I believed her,' Ellis says. 'Now even more.' He sighs. 'I went round there tonight because after she emailed me, she'd called me and told me she'd finally found it. She'd put it inside an old notebook and had only just come across it when she was packing to move house.'

'Just tell me,' Harper says. She will face whatever it is she needs to.

'The letter was exactly as Jennifer had said. A confession from a fifteen-year-old girl. Explaining she didn't want the affair on her conscience, and she wanted Jennifer to know what kind of man she was with. But the thing is – it wasn't Kate's handwriting.'

Harper's eyes widen. 'What? How can you tell? She was fifteen when she wrote it.'

'Handwriting doesn't change that much. This girl's writing was completely different to Kate's. The shape of the letter Y. It wasn't Kate's writing at all. Nothing about it was similar.'

'So who wrote it, then?'

'I managed to track down some old school friends of Kate's on Facebook. And they all kept coming up with the same name. Kate had a best friend called Mona Shaw. I found her on LinkedIn and messaged her. She didn't want to talk to me at first but I told her I had the letter she wrote, and that handwriting experts would be able to determine that it was hers. But she never got back to me. What if she's the one who attacked Kate? I think Kate might have threatened to finally tell the truth, and that's what this is all about. Maybe Jamie too.'

Harper can't see how. 'But Kate said it was a man.'

'She could have been mistaken. Or Mona could have got someone to do it for her.' The urgency is back in his voice. 'We need to find Kate now. Are you sure you don't know where she could have gone?'

'No! One minute she was going to bed – the next she'd rushed off.'

'It's got to be Mona Shaw,' Ellis says. 'I don't understand it but I need to find Kate!'

'How are we going to find her?'

Ellis stares at his feet. 'I'm ashamed to say this... but I never took family sharing off my phone – and if Kate didn't either then we should be able to see where she is. I'd forgotten we even had it on. So much has happened since we separated.'

'What are you waiting for?' Harper says. 'Check it now!'

Harper watches Ellis as he checks his phone, relieved when a smile appears on his face. 'Come on!' she urges. She's got to take a gamble and trust Ellis. 'Before it's too late.'

Kate's aware of Rowan watching her as she pulls out a kitchen chair and sits close to him. She's tempted to ram the knife into the expensive-looking leather, but holds back, aware that he could spring for the knife at any moment. She needs to be ready for that.

Rowan's eyes are devoid of warmth, darker somehow, as he stares at her. 'What exactly do you want, Kate? You want Daniella to find out about us?' He smiles. 'She won't believe you,' he whispers. 'You're a deranged ex-patient of mine, threatening to lie about me if I don't continue being your therapist.'

Kate stands, and moves closer to him. 'It's gone way past that, Rowan. I don't give a damn about you being my therapist. That's the last thing I want.' Words Kate never thought she'd utter.

Rowan flinches. This isn't what he's expected her to say. 'Then what are you doing here? Is this about us? It's been over for months. You know it was a mistake and I'm not going back there. I've got my wife and career to think about.'

The door opens and Daniella pokes her head in, forcing Kate to conceal the knife behind her back.

'I'm just off out now,' Daniella announces. 'See you later.' From the door, she blows Rowan a kiss then turns to Kate. 'Nice to meet you.'

Kate waits until the door closes, then draws the knife again. 'She's so trusting, isn't she? Leaving you here alone with me.'

'Daniella has nothing to worry about. I would never—'

'Never what? Cheat on her for months. Sleep with a patient? Tell a patient that you can't live without them. That's what you said to me, isn't it? Remember? I do. Every single time we were together. Those memories will never fade.'

Rowan stands up, and Kate holds up the knife. 'Sit down!'

'Woah, calm down.' He holds up his hands. 'Please, Kate, don't do this. I'm sure we can work something out. Just give me the knife.'

'Sit down!' she shouts.

Finally he sits back down, and Kate lunges towards him, coming up behind his chair and holding the knife to his neck. She senses his fear, and this is what she wants.

'Please, Kate. I'm sorry if I hurt you. I did really care about you. Those times we spent together meant a lot to me.'

It's as if he's reading from a memorised script, and Kate feels her body swell with rage. She thought she had a hold on her anger, but here it is again, erupting violently. She presses the blade against his neck, relishes his sharp intake of breath. Is this what Mona felt like when she killed Graham White? Kate will never know if it truly was self-defence, but she suspects otherwise. And now, ironically, Kate is in the same position.

She leans in close to Rowan's ear. 'Why the fuck did you do it?'

'I told you. I fell for you. I'm sorry, I shouldn't have acted on my impulses. That goes against everything I—'

'Stop!' Kate screams. 'I'm not talking about that!' With her free hand, she pulls out the sheet of paper from her coat pocket.

Rowan stares at her, and slowly she sees the moment everything becomes clear for him. Now he knows exactly why she's here.

Kate clutches the knife tighter.

'Hello, Jamie.'

Jamie tries to slam the door, but Rowan wedges his foot in the gap. 'What the hell? Get the fuck out.'

'I think we need to have a little chat, don't we?' Rowan forces his way in and shuts the door.

The blood drains from Jamie's face. 'I'll call the police,' he says, quickly realising that his phone is nowhere in sight; he probably left it on the bedside table.

'And what exactly will you tell them?' Rowan snorts. 'That you've taken fifty thousand pounds from me?' And you haven't even delivered the service I paid for. That's hardly fair, is it?'

Jamie shrinks against the wall. 'I'll get your money back,' he says. 'All of it. Just go.'

'And how will you do that? I'm sure it's already gone. And you're already drowning in debt.' Rowan steps towards him, glancing around. 'Nice place. You'll probably have to sell it.'

'I can't,' Jamie says. 'Renting this place out is my only income.'

'Not my problem,' Rowan says. He wanders into the living room as if it's his own apartment. He scans the room, then goes back into the hallway, peering into the two bedrooms. 'Want to tell me why Kate Mason isn't here?'

'I... She was here. I did what you asked and got her here. She was here for a few hours, but then she wanted to go home. What could I do? I couldn't force her to stay.'

Rowan nods, his top lip curling. 'You didn't give her the drugs, did you? If you had, then she'd never have been able to walk out of here on her own.'

'I... I couldn't do it. It's not right! Why the hell are you doing this?'

'You're asking me that now? You didn't seem to care when we made the deal. You agreed to all of it.'

Jamie needs to get this man out of there – he's dangerous, and has too much to lose. There's a wildness in Rowan's eyes that scares him. 'I was wrong. And that was before I met Kate. She's... she's a decent person. Why are you doing this?'

'Decent people don't sleep with their therapists. Or black-mail them and threaten to get them struck off.'

Jamie's eyes widen. 'What?'

'Oh, didn't you know about Kate and me? Guess that didn't come up in the couple of hours you spent with her. Not exactly small talk, is it? Oh, by the way – I slept with my therapist for almost a year.'

This revelation floors him; was he wrong about Kate Mason? Quickly he pulls himself together. None of this matters now – Kate will soon find out what Jamie has done and there'll be no hope for them to start any kind of relationship. 'It's... none of my business,' he says. Besides, Jamie has done far worse. 'It's up to Kate what she does.'

'True. But is it okay if she's killed someone?' Rowan's words echo around the hallway.

'What are you talking about?' This man will say anything, and Jamie just needs to figure out how to get him out of here.

'Kate killed a man when she was fifteen. That's why she

started having therapy with me. I guess it all finally caught up with her. I'm guessing this didn't come up in your conversation either.'

Jamie doesn't want to believe this, but as much as he liked Kate, the truth is he knows nothing about her. 'Even if that's true – why would you want to drug her? What were you planning to do to her?' He can't keep the contempt from his voice.

Rowan screws up his face. 'Not what you're thinking. I've already been with her – I don't need to force myself on her. She would have quite willingly come back to me any time.'

Jamie wants to pummel his fists into Rowan's smug face. 'Then why? Who's this man you're claiming she killed?'

'It's not a claim, it's a fact. His name was Graham White.'

Jamie glances past Rowan to the hallway If he's quick, maybe he could make a run for it. Through the front door. He knows this building well, there's a chance he could get away. 'So that's what this is all about? Revenge for what you think Kate did when she was fifteen?'

Rowan throws his head back and stares at the ceiling. 'I'm losing my patience here, Jamie. Graham White has got nothing to do with this.'

'Then what?' Jamie demands. 'If you want to see your money again, then tell me!'

Rowan stares at him. 'Don't suppose it matters now if you know.' He sighs. 'I suppose it's the least I can do.'

Jamie freezes, scanning the room for something he can use as a weapon. This man is unhinged, and with every passing second Jamie is realising he might not get out of here alive.

'She started blackmailing me,' Rowan says. 'After I ended our relationship and told her I couldn't be her therapist any more. Let's just say she didn't take that well. She threatened to tell my wife, and report me.' Rowan's eyes narrow. 'I can't lose my wife. And I've worked too hard for my career. Kate would destroy my whole life if she talks about our affair. I can't let that happen. Do you understand that, Jamie?'

'So she was forcing you to stay in a relationship with her?' Jamie can't get his head around this. He's no expert but Kate hadn't seemed the obsessive type.

'No, that's not what she wanted,' Rowan says. 'She wanted me to keep being her therapist. She didn't care at all about our affair being over.'

Jamie struggles to comprehend this. 'That doesn't make sense. Why would she force you to continue as her therapist?' *And why wouldn't she want this despicable man out of her life?*

'Because she developed an attachment to me. Not in a romantic way – I don't think she gave a damn about our relationship – it was never me she wanted, it was only ever my help. She was under the false impression that I was the only one who understood her, who could help her heal.'

'What were you planning with her? Why did you want her drugged?'

'I'm sorry, Jamie. You're just collateral damage in all this. I didn't want it to be this way. Any of it.' Rowan glances around the room. 'This wasn't exactly what I had planned, but it could still work. Kate was here for long enough to have left DNA evidence. And with her anger issues added to the mix... I'm sorry, Jamie. It's the only way I can make sure she can never hurt me, and make sure it never comes back to me.'

Jamie is confused again. Nothing Rowan says makes sense. But then, when Rowan steps towards him, pulling something from his coat, Jamie finally understands. 'No,' he says, as his palms begin to sweat. 'Don't do this. Please.'

Rowan moves closer towards him. 'Kate's already killed someone. It's not too much of a stretch for people to believe she could do it again.'

The last thing Jamie sees is the blade of the knife, and the last thing he feels is the cold chill as Rowan thrusts it in his neck. And his last thought is that Kate Mason doesn't deserve this.

FORTY-FIVE
SIX MONTHS AGO

Rowan feels as though his life's hanging by a fine thread, and Kate Mason has the power to pull on it and unravel everything. He's sick of the way she strolls into her appointments as though nothing has happened, as if equilibrium exists between them, and she isn't forcing him to sit there and listen to her. He didn't mind before – he wanted to help her, but the way she's made him feel powerless sickens him. He can't let her keep doing this. And Rowan might just have found a way to makes sure that happens.

Walking to the door of his office, he plasters a smile on his face and prepares to greet his next patient. Jamie Archer. Rowan quite likes him, he's an interesting man, but Rowan can't see how he's going to get himself out of the mess he's in unless he's willing to do some serious work on himself. After all, most of the time there's a reason we are the way we are if we search hard enough to find it. 'Hello, Jamie,' he says. 'Would you like to come in?'

Jamie nods and follows Rowan into his office, keeping his head low. Shame seems to surround him whenever he walks in here, and Rowan wishes he would shed it and fully embrace his therapy. Perhaps today will help.

'Take a seat, Jamie. How have you been this last week?'

Jamie sinks onto the sofa and shakes his head. He's leaning forward as usual, never at ease enough to sit back and relax. 'Not good. I don't know how to get out of this hole I'm in. I've got those women demanding their money back. I've tried to stop but I need to pay my debts. I promised Harper I wouldn't do it any more. I tried to stop... you know, with the women at the gym. But how else can I get out of the mess I'm in?'

Interesting. Will this change Jamie's susceptibility? 'Do you think there might be other ways to sort out your financial situation?' Rowan asks. 'There's always another way.'

Jamie shrugs. 'No job will clear my debts. And I'm not declaring myself bankrupt. The only reason I can afford therapy is because Harper insists on paying. She thinks it will help stop me going back to my old ways so we can save our marriage.'

Even though he shouldn't be – and wouldn't normally be – Rowan's silently pleased to hear about the mess Jamie's in. 'Are you sure it's just your financial situation that got you involved with these three women?' Rowan asks. 'Could there be another reason?'

Jamie wrinkles his nose. 'This isn't about the women. It's not about *sex*. Not at all. It's about me trying to claw my life back. For my family.'

Rowan's not convinced; if Jamie would open up about his childhood, there's sure to be something there that led him down this path, with no regard for the women he's conning. But from what he's learned about Jamie so far, his mother was a strong figure in his life. Hardworking and nurturing. His father too. Rowan's not quite sure what could explain it, and if he's honest with himself, what Jamie does disgusts him.

'I'm desperate,' Jamie says. 'This is affecting my whole life.'

'Do you believe that if your debts were all cleared, you'd be able to make a fresh start?'

Jamie nods. 'Yeah. Definitely.'

Rowan needs to test the waters. He leans forward and lowers his voice. 'Can I trust you, Jamie?'

Jamie frowns and shifts on his seat. 'Yeah. But what do you mean exactly?'

Rowan glances at the door. 'I'm taking a huge risk here. This is completely outside of my capacity as your therapist, and I'm risking my professional reputation.' He pauses. No going back now. 'But I want to help you, Jamie, and I don't think, for you, the answer to this particular issue lies in therapy.' Rowan takes a deep breath. 'What I'm about to tell you absolutely can't be spoken about outside these walls.'

Jamie's eyes widen. He must be confused that his therapist is having this kind of conversation with him. He has no idea that Rowan is just as desperate as he is. 'I might know someone who could help you,' Rowan says. There. It's said now and can't be taken back. This is the biggest risk of Rowan's life and he's taking it because of Kate. Rowan's hatred towards her intensifies. If only he hadn't stopped to have that drink with her. A dreadful mistake on his part. What had he been thinking? He's never done anything like that before.

'I don't understand,' Jamie says.

'It's simple,' Rowan explains. 'If you're prepared not to ask any questions, that is.'

'Okay.'

'This person needs a favour and is prepared to offer one hundred thousand pounds.'

Jamie's head jolts up and he stares at Rowan. Perhaps he's wondering if this is some sort of trap. 'What... what for?'

'No questions, remember? All you'd have to do is meet a woman. Just like you've already been doing. Get to know her and then take her back to your flat. That's it.'

Jamie frowns. 'That's all? For a hundred grand? I don't get it. Why would someone give me that much money just to take a woman back to my place?'

Looking across at Jamie, a flood of pity overcomes Rowan. If Jamie agrees to this, then he's signing his own death warrant. 'Remember I said the deal is you can't ask questions. Just follow the simple instructions.'

Jamie stares at him and Rowan can tell he's torn. Of course he's thinking that this is too good an offer to be true, too easy, and that there must be a catch. It feels like hours before Jamie responds. 'Okay,' he says, exhaling a deep breath. 'I'll do it. I don't have much choice.'

'Okay. Good. There's one other thing,' Rowan says. 'This woman will need to be drugged once you get her to your place. Or before. She needs to have no memory of how she got there or what she's doing there.'

Jamie's eyes widen. 'No! Is this... are we talking rape? No way. Never. I'm not being any part of—'

'It's nothing at all like that,' Rowan assures him. 'Not at all. Don't worry – this woman will not be harmed in any way whatsoever.' Rowan can picture it now: Kate waking up to find Jamie's dead body, blood all over her hands, her DNA all over him. And then a lifetime in prison, where she'll never be able to ruin Rowan's life.

'Then why? It doesn't make sense.'

'No questions,' Rowan repeats.

'I don't know about this,' Jamie says. 'Who am I doing it for? Is this illegal?'

'No more so than what you've been doing by defrauding all those women.' Rowan's voice softens. 'Look, I can't give you any names. I'm sorry. Will you just trust me, please?'

Jamie's head moves, and Rowan can't tell if it's a nod or an involuntary gesture.

'There's just one thing. Half the money upfront, and half once you've got her to your flat.'

There's another pause before Jamie nods. 'So fifty grand now, and fifty when she's at my flat.'

Rowan nods.

'Okay. I'll do it. I don't like it – but I have no choice. This will really help get me out of a hole.'

Rowan's body floods with relief – he hadn't expected this to go so smoothly. He walks to his desk and pulls out his mobile from the drawer, scrolling through his photos until he finds the one he took of Kate without her knowing. It was the last afternoon they'd spent together in that hotel. He shows it to Jamie. 'Take a photo of this with your phone, and then put the name and address I give you into your contacts. Her name's Kate Mason and she lives in Wimbledon. You'll need to follow her for a while, get a feel for her so that she goes back to your place with you.'

'That's miles from me,' Jamie says.

'You could move closer. You told me at our last session you needed to get out of the house you're in. This is a good reason to speed that up. It's really important that you get a good feel for this woman. Implant yourself into her life without her knowing.'

Jamie doesn't look convinced; but the lure of that money will ensure he follows through with this arrangement.

'If I'm taking her back home with me, it will have to be to my rental property,' Jamie says. 'We've been doing it up so it's empty at the moment.'

'Then luck is on our side,' Rowan says. 'Tell Kate it's your place, and that you're separated – she is too, so that might help you bond with her. I think that's all you need to know for now. I'll be in touch about the money.'

Jamie nods and stands up, pulling on his jacket as he heads to the door.

'Oh, and Jamie?' Rowan calls.

He turns around.

'I really think this will help you find the peace you're looking for.'

FORTY-SIX

TUESDAY 4 FEBRUARY

There's terror on Rowan's face as Kate pushes the knife against his skin. 'Tell me about Jamie Archer,' she says. She unfolds the receipt she found in the box of Jamie's things. 'This is a receipt from your practice – I know he was a patient of yours.'

Rowan says nothing and closes his eyes.

'Was it you who killed him?' Kate says. 'Talk!' She presses harder on the knife, feels his body tense underneath it. 'Why did you do it?'

'You should never have blackmailed me, Kate. Don't you get it? Everything that happened to Jamie is because of you. If you'd just left me alone and gone to another therapist, he'd still be alive now. I kept telling you I couldn't be your therapist any more. You're the reason we're all in this... this mess.'

Kate stares at him, open-mouthed. She'd wanted Rowan to tell her that she's wrong, that he had nothing to do with Jamie's murder and it's just a coincidence that he was one of Rowan's patients, just like she was. Wasn't it Rowan who'd insisted that coincidences happen? But looking at him now, Kate knows that's not the truth.

'Is this about Graham White?' she demands. 'Did you know

him? Are you something to do with him? All those times you tried to convince me that he could have nothing to do with Jamie ending up dead! That was all to protect yourself!'

'Please lower that knife so I can talk?'

Kate ignores him. 'It was you who set fire to my house, wasn't it? All of it... you did all those things. You're the one who took my house keys from Jamie's flat. And you attacked me this evening.'

'Accusations without proof are meaningless, aren't they? You should know that.' Rowan glares at her.

'My son was in the house. He could have died. And his friend too.'

'But he wasn't supposed to be in the house, was he? Whose fault is it that you changed your plans? Just lower that knife, Kate, if you want me to talk.'

'How... how did you know the plan changed?'

'Because I've made it my business to know every single thing you do.'

For a moment Kate doesn't move. Every move Rowan makes is cold and calculated – how could he have been the one person she trusted above anyone else? But if she wants him to talk, she needs to play along. She lowers her hand, but keeps a tight grip on the knife.

'You're so deeply traumatised by that man,' Rowan says, 'that it clouds your judgement. Jamie had nothing to do with Graham White, and neither do I.'

They'd still be alive now.

They?

Faye Held.

Before Kate can question him, Rowan thrusts his chair back, knocking her off balance. The knife crashes to the floor, landing by his feet. Kate lunges towards it, but Rowan is too fast, swiping it up and rushing towards her, plunging the knife into her stomach. Kate doubles over. Ignoring the searing pain, she picks up a vase of flowers from the table and hurls it at Rowan's face. It thuds against his head then smashes to the floor. Anger flashes across his face and Kate knows she has to run.

Making for the door, she reaches for the handle just as Rowan grabs her legs and drags her down, her bones crashing against the tiled floor. And for a fleeting moment it's not Rowan's face she sees but Graham White's. But unlike Graham, Rowan is guilty, and she will kill him if that's what she has to do to get out of here alive.

Rowan sits on her stomach, pressing down on her with all his weight, slamming his fist into her face, over and over until the edges of her consciousness begin to darken. And the pain in her abdomen in excruciating. She tries to kick out but he's over-powering her. Why isn't he using the knife? That would be quicker. And then she feels it against her neck. Kate closes her eyes and stays still. Her only hope now is to try and reason with him – maybe some minuscule part of him might care about her after what they had.

Someone is screaming. It must be Kate, but her mouth is closed. Rowan stops, the pressure of his body on hers easing.

More screams. Rowan shouting. A woman's voice, urgent, frantic. Then footsteps running.

Someone kneels beside her. 'Kate? Can you hear me? It's Daniella. Please, let me know if you can hear me.'

Kate opens her eyes to find Rowan's wife peering at her. It takes a huge effort, but she attempts to nod.

'Good.' Daniella stands up and grabs a kitchen towel from the worktop, pressing it down over Kate's stomach. 'You're safe now. I'm calling the ambulance. They'll be here any—'

The doorbell rings, and Daniella jolts up. 'That was too quick.'

'Don't let him in,' Kate says.

Daniella nods. 'Stay here.'

Alone in the kitchen, Kate pulls herself up, slowly making

her way to the door. She can hear familiar voices. Urgent and questioning. Then Harper is rushing towards her, grabbing Kate's arms to steady her.

Behind Harper, Ellis runs to Kate. 'Jesus! What did that monster do to you?' He glances at the trail of blood on the floor.

Kate can barely stand, but this is nothing compared to what Rowan would have done if Daniella hadn't come back. 'I'm okay,' she says. She falls into Ellis, and he manages to grab her before she falls to the floor.

Kate opens her eyes, disorientated until she focuses on the square tiles on the bright white ceiling, then the crisp white hospital sheets covering her body. It all floods back to her: Rowan. Daniella coming back to their house. Saving her life. Harper and Ellis turning up – how did they know where she was?

'Hey, you're awake.'

She turns to see Ellis sitting on the chair by her bed. 'Where's Thomas?' she asks. Right now, she wants nothing more than to see her son.

'Don't worry – he's fine. He's with Harper.' Ellis offers a faint smile. 'How are you feeling?'

'Like I've been stabbed in the stomach.' Kate tries to laugh but intense shooting pains fire through her body and instead she groans.

'It's not something to joke about, Kate,' Ellis says, reaching for her arm. 'You could have been killed.'

Kate tries to pull herself up. 'Where's Rowan? He killed Jamie. He might try to come here and—'

'He can't hurt you now.' Ellis gently squeezes her arm. 'After he ran from his house, he jumped off Chelsea Bridge. He's dead, Kate.'

Kate should be relieved to hear this, but she's not. Now

Rowan will never have to face the consequences of what he's done. Death was the easier option. And now she'll never have the answers she needs about Jamie.

'Why did he do that to you?'

'I don't know,' Kate says. 'We'll never know. But... I need to tell you something about Rowan.' Sick of all the lies, it's time for Kate to tell Ellis the truth about her affair.

He listens silently and then takes her hand. 'Is that why he killed Jamie?'

'Maybe.'

Ellis shakes his head. 'Let's only look forward now. You're free, Kate.' He takes her cannula-free hand. 'Harper told me you thought I was the one who killed Jamie. And that I attacked you. I can't bear the thought of you thinking that, even for a second. All I've ever done is try to protect you.'

Kate pulls her hand away. 'It was all those lies you told.'

Ellis buries his head in his hands. 'A while ago, I started looking into what happened with Graham White. It was after you said something weird in your sleep one night.'

Kate frowns. 'What?'

'You don't normally talk in your sleep, but this one night you were mumbling something about how Graham White had got away with what he'd done. Something like that. It was a bit garbled but that was the gist.' He looks at Kate again. 'It scared me, Kate. I... I thought you must have been lying to me about not knowing him and him just attacking you randomly.' He hangs his head. 'I needed to know. I thought you must have had some kind of relationship with him, and that maybe you'd killed him out of revenge for... for grooming you. I just needed to know the truth. And you'd never talk about it. I wanted to help you.'

'I was never seeing him,' Kate says. 'It was nothing like that.'

'I know that now,' Ellis says. 'But remember you'd never talk about it? It was eating away at me. But now I know it wasn't you who was seeing him.'

Kate stares at him. 'How?'

Ellis explains that Jennifer Seagrove showed him the letter from the girl Graham was supposedly sleeping with. 'It wasn't your writing, Kate. Do you know who wrote that letter?'

She nods. It's time Ellis knew the truth. 'I'm sick of all the lies. My whole life since I was fifteen has been a lie.' She hesitates. 'Apart from you and Thomas.' Kate tells him the truth about what happened that day, when Graham White threw her and Mona in his van. And how Kate has kept Mona's secret until now.

He listens, open-mouthed, until she's finished. 'Why would you protect her all these years? Everyone in your life believed you'd killed someone!'

'Because she blackmailed me. And threatened me. Plus I didn't know the truth. Initially I thought I was protecting her – she needed a break in life. She'd had a rough childhood, and then I thought she'd been raped by him. But I just found out that was all lies – he hadn't laid a finger on her. Mona had met him in the park and become obsessed with him, but he was having no part of it. It made her angry and she waged a hate campaign against him.' Tears slide down her cheeks. 'And I helped her, because I thought he was a paedophile.' Kate swipes at her tears.

'But he did kidnap you,' Ellis says. 'He hit you. Why did he do that? Maybe he did want to—'

'No, I think he'd just reached the end of his tether. Because of what Mona had done. He was desperate.' *Like Rowan, and Jamie too, people do desperate things when they're pushed to their limit.* 'I really believe he was just an innocent man. He took us away in his van to scare us, to tell us to leave him alone.'

Ellis listens, chewing over her words. 'Do you think Mona was lying about it being self-defence?'

'I'll never know. She'd never admit that now. And the only person who can answer that is dead.'

'But the truth has to come out, doesn't it?' Ellis says. 'For Jennifer's sake too. She needs to know that the man she loved was innocent.'

Kate knows this. 'I'll find a way,' she says. Her head flops back against her pillow.

'Speaking of the truth,' Ellis says, chewing his lip. 'I need to tell you something.'

Kate closes her eyes. What is she about to hear?

'I'm the one who put that photo of Jamie in Thomas's school bag for you to find. I did it after I picked him up so I knew he wouldn't see it.'

Kate stares at him. 'Why?'

'First, I was angry with you for ending our marriage over my affair, when I thought you'd had one yourself. But then I kind of hoped you'd be so worried about it that you'd confide in me. I just wanted you to talk to me about what was going on.'

'Does Harper know it was you who sent it?'

'No. I never told anyone. I'm sorry, Kate.'

What does it matter now? 'Well, we've both lied,' Kate says. 'Let's just move forward. All I want right now is to be with Thomas.'

'I'll bring him to see you in the morning,' Ellis promises. 'They said you should be able to go home tomorrow afternoon.'

Home. I no longer have one. 'And where exactly is home?' Kate says, more to herself than to Ellis.

'My home. It's always there for you and Thomas. I know there's no going back for our marriage, but we can move forward with a different kind of relationship. As Thomas's parents. That's all I want.'

Kate smiles, and prays Ellis means this. 'Me too. Maybe you and Maddy can—'

'No, that's not what I want. I'm moving forward, Kate. Do

you want some water?' Ellis doesn't wait for a reply but pours water into Kate's cup and hands it to her. 'Harper said she'd like to visit this evening. Is that okay?'

Kate nods. It's more than okay.

Harper hovers in the doorway, waiting for Kate to beckon her in. 'I wasn't sure you'd want to see me,' she says. 'It's hard to know anything really after all that's happened.'

Kate pulls herself up. Her pain medication is starting to wear off and she'll need more soon if she's going to get through the night. 'We're in this together, aren't we?' she tells Harper.

Harper comes in and sits by Kate's bed. 'But I wasn't there for you when you needed me. I'm sorry we didn't get to you in time. If Rowan's wife hadn't left her phone behind...'

'It's best not to think about that,' Kate says.

Harper nods. 'Actually, I think you would have handled him. You're a fighter, Kate. A survivor. And now everyone will know you didn't kill Graham White. Or Jamie. I've just read a post from Faye Held's younger sister – she's planning to take over the *Beneath the Surface* podcast in memory of her sister. I've already messaged her to see if she'll re-examine the Graham White story. Because of Mona's confession to Kate. And then there's Jamie too. Everyone should know who was responsible, even if the police will never be able to prove it.'

'But we have to be mindful of Daniella,' Kate says. 'She didn't deserve to be married to such a psychopath.' And Kate will always feel guilty about her affair with Rowan.

'People might wonder how she didn't know how disturbed he was,' Harper says. 'But I know from Jamie that people are too good at hiding what they don't want others to see.'

'I don't think it's as straightforward as saying Rowan was a psychopath,' Kate says, reaching for her water. 'I think he was just faced with losing everything in his life, and he did what he thought he had to, to keep it. My blackmail pushed him to his limit.'

'But there must have been something always there for him to have snapped that badly,' Harper counters.

'Yeah, you're right,' Kate agrees. *Unless we're all just close to the edge.* 'I'm sorry about... about me and Jamie.'

Harper sighs. 'You don't need to say that. Jamie was never mine. And actually, Dexter and I were never his, so it's all fine.'

'What do you mean? Dexter's his son.'

'That's a story for another day,' Harper says. 'If you don't mind?'

Kate frowns, searching Harper's face. Perhaps she doesn't want to know – she's had more than enough of lies and deception.

Harper stays for a couple of hours, filling Kate in on what Thomas and Dex have been doing on their extended playdate. 'They've really hit it off,' she says. 'We're doing homemade pizzas for dinner tonight. Hope that's okay? They never got to have them last time.'

Kate nods. 'Thank you.'

'And I... I asked Ellis if he'd like to stay for dinner too. I hope that's okay?' Harper's cheeks flush.

Kate smiles. 'Of course it is,' she says. Harper deserves some happiness.

Harper nods, and a silent exchange takes place between the two women. 'Well, I'd better go and make myself presentable.'

'Okay,' Kate says. 'Maybe wear your hair down.'

Harper nods. 'One step ahead of you,' she says, smiling.

And when she leaves, Kate finally lets herself exhale.

Now she truly is free.

A LETTER FROM KATHRYN

Thank you so much for choosing to read *The Last One to See Him*. This book had a couple of false starts, but hopefully I got it right in the end. Did the twists come as a surprise? I do try hard to keep readers guessing! And I hope it's clear that underlying the plot is the sense that we can survive whatever life throws our way. I was determined for Kate and Harper to both be fighters, protecting their sons no matter the cost.

If you'd like to keep up to date with all my latest releases, please do sign up at the following link. Your email address will never be shared and you can unsubscribe at any time.

www.bookouture.com/kathryn-croft

I really hope you've enjoyed reading this book and that it offered you some escapism in a world that can sometimes feel increasingly overwhelming, and where technology seems to be taking over our lives. Books really help us keep things simple, while still being powerful tools to teach and entertain.

If you did enjoy this book, and can spare a short moment, I'd really appreciate it if you could leave a review on Amazon. Reviews really are an important lifeline for authors as they help our books to be discovered by new readers.

If you'd like to, please also feel free to connect with me via my website, Facebook, Instagram, or X. I'd love to hear from you!

Thank you again for all your support – it is very much appreciated.

As Ernest Hemingway said: 'There is no friend as loyal as a book.'

Kathryn x

www.kathryncroft.com

facebook.com/authorkathryncroft
instagram.com/authorkathryncroft
x.com/katcroft

ACKNOWLEDGEMENTS

Once again, I'm beyond grateful to every single person who chooses to read my books, whether it's for pleasure or to review them. Time is so precious, and I appreciate everyone who gives up theirs to escape into worlds I've created.

Lydia Vassar-Smith – thank you for tirelessly working to get this book into better shape than I would have managed on my own. It's such a pleasure to work with you and I truly value your insight and advice.

Hannah Todd – thank you for everything you've done for me over the last three years. I appreciate all your support and enthusiasm.

The publishing team at Bookouture – all your hard work makes magic happen, so thank you for everything you do for all of your authors.

Jo Sidaway and Michelle Langford – once again a huge thank you for your police advice – always a pleasure picking your brains!

To my parents – I'm truly blessed to have you and thank you for everything you still do for me.

To my children – No, you can't read this book yet, but I hope you're proud of me – everything I do is for you and Daddy!

To my husband – thank you for never once complaining when I have to escape upstairs to write (which is a lot!).

PUBLISHING TEAM

Turning a manuscript into a book requires the efforts of many people. The publishing team at Bookouture would like to acknowledge everyone who contributed to this publication.

Audio
Alba Proko
Melissa Tran
Sinead O'Connor

Commercial
Lauren Morrissette
Hannah Richmond
Imogen Allport

Contracts
Peta Nightingale

Cover design
The Brewster Project

Data and analysis
Mark Alder
Mohamed Bussuri